What People Are ~~Saying About~~
Penny Zeller ~~and Hailee~~

Hailee warms the heart and promises the reader a walk through the fire and into the arms of love. This cozy-weekend read weaves a romance filled with all the elements of a winner—love, strife, joy, and trust. A must-read.

—**Cindy Sproles**
Editor, ChristianDevotions.us, and coauthor,
He Said, She Said: A Devotional Guide to Cultivating a Life of Passion

Engaging characters and heartfelt faith messages make Penny Zeller's *Hailee* a memorable conclusion to the Montana Skies trilogy.

—**Amanda Cabot**
Author, *Tomorrow's Garden*

If you enjoyed *McKenzie* and *Kaydie*, you'll adore *Hailee*. You will laugh, cry, and fall in love with Penny Zeller's vibrant characters.

—**Shellie Neumeier**
Author, *Driven*

Penny Zeller has penned a heartwarming conclusion to her Montana Skies series. *Hailee* grabbed my attention from page one and kept it as I prayed for Hailee not only find her two missing brothers but also to find happiness and love in Montana.

—**Laura V. Hilton**
Author, The Amish of Seymour series (*Patchwork Dreams, A Harvest of Hearts,* and *Promised to Another*)

To my husband, Lon.

Thank you for your love, encouragement, and support, all of which make my writing ministry possible. I couldn't do it without you!

Hailee

Penny ZELLER

WHITAKER
HOUSE

HAILEE
Book Three in the Montana Skies Series

Penny Zeller
www.pennyzeller.com

ISBN: 978-1-60374-218-4
Printed in the United States of America
© 2011 by Penny Zeller

Whitaker House
1030 Hunt Valley Circle
New Kensington, PA 15068
www.whitakerhouse.com

Library of Congress Cataloging-in-Publication Data

Zeller, Penny, 1973–
  Hailee / by Penny Zeller.
     p. cm. — (Montana skies ; bk. 3)
  Summary: "When Hailee Annigan comes to Pine Haven as the new
schoolteacher, an unexpected romance arises, but she needs to forgive
herself, with the help of God, for some parts of her past before the
relationship can be realized"—Provided by publisher.
  ISBN 978-1-60374-218-4 (trade pbk.)
1. Montana—Fiction. I. Title.
 PS3626.E3565H35 2011
 813'.6—dc23
                                                          2011030188

1 2 3 4 5 6 7 8 9 10 11 **W** 18 17 16 15 14 13 12 11

CHAPTER ONE

*H*ailee Annigan removed the discolored sheet of paper from the community board in the train depot. Time and weather had faded the poster, so the message was barely readable, but she had memorized the words:

Looking for Philip and Reuben Annigan.
If you have any information, kindly respond to:
Hailee Annigan
c/o Dot Pangbourn's Boardinghouse
West Eberlee Street, Cincinnati, Ohio

She crumpled the paper in her hand and stuffed it into her purse. In its place, she posted the notice she'd written that morning, then stepped back to make sure it would be conspicuous to people passing by or preparing to board a train.

Looking for Philip and Reuben Annigan.
If you have any information, kindly respond to:
Hailee Annigan
c/o Pine Haven School
Pine Haven, Montana

For the past several years, she had replaced the posting every month, two times in order to alter the address where she could be located if someone knew of her brothers' whereabouts.

Hailee swallowed hard to hold back her tears. She didn't want to leave Cincinnati and diminish her chances of ever finding her younger brothers. However, she knew that a change in location would do her heart good, and that she was following God's prompting to fulfill the dream she'd had in her heart since she was a young girl.

Tomorrow, Hailee would begin her journey of nearly two thousand miles to a place she'd never been, where she had accepted a job as the schoolteacher. Yes, such a drastic change would help her to leave the past behind and start life anew.

She turned and trudged the short distance from the train depot to Austin Street. Her feet ached from all the walking she'd done in the past few hours, replacing each of the seven postings in varied locations around the city. Now, she had one more place to visit—one more person to see—before leaving Ohio.

Hailee sat on the wooden bench and waited for the horse-drawn hansom cab to round the corner during one of its many scheduled stops. Hoping she had read the schedule for the cab correctly, she counted the money in her coin purse. She'd ridden in a hansom only a handful of times due to the cost, but today was an exception. Today, she would travel to a distant part of the city to say a final good-bye to an important part of her life. She needed to put a period at the end of the sentence that had affected her more than anything else in her nineteen years.

Within minutes, Hailee spied the carriage. She rose to her feet as the hansom cab slowed to a stop.

A short, husky man with a mustache that was black, peppered with gray, and that curled up in swirly loops at the ends stepped down from the back of the carriage. He removed his top hat and greeted her with a bow. "Good afternoon, ma'am. Ambrose Peters at your service. Where may I take you today?"

"Hello, Mr. Peters. Would you please take me to The Sanctuary of Promise?" Hailee smiled at the driver.

"My! A ways away, is it not?" said Ambrose. "But, yes, I can take you there." He extended a white-gloved hand and helped Hailee into the cab. "If you need anything, anything at all, please don't hesitate to let me know. I can hear you through the open window in the roof."

Hailee nodded and glanced up at the small window with a hinged cover that was open. As she settled into her seat, Ambrose prepared to close the door. "Are you comfortable?" he asked.

"Yes, thank you."

"Very well, then. We shall be on our way." He bowed again, placed his hat back on his head, and closed the door. Moments later, they lurched forward with the clatter of horses' hooves.

"Are you from Cincinnati, miss?" Ambrose asked sometime later.

"Yes, I've lived here all my life," Hailee replied. She appreciated the driver's small talk. It took her mind off of the nervousness she felt.

"As have I," said Ambrose. "Do you have family here?"

Hailee wasn't sure how to answer that question. Were her brothers still in Cincinnati? Or, had they traveled far from this city, which held so many memories? "My parents have gone to be with the Lord, but I do have two brothers," she finally answered.

"I'm sorry to hear about your parents, miss." Ambrose paused. "It sure is a lovely time of year, isn't it, with the flowers blooming and the trees with all their leaves? I have to admit, I enjoy every season, but winter gets a mite cold at times driving the cab."

Hailee smiled and nodded. She could only imagine how a cold Cincinnati winter might affect cab drivers. She wondered about the winters in Montana. Were they similar to those she had experienced her entire life in Ohio? Would she still love summer the best of all the seasons once she was settled in her new home? She watched in silence as they passed by the tall buildings, some dating back to the turn of the century, and dozens of other buggies traversing the crowded avenue. Would Pine Haven match the hustle and bustle of Cincinnati? Would it have streets lined with storefronts offering a wide variety of goods? Somehow, she doubted it. From what she had heard, Montana was rugged and wild, Pine Haven nothing like a big city. *A change will do you good, Hailee*, she reminded herself. *Even if that change is a drastic one.*

"We're almost there," Ambrose announced. "It's been a while since I've traveled out this way. I'd forgotten how beautiful this road looks, lined with trees as it is."

"It is beautiful," Hailee agreed. The buildings became fewer and farther apart, while the buckeye trees grew more numerous. They folded out their branches as if to welcome Hailee to the place she would never forget, a place where God had molded her into the type of woman He desired her to become.

In the circular driveway in front of The Sanctuary of Promise, the cab slowed to a stop. The door opened, and Ambrose peered in. "Here we are, miss." He held out an arm to assist her out of the cab. "When shall I return for you?"

"In about an hour, if it's convenient. Thank you, Ambrose." Hailee climbed out, then handed him her hard-earned money for the fare.

"See you shortly, miss."

"Yes, indeed!" She bid him farewell as he climbed back onto the cab and picked up the reins. Then, she turned around and surveyed the mammoth building before her. The brick structure had four stories and two wings, the third- and fourth-floor windows of which were covered with curtains, and a covered porch held up by four faded white pillars. The building was surrounded by a well-manicured lawn, and Hailee spied the familiar tiered birdbath under an oak tree. To the left of the tree was the fenced-in garden where she had learned much about farming.

Looking back at the building, Hailee could see the heads of students inside the first floor windows, and she recalled the many hours she'd spent in its classrooms. A little girl turned her head and peered out at her with a look of curiosity.

Hailee smiled at her and urged her feet to move toward the front door. Had there really been a time when she'd spent almost every waking moment in this looming fortress of a building? It felt as if she'd stepped back in time; while everything around her had changed in the past two years, and while dozens of children from entirely different backgrounds had lived within its walls and played on its grounds, The

Sanctuary of Promise had undergone no observable alterations, at least on its exterior.

On the porch now, Hailee sucked in her breath and turned the doorknob. As she stepped inside the vast entryway, a mix of emotions stirred within her.

"I'll be right with you," a woman called from an adjacent room.

Hailee recognized the voice and smiled. "Ella?"

"Hailee Annigan, is that you?" Ella Fanshaw rushed through the door toward Hailee and wrapped her arms around the much younger woman. "It's been the better of three months since we last saw each other. How have you been?"

"I've been well, thank you."

"Please, come into the dining area," Ella invited her.

Hailee followed her and sat down at the long, worn wooden table—quite possibly for the last time in her life, she realized—where she had once taken every meal. Gazing around the room, she recalled the first day she'd entered The Sanctuary of Promise, at fourteen years of age....

"I don't belong here!" Hailee shouted at Officer Ulmer, who had taken her inside the large, frightening building.

"The judge ordered for you to come to The Sanctuary of Promise, so that is where you'll stay," Officer Ulmer said firmly. "Had you not done what you did, you wouldn't have found yourself in this predicament." He paused and shook his head. "Just about every child I remand to The Sanctuary of Promise makes the same claim about not belonging

here. When will you street children come to learn that crime doesn't pay? It never has and never will."

"But I don't belong here!" Hailee stamped her feet.

"If you don't belong here, then why do you have a reputation for thievery among the storefront owners in East Cincinnati?"

"A reputation?"

"Yes, a reputation. There's nary a storekeeper who hasn't fallen victim to your thieving ways and lying tongue."

Hailee ignored the officer's insinuations. Yes, she had stolen; yes, she had lied; and, yes, she had deceived. What of it? It had been out of necessity that she had done such things. Had she not needed to provide for her younger brothers, she wouldn't have dreamed of lying, stealing, and deceiving.

"You don't understand. I need to be with my brothers!" Without forethought, Hailee pushed past the man, rushed out the door, and raced across the vast lawn. Spurred on by the rhythmic thumping of her heart within her chest, she ran with all her might, willing her eyes to adjust to the darkness of night so that she could make out her path.

"You come back here, young lady!"

Hailee stole a glance over her shoulder and saw Officer Ulmer running after her, but the thickset man was no match for her speed. "Stop that girl!" he yelled as the gap between them continued to widen. "Stop her!"

As Hailee rounded the corner of East Seventh Street and Holmes, a strong hand grabbed her arm and stopped her in mid-stride. "Not so fast," the officer said sternly.

"Let me go!" Hailee wailed as she tried to wriggle out of the officer's grasp.

"Not this time," he said. "Another runaway?"

Hailee looked around. Officer Ulmer was stumbling toward them, gasping for breath.

"Yes," he managed, still panting. "Ten years ago, I could have caught her"—he expelled a loud breath—"but my best years of chasing street urchins are behind me."

The other officer chuckled. "That's true of a lot of us, Quincy."

"That's why I requested this post, delivering wayward juveniles to The Sanctuary of Promise," Officer Ulmer continued. "It's supposed to be easier and less eventful. But then, spitfires like this Hailee Annigan come along and make my job almost impossible." He breathed in and out, in and out. "Still, children like Hailee give me reason to pray even harder. Yes, I lift every lost child I meet to my Father's throne, asking Him to take care of their needs, and—"

Out of desperation, Hailee leaned forward and bit the officer who held her on the arm. Yelling in pain, he immediately released his grip. Hailee stepped back and was ready to run, but Officer Ulmer grabbed her arms and held her fast. "She really doesn't think she belongs in The Sanctuary of Promise, Officer Edwards," he said.

"Humph. Do any of them?" Officer Edwards scowled and rubbed his arm where Hailee had bitten him.

She glanced around, hoping for another way to escape her captors. She would not give in and be taken to The Sanctuary of Promise. Sure, it was a big brick mansion, but it was just a fancy jail. Besides, she had her brothers to care for. Why couldn't these officers see that?

"You don't understand," she whined. "My brother Philip, he has to walk with a crutch." She pasted a sad look on her face in hopes of eliciting their pity. One thing she had learned on the streets was how to manipulate others through emotional appeals.

"Right. And I'm the president of the United States," Officer Ulmer said with a chuckle. "Let's get moving." He started walking and pulled her along.

"I'm telling the truth," Hailee insisted, trying to keep her voice low and her tone mournful.

"Are you aware of the alternative of going to The Sanctuary of Promise?" Officer Ulmer asked.

"What?" Hailee demanded.

"You would be put in jail."

"The Sanctuary of Promise is a jail—just a fancy one," she retorted. "Nothing good ever comes from being in a place like that."

"I think you'll find The Sanctuary of Promise quite different from the jail where you were held until the judge heard your case."

"I don't want to be in any jail. I want to be free!" Hailee gritted her teeth and tried to pull her arms out of Officer Ulmer's grasp, but Officer Edwards held fast to her shoulder as he walked alongside. She was no match for two grown men.

"You know, most kids at The Sanctuary are released after about a year and a half," mused Officer Ulmer. "With the little shenanigan you just pulled, you're likely to spend more time there, though."

"I won't stay there," Hailee insisted. "I'll just escape. I have to. My brothers are depending on me. Who'll make them dinner? Who'll tell little Philip the story about baby Moses in the basket?"

"I'm sure someone will see to it that they're taken care of," Officer Edwards muttered. "If they even exist."

"You don't believe that I have brothers?" Hailee was shocked at what she was hearing. Why would she make that up?

"You couldn't imagine the stories we hear," Officer Ulmer chuckled. "Do you think you're the first wayward juvenile to insist she has younger siblings to care for? And we've heard the brother-with-a-crutch story one too many times."

"But it's the truth! One of Philip's feet is turned the wrong way. He was born like that. And it makes it hard for him to walk, so he has to use a crutch."

"And just how old is this Philip?" Officer Ulmer asked as they entered The Sanctuary of Promise grounds.

"He's only six."

"What about your other brother? I'm sure he can care for him just fine," Officer Edwards said dryly.

"Reuben?" Hailee was getting angry. "Reuben can't care for him—not like I can. He's only twelve. And, sometimes, Reuben is...well...grouchy."

"And where do these brothers live?" asked Officer Ulmer.

"Over on Gardner St—wait, why?"

"Gardner Street?" asked Officer Ulmer.

"No, not Gardner Street," Hailee said. "I meant to say Garrison Avenue."

"Either way, we'll find them," said Officer Edwards. "Again, assuming they exist."

"Why doesn't anybody believe me?" Hailee demanded.

"With the crimes you've committed and the lies you've told, it is a bit difficult to believe you," Officer

Ulmer reasoned. He reached out with his free hand and opened the front door of The Sanctuary. "Good evening Miss Torenz," he said as they stepped inside and were greeted by a young woman. "We've got one who insists on escaping."

"Don't worry, she won't be escaping," the woman assured him. "Please bring her upstairs to the Yellow Flower Room."

Still fighting to be released, Hailee kicked and wriggled as the officers dragged her up the stairs. Miss Torenz opened a door, and the officers shoved Hailee inside and quickly shut the door.

"Let me out!" she shouted, beating on the door with her fists. She had to get out of here—her brothers' lives depended on it! No doubt, little Philip was hungry right now. It was bad enough that she'd spent last night in jail and left Philip and Reuben all alone. But two nights in a row? Hailee cringed at the thought.

"It'll do you no good to pound on the door," said Miss Torenz through the door, her voice firm. "We'll bring you some breakfast in the morning."

"No, wait! You can't leave me here!" Hailee resumed pounding on the door. After a while, her fists sore, she turned to assess her whereabouts. A tiny window on the far wall allowed a minute amount of moonlight into the room. With the exception of a bed with a faded quilt, the closet-sized room was empty. Hailee squinted. Was the wallpaper yellow with large sunflowers? It was difficult to tell in the dim light, but she supposed it was, which would account for the name of the room.

One last time, Hailee pounded on the door and screamed until her throat hurt. Finally, she gave up, turned, and leaned back against the door. She slid *down into a seated position, buried her face in her hands, and began to sob. While she'd never been one to give up, no matter how harsh the circumstances life had dealt to her, this was the exception. She was trapped, and there was nothing she could do about it....*

"Hailee?" Ella asked.

"I'm sorry, Ella. I was just remembering my first day here."

"I wasn't here that night, but I recall hearing that you put up the fight of the century," Ella said, laughing.

"It seems so long ago now, almost a different lifetime."

Ella sighed. "It was only five years ago, but you were so different then. I could tell when I first met you that you were frightened and feeling alone. And so thin and malnourished.... My heart broke for you."

"I will forever be indebted to you for all you've done for me," Hailee said.

Ella smiled. "I prayed that very morning for God to send me someone I could encourage. I didn't real- ize that He would make good on my prayer right away by sending me someone the same day! And a chal- lenge, too—that's what you were, Hailee Annigan. A challenge."

Hailee had thanked the Lord many times for Ella. In the years since she'd left The Sanctuary, she had maintained contact with her former teach- er, although their visits had not been as frequent as she would have wished due to the busy lives of both of them. However, Hailee had treasured the times when Ella had met her at the boardinghouse where she lived. They would have tea and catch up on the happenings in their lives, and, many times, Dot Pangbourn, the boardinghouse proprietress, would join them.

Sitting across from Ella, Hailee realized how much the past five years had altered her friend. Her auburn hair was beginning to gray, her lovely face had gained a few more wrinkles, and, behind her thick glasses, her eyes looked more tired than ever. Hailee knew she was responsible for some of those wrinkles, and that she and others like her had been sources of the weariness her dear friend's face showed. "I am deeply sorry about having been a challenge," she said.

Ella smiled. "Oh, pooh. That's in the past. What matters now is what you do with the second chance the Lord has given you." She paused. "Would you care for a cup of tea?"

"I would love a cup of tea, thank you."

Ella stood up and left the room, then returned a few moments later with two steaming teacups. She set one down at each of their places and then took her seat again. "So, tell me, Hailee, what is new in your life?"

"Well, I actually came here to tell you that I am moving…to Montana. I've been hired as the new schoolteacher in Pine Haven."

"Pine Haven? That's wonderful! From the moment you told me of your intent to apply, I had no doubt that you would get the position. I clearly remember the day you showed me the newspaper advertisement." Ella took a sip of tea. "However, I must say…Montana? That's pretty far west!"

"It is quite far from here," Hailee conceded. "At first, I was hesitant because of my brothers. What if Philip or Reuben finally sees one of my postings? It will take weeks for me to receive word, and then there is the matter of the travel time. But you know my dream of becoming a teacher, and Pine Haven was the only place where the incoming teacher was not expected to have several years of experience."

"If your brothers see one of your notices, they will contact you, wherever you are," Ella assured her with a pat on her arm. "This will be an adventure, and you are smart to take advantage of it."

"I have prayed about it so much, Ella. I prayed that God would open a door for me to be a teacher, and He did."

"He's had a plan for your life all along."

"Even when I was causing so much trouble here?"

"Even then." Ella smiled. "Now, besides the good news of your teaching position, what brings you to The Sanctuary?"

"To see you," said Hailee. "I couldn't very well go without saying good-bye, and I'm leaving tomorrow. I will arrive in Pine Haven on July twenty-seventh, with plenty of time to get settled before school starts."

"My, things are happening fast."

"They certainly are." Hailee bit her lip. "I also felt that I needed to see this place one last time."

"Not much has changed since you lived here, Hailee, although many lives have been changed—for the better, I might add."

"God has used you in wonderful ways to touch the lives of so many children. I can only pray that He will use me in the same way with my students."

"I know He will." Ella paused, looking pensive. "Do you remember the first Bible verse I asked you to look up?"

"Of course!" Hailee had all but forgotten that there had been a time when she was not familiar with the Scriptures. Ella had opened God's Word to her, and the first verse she'd learned had become one of her favorites. "Jeremiah twenty-nine, verse eleven," Hailee began, and Ella's voice joined with hers as the two women recited together: "*'For I know the thoughts that I think toward you, saith the* LORD, *thoughts of peace, and not of evil, to give you an expected end.'*"

"Hailee, do you finally understand that God has always known the plans and thoughts He has toward you?" Ella said. "He hasn't changed. The Lord has been laying the foundation for those thoughts and plans, and, now, they are coming to fruition."

"Thank you." Hailee squeezed the hand of the woman who had become a second mother to her. "I'm just a little nervous about going all the way to Montana."

"I can see that. Just remember that there is no place you can go where the Lord is not there with you. Lift your eyes to Him, Hailee, and He'll be your comforter."

Hailee nodded. Ever since she'd come to know the Lord, He'd never turned His back on her.

"I'm sure Dot will be sorry to see you go."

"I will miss her so. She's been so kind to me, almost like a grandmother." Hailee paused. "And, more than anyone, Ella, I'll miss you."

"I'll miss you, too, Hailee. But you have prayed about this decision, and I do believe it is the Lord's calling for your life. Besides, I'm only a train ride away."

"A *long* train ride."

"Nonetheless, we will correspond regularly, which shall be a source of encouragement to both of us."

"I promise to write if you will," said Hailee.

"It's a promise," Ella agreed.

"Well, we've talked enough about me. Please, Ella, tell me how you have been."

"Oh, I've been well." Ella paused, her eyes suddenly glowing. "I do have a tidbit of information you might find amusing, if not exciting."

"Do tell!"

"Do you remember Officer Ulmer?"

Hailee feigned a grimace. "How could I forget him?"

"Well, he has asked me to marry him."

Hailee almost choked on her tea. "I beg your pardon?"

"It's true. He has been courting me for the past several months, and it happened rather quickly—"

"Officer Ulmer, the man who brought me here?"

"The one and the same."

"I don't believe it!" Hailee immediately regretted her words, for Ella looked stricken. "Oh, do forgive me, Ella. Congratulations are in order!" She reached out and clasped her friend's hand. "I am happy for you."

"I know you saw only the authoritative side of him, Hailee, but Officer Ulmer—Quincy, rather—is a kind, gentle, and godly man. He's loving, thoughtful, and...." Ella blushed. "Handsome."

"You're right, Ella. I knew him only as a policeman, and we didn't meet under the best circumstances. He treats you well, doesn't he?"

"Yes, he does. He's exactly the type of husband I have been praying for all along. You see, I thought I was much too old to get married, but the Lord had other plans. He placed Quincy in front of me all these years, and we've been good friends for so long. It was just recently that we both began to see each other as something much more than a friend." Ella giggled shyly. "It took us many years, but we finally realized our love for each other. I couldn't be happier, Hailee."

"And I am happy for you. Have you selected a wedding date?"

"Sometime this fall. And, although I don't like to wish time away, autumn can't come soon enough!"

"I only wish I could be here for the happy event." For a moment, Hailee considered staying in Cincinnati, if only to see one of her dearest friends get married.

But Ella knew her so well that she read her thoughts. "Now, Hailee, you must go. I know how you have searched for a permanent teaching position for some time now. I also know how humbly you have asked God to use your gift of teaching. I believe He has answered that prayer. Had He wanted you to teach in Cincinnati, the opportunity would have arisen."

"You're right, Ella. Still, I shall miss you so."

"And I shall miss you."

"I suppose I should go," Hailee said. She stood to her feet and gave Ella a warm hug.

"Take care, dear one. Write and let me know that you have arrived safely."

"I will."

"And don't worry. You'll do fine in Montana."

"Good-bye, then."

"No, never good-bye," said Ella. "As my grand-mother Fanshaw was fond of saying, 'It's never "Good-bye" but instead, "So long."'"

"So long, then, Ella."

Hailee hoped that Ella's conviction about her doing fine in Montana would prove true. She took one last look around the room. With the adventure that lay before her, she might never get another chance to see the place that had housed so much of her past.

CHAPTER TWO

Seated in his small office, Reverend Nate Adams tapped his pencil on his desk as he tried to think of the right way to make a particular point in Sunday's sermon. He glanced down at the sheet of paper. Although he'd been working for the past hour, all he had written so far was the central Scripture, Galatians 5:22–23, and the words "The Fruit of the Spirit." *Lord, please give me the words to write so that I may preach them according to Your will this Sunday,* he prayed silently.

Maybe he needed a break. Standing, Nate clasped his hands behind his back and stretched as he stared out the lone window in his office. The main street of Pine Haven was busy, as it usually was at midday, even with the hot July sun beating down. Townsfolk bustled about, greeting one another as they tended to their business. In recent years, Pine Haven had grown substantially, reaching a population of nearly four hundred. Prime grazing land, combined with the railroad expansion, had brought people from all over the United States and beyond to settle in the friendly Western town.

Nate had moved here from Boston nearly a year ago to accept the position as pastor. Of course, from the first time he'd set foot in the town for the wedding of Aunt Kaydie and Uncle Jonah, he'd known that he'd live here someday....

"I'm so glad you could make it," Aunt Kaydie said to Grandmother—her mother, Florence Worthington.

"Yes, well, traveling here was not first on my list of things to do, but I did not think it proper for you to get married without at least one parent present. By the way," Grandmother said, "this is my grandson, Maxwell Nathaniel Adams Junior."

Nate nodded at Aunt Kaydie's new husband, Jonah, who returned the gesture with a smile.

"I was not about to travel so great a distance on my own again," Grandmother continued, "and since Kaydence's father cannot travel, I decided to take young Maxwell Junior with me. He's far better company than our chauffeur, Lawrence, and it was time he saw the uncivilized West."

"It's a pleasure to meet you, Maxwell," said Jonah, extending his arm for a handshake.

"You can call me Nate." Nate had heard men introduce themselves that way, and it made him feel older to say it, himself. He looked around, thinking that Pine Haven was hardly as "uncivilized" as Grandmother had indicated. "This place isn't so bad. You made it sound like the pits of the earth, Grandmother."

"Pish posh," Grandmother said. "It is the pits of the earth, as far as I'm concerned."

"I don't think so," Nate insisted. "I think I'd like to live here someday." Where did that come from?

"And you can say that after spending a mere thirty minutes in this place?" she asked, raising an eyebrow.

Nate nodded, even though he himself was surprised at how comfortable he felt here. "I sure can, Grandmother. You'll see. Someday, I'm going to live here. I like it because the folks are nice, and it's not crowded like Boston. I can see it now, Grandmother—living out in the Wild West, with my own ranch, a buggy, and a team of horses, and—"

"Nonsense, child," Grandmother cut in.

"I even like this church," he continued, ignoring her attempts to stifle him. Then, he walked back up the front steps and down the aisle to the well-worn wooden podium. "Hello, and thank you for coming today," he said with deepened voice. "Would you please turn to page one forty-five in your hymnals?" He looked down and picked up a tattered hymnal. As he ran his fingers along the edges of the pages, he wondered how one little book could hold so many hymns. Of course, he didn't have much experience with hymnals, or hymns, for that matter. He and his family attended church on occasion, but it seemed to him that they went out of a sense of duty and social obligation. And Nate had never cared enough to memorize the rich words of worship.

"Maxwell Nathaniel Adams Junior! Come down from there this instant!" Grandmother screeched.

Nate looked up and saw his grandmother walking briskly toward him. "I really would like to live here someday, Grandmother," he told her.

"There will be no more talk of that, young man. I've already lost two daughters to this uncivilized place. I'm not about to lose a grandson to it, too!"

After that first visit, Nate had found that there was no place else he'd rather live than Pine Haven, even if his grandmother had called it the "pits of the earth."

What Nate hadn't known when he'd first set foot in Pine Haven ten years ago was that God would call him back there to spread the gospel in a place where so many still hadn't heard about the saving grace of Jesus Christ.

Nate turned and peeked out through his office door at the sanctuary. It was a rustic space, with ten rows of pews facing the front, where there was a podium and an old piano. There was no carpet or fancy stained-glass windows, as there were in most of the churches in Boston. There was no intricate wrought-iron railing leading into the Pine Haven church; instead, only three wooden stairs in need of painting led to the double-door entrance. A steeple and a cross made of rough-hewn wood provided the only decoration for the exterior.

Yes, it was the Lord's house, and it was Nate's church. With the guidance of his heavenly Father, he had embarked on a mission to bring lost souls to Christ, as well as to assist those already within the Father's hand to grow in their walks with Him. Nate was their shepherd, and, by God's grace, he would lead his flock.

Nate felt a range of emotions, as he always did whenever he paused to take in this place where God had called him. He was humbled that he'd been chosen for such an important job, and that the townsfolk of Pine Haven had even accepted him in the first place when the former pastor, Reverend Eugene, and his wife, Myrtle, had moved to California.

It probably had helped that he had so many relatives in the area. There were the Sawyers—Aunt McKenzie, Uncle Zach, and cousins Davey and Chloe—and the Dickensons—Aunt Kaydie, Uncle Jonah, and cousins Bethany Ethel, Tommy, and Clint. Still, a young pastor fresh out of seminary with no preaching experience was not exactly in high demand. "Don't limit what God can do," Uncle Zach had told him. "Apply for the position and watch as God opens doors that you thought could never be opened."

And Nate had done just that. After receiving the letter from Uncle Zach about the position, Nate had prayed, then applied. He'd written thoughtfully about why he wanted the position and how he planned to provide spiritual leadership for the fine citizens of Pine Haven. Not long after he'd sent his letter, he received one back—a formal offer for the Reverend Maxwell Nathaniel Adams Jr. to become the pastor of Pine Haven Chapel.

Nate turned back to the window and looked out at the street, trying to identify anyone he saw. He was proud of how quickly he was learning the names of the citizens of Pine Haven. Granted, it would take a while for him to learn them all, but he'd made good progress in the past nine months. As a matter of fact, of the ten or so people in the street at that moment, he could probably name eight. He listed off the people he recognized: Uncle Jonah; Wayne Waterson, the blacksmith; Sheriff Clyde Kinion and his wife, Marie; Anders Nash and his daughter, Etta Mae; the widow Marlen; and Lucille Granger.

Lucille Granger. What was she doing? Nate squinted to improve his view of the town busybody, who, with her husband, Fred, owned and operated Granger Mercantile. She stopped on the boardwalk between her store and the post office and held up what appeared to be an envelope toward the sky, tilting her round head back to gaze at it. She rotated it slightly, then turned it over, and it looked to Nate like she was trying to read the contents of whatever was inside! He shook his head. Never had he met someone as nosy and prone to gossip as Lucille. And she never changed, no matter how many sermons he preached on the dangers of gossip.

Nate exited his office, walked down the aisle, pulled open the door, and stepped out into the sunshine. *Perhaps a stroll down the street will provide me with some inspiration,* he thought. He closed his eyes and lifted his face to the sun's warm rays.

"Reverend Adams! Oh, Reverend Adams!"

Nate opened his eyes to see Lucille rushing toward him, propelled by her short legs and waving the envelope wildly. "Oh, Reverend!" she squealed.

Nate walked down the church steps to greet her. "What is it, Lucille? Is something wrong?"

"Is something wrong?" she repeated, looking confused.

"Yes, is something wrong?" Nate asked again.

"No, nothing's wrong; I have something for you." Lucille began to fan herself with the envelope. "I was just chatting with Mr. Victor in the post office and saw this envelope on his desk. While I always try to keep my eyes from wandering beyond what they should see, I did notice that it was addressed to you."

Nate nodded and waited for her to continue. What would Lucille think if she knew that he'd seen her trying to read the contents of his envelope moments earlier?

"Anyhow, I asked Mr. Victor—I said, 'Mr. Victor, would you like for me to take that letter to Reverend Adams? It looks mighty important.' And Mr. Victor, he said, 'Why, Lucille, you are always such a helpful sort. Yes, I would appreciate it very much if you would take it to the reverend.' And, ever glad to accommodate others, I said, 'Very well, then, Mr. Victor. I'll take it to him. I'm heading over toward the church, anyway.'" Lucille's eyes widened as she paused, probably waiting for an accolade from Nate.

He decided to humor her. "Thank you, Lucille. I appreciate your taking the time to deliver that to me," he said, suppressing a grin.

"Oh, it's no problem at all, Reverend. You see, I noticed that the return addressee is a Miss Hailee Annigan from Cincinnati, Ohio, and I just knew it was important, because she was our first choice to be the new teacher." Lucille held her head high and puffed out her chest with pride. "Yes, here is the return address, up here in the left-hand corner," Lucille said, pointing at the spot she indicated. "She has nice penmanship."

"May I have the envelope, Lucille?" Nate asked.

"The envelope? Oh, yes, the envelope. Do forgive me, Reverend." Lucille handed it over—reluctantly, Nate thought. "Do you think she accepted our offer?"

Lucille just had to be the first to know. Well, if not the first, then the second, for Nate would be the first.

"There's no way of knowing until I open the envelope," he said.

"Yes, well, go right ahead. Don't let me stop you." Lucille smoothed down her already too-smooth, too-tight, and too-severely-slicked-back hair, which had been pulled into a bun on the very top of her head like a Christmas tree ornament.

"Thank you again, Lucille. You have a blessed day in the Lord."

"And you do the same, Reverend."

Nate turned his back to her and opened the letter. *Please let Miss Annigan have said yes*, he prayed. The last thing he wanted was to be obliged to offer the position to their second choice—the only other applicant—an impatient- and strict-sounding woman from Wilmerville, Montana, who didn't seem to be a good option.

Nate tore open the envelope, unfolded the letter, and began to read. His eyes had scanned only the date and the words "Dear Reverend Adams" when he felt a soft wisp of air on his neck. He turned his head to look over his shoulder and nearly collided with a forehead—Lucille's.

"Lucille?" He raised his eyebrows. "What are you doing?"

"Nothing! Nothing at all." She clasped her hands behind her back and smiled sheepishly at him.

"Were you reading over my shoulder?"

"I...well, I...you see, I was...."

"Lucille, this is a private letter," Nate gently reminded her.

"A private letter? Oh, dear. Do pardon me. I was merely trying to see if she had accepted our offer of the position of teacher of the fine children of Pine Haven."

Nate grinned. "Lucille, I need to read the letter first. Regardless of Miss Annigan's decision, we'll have a school board meeting tomorrow night to discuss the teaching position and the next steps we need to take."

"Does that mean she said no?" Lucille looked horrified.

"I haven't gotten to her answer yet," Nate said. He wondered if Lucille realized how nosy she was being.

"Well, go ahead and read it. Don't let me delay you." Lucille took a step back and put her hands on her hips.

Nate truly admired Uncle Zach's patience with this woman. He didn't think he could ever match it. "Lucille, would you please do me a very important favor?"

"A favor?" Lucille's expression brightened. "You know that, as the owner of the finest mercantile in Pine Haven, I strive to do my best to accommodate others."

"Yes, I do know that," said Nate. *It's the only mercantile in Pine Haven*, he almost said. "This is extremely important, Lucille."

At Nate's declaration, Lucille leaned toward him, her eyes wide with anticipation. They looked even bigger magnified by her thick glasses. "What is it that you need me to do?"

"Would you please remind the school board members of the meeting at six thirty tomorrow evening?"

"I will do that," Lucille answered solemnly. She adjusted her glasses on her nose. "See you tomorrow, if not before."

"So long," said Nate. He watched as Lucille hurried off to tend to her assignment. Returning his focus to the letter in his hand, he began to read:

July 2, 1893

Dear Reverend Adams,

Please convey my gratitude to the school board for offering me the position as teacher in Pine Haven. I would be honored to accept the position. As you requested in your recent correspondence, I will make arrangements to arrive there on July 27.

Sincerely,
Hailee Annigan
Cincinnati, Ohio

Nate sighed with relief. *Thank You, Lord*, he prayed. He wanted only what was best for the pupils of the Pine Haven school, not only because several of them were related to him, but also because he truly cared about children. While there had been only two applicants for the teaching position, he, as well as the other school board members, had clearly agreed that Hailee Annigan was the better choice. Based on her letter of interest, she sounded like a kind woman with a love of teaching and a heart for children.

Nate glanced again at her letter of acceptance. Yes, Miss Annigan was likely a spinster in her late forties with smooth black hair pulled tautly into a bun at the back of her head. She was probably tall, thin, and sure-footed; wore glasses; and dressed in plain, brown cotton tweed dresses. It was doubtful she'd ever broken a law in her life, and she probably strived to make sure none of her students did, either. Nate then laughed to himself. He had just described one of his favorite teachers from the boarding school he had attended years ago. Still, he expected Miss Annigan to be a lot like her.

CHAPTER THREE

After brushing her long, blonde hair and tying it back with a ribbon, Hailee put her comb in her trunk, closed and secured the lid, and took one final look around the room she'd called hers. She would miss the humble space and, even more, the woman who owned the house. When Hailee had left The Sanctuary of Promise at the age of seventeen, she'd had nowhere to go. She thanked God for leading her to Dot Pangbourn's Boardinghouse. Dot had taken Hailee under her wing and had even reduced her monthly rent until she'd found a permanent job, working in the same factory where her mother had worked several years prior.

Hailee stepped aside when the doorman came to carry her trunk to the carriage. She followed him out the door and down the stairs, then turned and entered the sitting room, where Dot was seated at the solid wooden table, mending some clothes. She glanced up and smiled warmly at Hailee.

"I shall miss you, Dot," said Hailee, trying to hold back her tears.

Dot stood to her feet. "And I shall miss you, Hailee. Just remember that if things don't work out in Pine Haven, you are welcome to come back here. There will always be a room for you."

Hailee swallowed hard. "Thank you, Dot. For everything."

"You've brought much happiness to my life, Hailee, and you are more than welcome."

"Dot? Do you...um, do you think I'm doing the right thing by moving to Pine Haven?"

"Come here, dear." Dot opened her arms wide, and Hailee walked into them, returning the embrace. "Do I think you are doing the right thing?" Dot whispered into Hailee's ear. "Absolutely."

Hailee took a step back and reached up to wipe a tear. "But...but how can you be so sure?"

Dot smiled. "Remember the day when you saw the advertisement for a teacher in Pine Haven, and we prayed that God would lead you in the right direction?"

"Yes."

"That's how I know. God has opened this door for you, Hailee. He has given you the chance to shape young minds, just as you've always wanted to do. Granted, it would have been nice if the job had been here in Cincinnati or some other city in Ohio. But that wasn't His plan. He wants you to grow. He wants you to spread your wings and go where He leads you."

"But what if I don't like it in Pine Haven? What if the children are so naughty that I want to turn and run? What if I'm not cut out for teaching, after all? What if Philip or Reuben sees one of my postings the second I board the train to Montana—"

"My dear, that's enough 'What if?' questions." Dot patted Hailee's arm. "You asked the Lord to lead you where He wanted you to go, and He has. Will it be challenging? Yes. Will it be different from everything you are accustomed to? Yes. Will you wonder whether you discerned God's promptings correctly when you made your decision? Likely, more than once. But you will never know what it's like to depend fully on God until you make the decision to do so."

Hailee smiled weakly. "But what if they find out about my past?"

"Nonsense!" Dot shook her head. "You are forgiven, are you not?"

"Yes."

"You're no longer living the way you once lived, correct?"

"Correct."

"Then, go and let the Lord use your past experiences to help other children who have made mistakes, as well. You're so concerned about what *might* happen." Dot paused. "The Lord has plans for you, and He will fulfill those plans, in spite of your doubts. Give your concerns to Him and watch as He guides you down a path you never could have expected."

"You're right, Dot," Hailee agreed. "I just had to be certain." *Surely, I can feel assured of my plans, since both Ella and Dot have confirmed them*, she thought.

"I understand your desire to be certain. Remember when I told you about how frightened I was to open the boardinghouse after my sweet Paul died? I kept trying to argue with God. I said, 'What if no one comes to board here, and I can't make a living?' 'What if someone comes to board here and robs me blind?' And on and on I went with those silly statements. I felt the Lord say to me, 'Now, Dot, are you relying on Me, or are you trying to control your future?' Well, once I really thought about it, I could answer honestly that I was trying to control my future. I decided then and there to surrender the fate of the boardinghouse, as well as my future, to God. When I did that, He directed my path in accordance with His will. On top of that, He allowed me to fulfill my dream of operating a boardinghouse. He's also provided me with the most wonderful boarders over the years."

Hailee nodded. "If Philip or Reuben—"

"If Philip or Reuben comes here looking for you, I'll tell him where you are, and then, just as fast as lightning, I'll run to the telegraph office and send you a telegram."

"Thank you, Dot." Hailee opened her arms again to hug the woman once more.

"You are most welcome. Now, off with you, before you miss the boarding call!" With tears in her eyes, Dot gently shoved Hailee toward the door.

Hailee gazed out the window as the train began to move. After a few minutes, she closed her eyes and wondered again what Montana would be like. Did it look anything like Ohio? Pine Haven sounded as if it would be less populated, perhaps with only a few thousand people, instead of the nearly 300,000 residents of Cincinnati. Would the townsfolk welcome her? Would she make new friends quickly? And where would she live? Reverend Adams had mentioned that, in addition to her small stipend, she would earn room and board. Would she stay with his family? She imagined Reverend Nathaniel Adams to be an elderly man—a grandfatherly sort, graying and crouched over—with a soft-spoken wife and several grown children. If that was the case, she wouldn't mind living with the Adamses. It would be a similar arrangement to the boardinghouse, where Dot had become like a grandmother to her.

Hailee would miss Dot a great deal, she knew. She'd miss Ella, too, and she giggled at the memory of the announcement she'd made yesterday about her engagement. If she hadn't heard it from Ella's own mouth, Hailee never would have believed it.

She sighed. Those first few days she'd spent at The Sanctuary of Promise seemed so long ago now. In her mind, she revisited her first impressions of the place where she'd been sent to be transformed into a productive member of society....

"I have your lunch," came a woman's voice from outside the Yellow Flower Room. Hailee rose from where she was seated on the floor and sat on the bed, instead. It was only her fifth day at The Sanctuary of Promise, and already she detested it.

The knob turned, the door opened, and Ella Fanshaw entered the room. She was the teacher who always brought Hailee's meals to her. Hailee glanced out into the hallway and saw two other teachers standing guard, as they always did whenever Miss Fanshaw brought her a meal. It had been this way ever since her first escape attempt. Her seventh try, yesterday afternoon, had been extremely close. But

Officer Ulmer had been checking on things at The Sanctuary and had caught her the second she had opened the front door. Poor timing on her part. Next time, she would try another door and hopefully make it through the large yard, past the buildings nearby, and out onto Gardner Street.

"Hello, Hailee." Miss Fanshaw shut the door with her foot and carried the tray of food toward her. "Lunch today is chicken noodle soup."

Hailee stared at her. Why did she have to be so chipper?

"I'm going to set your meal right here." Miss Fanshaw lowered the tray to the small desk next to the bed. "It's very good, so I hope you won't waste it."

Hailee said nothing but continued to stare at Miss Fanshaw. Why should the teacher at The Sanctuary of Promise care whether or not she wasted her food? What business was it of hers?

"Oh, I nearly forgot! I brought you something." Miss Fanshaw dug inside her pocket and pulled out a folded piece of paper. "It's a Bible verse I'd like you to look up and read."

"What would I want with a Bible verse?" Hailee demanded.

"Well, I thought I would bring you a different verse each day, and that you could look it up in the Bible and read the four verses that precede it, as well as the four that follow."

"Why?" Hailee didn't see the point. Yes, she was bored, but not bored enough to read the only book in the Yellow Flower Room.

"It'll prepare you for when you begin regular Bible studies," said Miss Fanshaw. "In addition, you'll see what a treasure the Word of God truly is."

"I don't think so," said Hailee. "God abandoned me long ago. Why would I want to read His Word?"

"God abandoned you?" asked Miss Fanshaw.

"I don't know what else to call it." Hailee shrugged. "First, He made my little brother Philip be born with a foot that faces the wrong way. Then, He took my pa from me when I was eleven and my ma when I was thirteen. And then, He allowed me to be caught and put in this horrid place, where I can't take care of my little brothers." Hailee sighed. "I think God has so many people to worry about that He just forgot about me, or maybe He just didn't care about me to begin with."

Miss Fanshaw looked thoughtful but said nothing, so Hailee decided to change the subject. "I saw those two teachers standing guard in the hallway. Are you afraid I'm going to try to escape again?"

"I suppose it's not unreasonable to expect you to try again, since you've made seven attempts thus far," Miss Fanshaw said with a smile. She sat down on the edge of Hailee's bed and studied her.

Hailee grew uncomfortable under her scrutiny. She was unusually skinny, she knew, and tall for her age; her body was gangly, her movements far from graceful. Her hair felt greasy and surely looked to be in need of a good washing, and she'd bitten her fingernails down to the skin. Yet Miss Fanshaw didn't look the least bit repulsed. Still, Hailee didn't like the attention.

"I don't see why you care so much whether I stay here or not," said Hailee, rolling her eyes.

"For one thing, you were ordered by a judge to be kept here until you straighten out," Miss Fanshaw replied, her voice firm yet kind. "For another, we care about you, Hailee, whether you realize it or not."

"Why would you care about me? I'm just another kid off the street who messed up and got herself caught. I'm just another kid who has to be trapped in this fancy jail."

Miss Fanshaw laughed softly.

"What's so funny?" Hailee gave her meanest glare.

"I've never thought of this place as a jail, fancy or not," said Miss Fanshaw. "Most of the children like it here."

"I'm not like most of the children," Hailee retorted. "Not only do I enjoy my freedom, but I also have mouths to feed—mouths that probably haven't been fed since I've been penned up here."

"Tell me about your brothers," said Miss Fanshaw. She folded her hands in her lap.

"Why do you care?"

Miss Fanshaw merely smiled. "How old are they?"

Hailee thought for a moment and narrowed her eyes. Why was Miss Fanshaw being so nice to her? Hailee knew better than to trust anyone, especially a teacher at The Sanctuary. "Reuben is twelve," she finally said, "and Philip is six. He's the one who has a foot that's turned the wrong way, and so he has to walk with a crutch."

"You are the oldest, then? I'm the oldest in my family, too."

"I'm supposed to be caring for them."

"I bet you were good at taking care of them."

"I was, but now I can't, since I have to stay here." Hailee folded her arms and pouted.

"Perhaps I can check on them."

"Why would you want to do that?"

"Because I care about children, especially little ones who have to walk with a crutch."

"They...they live on Gardner Street." Hailee hadn't wanted to tell, but maybe it wouldn't hurt. Maybe Miss Fanshaw would find her brothers and bring them to The Sanctuary, too.

"Gardner Street? That's not far from here." Miss Fanshaw looked thoughtful. "Did you know that The Sanctuary of Promise is not just for children who get caught breaking the law?"

"No," Hailee admitted.

"It's true. The Sanctuary was founded by Reverend P. L. Davidson. He wanted it to be a place where orphans and other struggling children could get their lives on the right track. We have many children here under the age of ten. As a matter of fact, we have more orphans than we do children who have been caught breaking the law."

Hailee raised her eyebrows.

"What's more, Reverend P. L. Davidson wanted this to be a place where children were educated—not only in the disciplines of reading, writing, arithmetic, Bible studies, and so forth, but also a trade. Some of our older boys are learning how to work in masonry, carpentry, and assisting with the upkeep of the building and its grounds. Girls are taught sewing, cooking, and taking care of the younger children. You see, Hailee, it's not like a fancy jail at all. It's more like a home away from home."

Hailee wasn't so sure. She hadn't seen much of anything but the Yellow Flower Room.

"Once you stop trying to escape, we can allow you to leave the Yellow Flower Room, and you will be able to join in the activities and make new friends. I think you'll find that you like it here at The Sanctuary." Miss Fanshaw paused. "Now, that being said, why don't I go see if your brothers are still at Gardner Street? Perhaps they would like to come here, too."

Hailee hesitated a moment. "All right," she finally agreed.

"I will search for your brothers...and I need you to do something for me."

"What's that?" asked Hailee. She should have known there were strings attached. Still, it would be wonderful to see her brothers again, even if it was at The Sanctuary.

"You have to promise not to try to escape again."

Hailee took a deep breath and considered her request. Maybe she could make the promise with her fingers crossed.

"I'll know if you're lying," said Miss Fanshaw, as if she'd read Hailee's thoughts.

Hailee narrowed her eyes again at the woman. She supposed Miss Fanshaw seemed innocent enough.

In the end, Hailee figured it was worth promising not to run away if it meant she might see her brothers again. And if they came to live at The Sanctuary with her, it probably wouldn't be so bad. After a while, she would find another place for them to live.

"All right," Hailee said. "I promise."

"Good! I'll let you know what I find out. In the meantime, your soup is probably already cold. You might as well start eating."

Hailee lifted the bowl of soup from the tray and brought it to her lap. Then, she picked up her spoon and delved in, ravenous from going days with so little food.

"You must be hungry! There's enough for seconds, if you'd like," said Miss Fanshaw. "You know, Hailee, now that you're no longer confined to the Yellow Flower Room, you'll be able to take a nice, hot bath, and we have some new clothes for you to wear. You'll be able to eat as much as your stomach can hold."

Hailee looked around. Yes, it would be nice to be in a different room and to enjoy tasty meals with the other children. She swallowed a bit of soup. "Will I wear a uniform like the ones I see the other kids wearing?" she asked.

"Yes. As a matter of fact, I can bring you a nice white blouse and long blue calico skirt after you've had your bath, if you'd like."

Hailee nodded. "I'd like that, I think," she said.

Miss Fanshaw grinned and stood up. "Well, I'd best go now, as I have to assist with kitchen duties. Be sure to look up the Bible verse I gave you, and I'll see you soon, Hailee. We'll get you settled in the girls' room tomorrow."

"Will you go check on my brothers?"

"Bright and early in the morning," Miss Fanshaw assured her.

Hailee would delay her thank-you until Miss Fanshaw had actually located her brothers. She finished her soup and handed Miss Fanshaw the tray with the bowl and spoon. "I think I'd like that second helping."

"I'd be delighted to bring it to you."

The next day at noon, Hailee heard a knock on her door. "Lunchtime," Miss Fanshaw's voice announced. Then, the knob turned, the door opened, and she walked into Hailee's room, as usual.

Hailee looked past her into the hallway, but she didn't see any teachers acting as guards. "Where are the guards?" she asked.

"You promised you wouldn't try to escape," Miss Fanshaw said.

"And you believed me?"

"Of course, I believed you." Miss Fanshaw handed Hailee a sandwich, then fished inside her pocket and pulled out a folded piece of paper. "Here's your Bible verse for today. Did you look up the verse I gave you yesterday?"

Hailee wanted to lie and say she had, but she decided against it. Miss Fanshaw would probably believe her, and then, when she found out the truth, she would really think that Hailee was a liar. "No."

"Well, please do, and look up this one, too."

"I told you, I don't really care about reading the Bible. God abandoned me, remember?"

"God didn't abandon you, Hailee. He's never left your side." Miss Fanshaw took a seat on Hailee's bed as Hailee hungrily took a bite of her sandwich and chewed. After swallowing, she asked, "Did you find my brothers?"

"I need to talk to you about them," said Miss Fanshaw.

"What's wrong?"

"Hailee—"

"Are they all right?" Hailee was nearly screaming. She hoped desperately that nothing had happened to Philip and Reuben in the week that she'd been away from them.

"Hailee, they aren't at the Gardner Street place anymore."

"Did you look everywhere?"

"I looked in the vacant building. There really is nothing else on Gardner Street except the dry goods store and the shoe store."

"Yes, the vacant building is where we lived."

"I'd figured as much."

"Where could they be?"

"After I checked the building, I asked around and discovered that Philip had been sent to live with a family. I'm not sure where, as they couldn't tell me. They said only that he had gone to live with a family somewhere in Cincinnati. Reuben has been sent to live with a family on a farm outside of Cincinnati. Again, they couldn't give me any details, but they reassured me both boys are fine. I believe they're going to be adopted."

"Adopted?" Hailee shrieked. "That's terrible news! You told me you would find them!"

"Hailee, I'm sorry. I couldn't get any more information. But this isn't terrible news. On the contrary, it's good news. They are both going to be adopted, and they'll have shelter, food, clothing, and families to live with."

"Why were they separated from each other?" asked Hailee. She threw the remains of her sandwich on the floor.

"I'm not sure. Sometimes, folks don't want to adopt more than one child due to financial reasons."

"What about me?" asked Hailee. "Maybe I would like to be adopted, too."

"Folks come here all the time to adopt children. You have as good a chance as anyone of being adopted."

"Well, I guess I don't really want to be adopted," Hailee grumbled. "No one would want me, anyway.

Only the small, cute ones get adopted. What I really want to know is where my brothers are!"

"I will try my best to find out more information, Hailee."

"Maybe I could go down there and ask. After all, I'm their sister!" Hailee stood up and stormed over to the tiny window. It wasn't fair. If she hadn't been caught stealing that loaf of bread, she would still be with her brothers right now.

"Even so, I don't think they can tell you anything more," said Miss Fanshaw. "I know it doesn't seem right—"

"It's not right. Not right at all!" Hailee began to cry, unable to stop the choking sobs.

Miss Fanshaw stood up and walked toward Hailee, her arms outstretched. When she reached her, she took her in her arms and held her. At first, Hailee resisted, but she quickly relented and buried her face in Miss Fanshaw's shoulder, allowing her pent-up tears to fall.

"I will do whatever I can to help you, Hailee," Miss Fanshaw whispered as she patted Hailee's head. "I will help you in whatever way I can, and I will be here for you."

"Everyone who says that leaves!" Hailee sobbed....

Hailee opened her eyes and realized that her cheeks were wet with tears. She'd never found Philip and Reuben, even though she had prayed that she would and had posted signs all over the city with her contact information. Miss Fanshaw had done everything she could to locate the boys, as had Officer

Ulmer. The adoption agencies didn't seem to have any records of them. In the end, it was as though her brothers had vanished without a trace, leaving only tender memories in her mind.

Now, she was embarking on a trip to a place she'd never been before. She had learned so many things at The Sanctuary of Promise, including the fact that God hadn't abandoned her and that He loved her and always had. Hailee had received superior schooling there, and, after finishing her studies at the top of her class, she had assisted many children in finding direction for their own lives, just as Miss Fanshaw and Miss Torenz had done for her. She had helped in their classrooms once she'd graduated from The Sanctuary, meanwhile pursuing her teaching certificate under the auspices of Miss Fanshaw, who had become Hailee's friend and mentor, someone she could trust.

Hailee reached up and wiped a tear that slid down her cheek. *Lord, it frightens me to leave Cincinnati and all that I know and love. How will I find my way around a new town? And, Father, I still miss my brothers dearly. I have prayed so many times that You would bring them back to me. I know that I must be patient, but waiting is so difficult. Please, Lord, comfort me in this journey and give me assurance that my brothers are fine. I love You, Lord, and I thank You that You never did abandon me, that You are with me even now.*

As Hailee turned and gazed out the window again, a sense of peace washed over her. She somehow knew that, while it wouldn't be easy, her heavenly Father would equip her with whatever she needed to survive this new adventure He had called her to.

CHAPTER FOUR

$\mathcal{R}$everend Adams?"

Nate looked up from his desk at the familiar, syrupy voice of Etta Mae Nash. Not again!

"I'm in my office," he called back, then stood up.

Moments later, Etta Mae came into view, strutting toward his office in an expensive-looking azure dress that accentuated her shapely figure. He focused instead on her face, framed by her long, wavy blonde hair.

"I brought you something," she said as she entered his office, smiling broadly to reveal her perfectly straight white teeth. She thrust a plate of cookies at Nate. "I baked these just this morning."

"Thank you, Etta Mae." He set the plate on his desk. "These look delicious."

"They are." She eyed Nate and gave him a seductive smile, which he tried to ignore.

The folks in Pine Haven had been so generous to him, especially with gifts of food, that if they continued to feed him as they had for the past several months, it wouldn't be long before he'd need a new wardrobe. Not that he minded. The plates of baked goods and the dinner invitations were welcome substitutes for preparing his own food, which was never very palatable. "What brings you to town on this beautiful day?" he asked.

"Oh, I just wanted to bring you these cookies," Etta Mae crooned. "I surely don't want you to go hungry."

"Thank you. I appreciate that."

"Also, Mother asked me to invite you to dinner tonight." Etta Mae paused. "Please, Reverend, don't say no, because it would just break Mother's heart, and we don't want to disappoint her."

"Dinner sounds fine," said Nate. He prayed often for Mr. Nash's salvation and welcomed the opportunity to be a godly example to the wealthy ranch owner.

"Very well, then. I'll see you at six o'clock tonight."

Nate nodded. "I'll be there."

Etta Mae batted her eyelashes, though he wasn't sure why. It failed to make her more attractive and merely looked as if she had something in her eye. "The summer's nearly over, and I have yet to picnic at the lake."

"Is that so?" Nate knew what Etta Mae was hinting at. She made similar insinuations every time they met, which was often.

"Yes, that's so," said Etta Mae, her voice dripping with self-pity.

"I hope you get the chance to go sometime," said Nate. He wasn't sure how to handle Etta Mae without hurting her feelings. He knew she liked him and wanted him to court her. Unfortunately for Etta Mae, the attraction wasn't mutual.

She gave him a smile that seemed forced. "Well, then, I must be on my way. I'll see you tonight."

"Thank you again for the cookies," said Nate.

Etta Mae fanned her fingers in a feminine wave, then turned on her heel and walked out of his office.

Nate watched her exit the church. He'd seen more than his share of women like her in Boston. As a matter of fact, his own mother reminded him of Etta Mae. And she wasn't the type of woman who would ever win his heart. He prayed that the Lord would provide him with a wife who was kind and thoughtful, and who loved others more than she loved herself.

Nate thought about his parents, back in Boston. Had it really been several years since he'd first told them of his plan to become a pastor? Memories of that day flooded his mind....

"Mother and Father, there's something I need to speak with you about," Nate said when the servants had cleared the dinner table.

"What is it?" his mother asked, readjusting her already perfect posture. "You seem distressed."

"Now that I'm out of boarding school, I've been thinking a lot about my future."

"That's wise, son," said his father, a thin, soft-spoken man with receding blond hair.

Nate sucked in his breath. It wouldn't be easy telling his parents what was on his heart. It had never been easy to talk with them, especially when his opinion differed from theirs. Still, he knew he needed to inform them of what he had decided to do. "Mother and Father," he began, then paused to send a quick prayer heavenward.

"What is it, Nate?" Mother asked, setting her tea-cup in its saucer.

"I've decided to become a pastor." There, he'd said it. He braced himself for his parents' reactions.

His mother nearly choked. "I beg your pardon?"

"I've decided to become a pastor," Nate repeated, trying to keep his voice steady.

"A pastor?" his father said with a confused look on his face.

"Yes, Father, a pastor," said Nate. "I feel it's what God has called me to do."

"What do you mean, God has called you to become a pastor?" His mother's voice had risen in pitch. "Did He send you a telegram?"

"No, Mother." Nate sighed in frustration. "It means that, after much prayer, I feel that God is leading me to a vocation of bringing others to Christ."

"I don't understand a word you're saying," his mother said curtly. She turned to her husband. "Do you understand him, Maxwell?"

"I'm afraid I don't. Are you saying you would rather be a pastor than a lawyer?"

"If that's what he's saying, then he's mistaken," his mother announced. "I can't believe we are even discussing this. Whoever heard of such a ludicrous career choice?"

"I have to agree, son," his father put in. "No man in his right mind would walk away from a life of privilege, such as you have, to become a pastor. Can you imagine the gossip that will circulate in our social circles?"

"I'm not mistaken, and it's not a ludicrous choice, Mother. And with all due respect, Father, I don't care about the opinions of the people in our social circles. I want to make a difference for eternity." Even as he tried to explain, Nate knew there was no way his parents would understand until God softened their hearts.

"Pish posh!" Mother exclaimed. "Your future has been planned for you since you were born. Tell him, Maxwell, about our plans for him."

"She's right," his father affirmed. "We've long expected you to work at Worthington and Worthington Law with your grandfather and me. You know that, Nate. We've discussed this many times over the years."

"Yes, Father, I know your plans for me. But I also know that the Lord has plans for me."

"The Lord has plans for you?" His father looked dumbfounded.

"Yes, Father. And I believe those plans include my attending seminary and becoming a pastor."

"I have heard enough!" his mother exclaimed dramatically. "No son of my mine is going to take a job that pays next to peanuts. Do you realize the kind of future you would have?" Without allowing Nate time to respond, his mother continued, "I realize that you will someday inherit the entire Adams fortune, but still...don't you think you should pursue a reputable career that will enable you to make a name and amass a fortune for yourself?"

"Money doesn't really matter to me," Nate explained.

"Money doesn't matter to you? Did you hear that, Maxwell? What has become of our son? Where is the real Maxwell Nathaniel Adams Junior? Surely, you are an impostor, as this is not how we raised you to be."

"Mother, I am your son," Nate insisted. "And I love you and Father very much. However, I feel I must respond to God's call for my life. I don't expect you to understand, although I pray that you will, someday."

"No, I'm afraid we don't understand," his father said, folding his hands on the table.

"I can't bear it. I just can't!" Mother began to sob.

Nate sighed. This was turning out to be even more arduous than he'd thought. "Mother, please don't cry. It's not that awful."

"That's easy enough for you to say." His mother blew her nose noisily into her handkerchief. "It's beyond awful to have but one child for whom to plan a life, and then to have that child go about creating a life for himself that is completely contrary to everything you had hoped for him, and without so much as a thank-you. Oh, Maxwell!"

Father pushed away from the table, positioned himself behind Mother's chair, and patted her on the shoulder. "There, there, Peyton. It's all right."

"Where, oh where, did we fail our son, Maxwell? What did we do wrong for him to make such an unfortunate decision?"

"I don't know, Peyton. I honestly don't know. We did everything right, as far as I know—provided him with the best nannies, sent him to the best boarding schools, gave him every privilege a boy could ever hope for...."

Nate scrambled to find something to say to appease his parents. "Mother, Father, please...if seminary does not work out, I'll seriously consider coming back here to attend law school. I give you my word."

At that, his mother's head jerked up, and she blinked at him. "What do you mean, you'll come back here? Where are you going?"

Nate braced himself for her response to his next piece of news. "Well, after seminary, I've decided to pursue a position as reverend in Pine Haven."

"Pine Haven? As in, Montana?" his mother screeched.

"Yes. I've been in correspondence with Aunt McKenzie. She tells me that the current pastor, Reverend Eugene, is preparing to retire and move away from Pine Haven in the next few years. If all goes as planned, I will take his place and assume his responsibilities."

"I should have known McKenzie would put you up to this. As if she hasn't ruined her own life, and Kaydie's, too, now she has to ruin your life! It's despicable!"

Nate knew that his mother had never gotten along well with either of her younger sisters. The two of them had relocated to Pine Haven—McKenzie first, as a mail-order bride, and then Kaydie, when she reunited with McKenzie and fell in love with an employee of McKenzie's husband, Zach.

"Mother, more than anything, I desire your blessing. Again, if it doesn't work out in seminary or in Pine Haven, I will return to Boston and consider preparing for a career in law." Nate didn't want to dishonor his parents, but he knew that doing the Lord's work was far more important than following his parents' plans for his life.

"He does have a point, Peyton," Father said, his voice low. "Nate is young, and he may just need a chance to see that being a reverend is not what he should do with his life. When he figures that out, he'll be back to pursue the plans we've made for him. At that point, he'll still be young, and there will be plenty of years for him to become a partner in the law firm."

Mother closed her eyes and sighed. "I suppose you're right, Maxwell—as usual, I might add." She opened her eyes and looked at Nate. "Go to seminary, Nathaniel, and fulfill your childish fantasy of becoming a reverend. Then, when you realize it's not for you, come back to Boston and secure a real future with a reputable career in law."

"And I must insist that you attend only the finest of seminaries," his father added.

"It's a promise on both accounts," said Nate, although he could not see himself as a lawyer. The Lord had planted too great a desire in his heart to further the kingdom. His parents had no inkling of the importance of following the Lord, yet he hoped that they would someday attend church—not to keep up with society's expectations but to worship the Lord in spirit and in truth....

Suddenly conscious of a bird chirping outside, Nate was brought back to the present. Yes, his parents had reluctantly given him their blessing to attend seminary and become a reverend, even though his mother had tried to talk him out of his decision no fewer than twenty times during the two years he spent in seminary.

Now, at twenty-one years of age, Maxwell Nathaniel Adams Jr. was known as Reverend Adams to those who called Pine Haven home. While he longed to bring those in the small, rustic town to the Lord, he had an even bigger longing—to see his parents surrender their hearts to Jesus Christ. Not a day went by that he didn't pray for their salvation.

CHAPTER FIVE

One day later that week, Nate decided to spend the afternoon painting the wooden steps and railing of the church, which had been splintered and peeling ever since his arrival. He worked for several hours, until the train whistle caught his attention. He balanced his paintbrush on top of the pail and then pulled out his pocket watch. *A quarter to four already? Where did the day go?* Without a second to waste, Nate cleaned up his supplies and rushed into his office to make himself presentable. He tucked his button-up plaid shirt into his trousers, regretting that he didn't have enough time to go home and change into his standard pastor attire. He needed to meet the new teacher at the train depot, and he didn't want to make a poor impression by arriving late. Dusting off his trousers, he checked them for any signs of brown paint, and then he wiped his face on his sleeve. Why had he lost track of the time? He sighed, yanking the cuff of his right pant leg out of the back of his leather boot, where it had gotten caught.

Nate slipped out the back door and locked it just as the train whistle sounded again. Then, he set off toward the train depot, thankful that it was only a few blocks away. Still, he quickened his pace, hoping to arrive before the train pulled into the station. He hadn't told anyone the exact time Miss Annigan was expected to arrive, as he didn't want her to be greeted by a mob of curious Pine Haven residents.

A cluster of folks had already gathered on the platform. Some were probably there to meet one of the few travelers who would arrive, while others were likely just curious to see any newcomers. Nate found a vacant spot on the platform and watched the train approach. He hoped he would be able to find Miss Annigan quickly. It wouldn't be too difficult, he figured, considering no more than a dozen passengers would get off the train, and it was unlikely that more than one of them would be a spinster schoolmarm.

Her heart pounding, Hailee wondered for the one hundred and fifty-sixth time if she was doing the right thing by coming to this unfamiliar place to teach the local children. At the sound of the train whistle, she focused her attention on the scenery outside her window. The area looked to be sparsely populated, nowhere near as dense as Cincinnati. During the course of her journey, she had formed a picture in her mind of how Pine Haven would look, and the reality didn't exactly match. She'd expected a population of 5,000 or so, and, while she'd known that Pine Haven would be much smaller than Cincinnati, she'd anticipated at least a few tall buildings and cobblestone streets. Instead, the tallest building was perhaps four stories, and the streets looked to be dirt. And Pine Haven was apparently home to no more than a thousand residents.

Hailee shrugged. She didn't mind that Pine Haven wasn't anything like she'd imagined it would be. She'd hoped only to find in this town some friendly, God-fearing folks who would help to ease her adjustment to her new life.

As the train slowed to a stop, Hailee searched the small crowd that had gathered on the platform. When her gaze fell upon a kindly-looking older man who stood beside a woman who must be his wife, Hailee breathed a sigh of relief. *There you are, Reverend Adams!* She was so thankful that someone had come to meet her. It would be a nightmare to try to navigate the streets of Pine Haven and locate the reverend without any help.

The aisle was blocked by several passengers preparing to disembark. Although Hailee was anxious to set foot on solid ground again, she decided to wait in her seat until everyone else had exited. She watched as the conductor assisted the passengers off of the train, then looked out her window and saw the excited faces of the travelers, as many of them embraced someone standing on the platform. Hailee felt a twinge of envy for those who were reuniting with family members. How she missed her parents and longed to be reunited with her brothers! She had prayed countless times for that reunion to occur, and she would not allow her faith to fail, no matter how long she had to wait.

Hailee rose to her feet. She reached up to make sure her hair was still secured in its ribbon, then reached down and smoothed her dress. Finally, she

grasped the handle of her carpetbag and moved into
the aisle. The conductor offered her his hand, and
she accepted his help to descend the steps—grateful-
ly, as she had never been sure-footed. Hailee could
run like the wind, if she had to, yet if there was an
obstacle in her way, or sometimes no obstacle but her
own two feet, she tripped very easily. She thanked
the conductor, then turned and spotted her trunk,
which sat amid several other pieces of luggage on the
platform.

Moving toward it, she glanced up to locate the
man she had presumed to be Reverend Adams. To
her dismay, he had turned his back and was walking away, engaged in animated conversation with his
wife and one of the other passengers from the train.
She must have been mistaken. Standing beside her
trunk now, she nervously scanned the thinning
crowd, yet no other nicely-dressed elderly men were
in sight. Had Reverend Adams forgotten his promise
to meet her at the train depot? Perhaps, he had fallen
ill and hadn't been able to send someone else in his
place. If that was the case, where would she go? With
whom would she stay?

Hailee began to circle her trunk, trying to get
a better view of the people around her. After several
steps, she stumbled and began to teeter. Just when
she feared falling on her face, she felt someone's
hands catch her. "Careful, there!" said a man's voice.

I am such a clumsy fool! Hailee thought as she
regained her footing. Then, she looked up and met
the eyes of the man who'd kept her from making a
terrible first impression on the citizens of Pine Haven.
Still, her legs felt weak from her embarrassment,
made worse by the discovery that the man who had

caught her fall was extremely handsome, with sandy hair, striking blue eyes, and a gentle smile. "Thank you," she said, her voice barely above a whisper. "I'm afraid I'm rather clumsy."

"Not at all," the man replied. "This platform isn't exactly the smoothest surface to walk on."

"I suppose my mind was on anything but walking," Hailee admitted. "Thank you again. It would have been quite embarrassing to fall."

The man grinned, making her knees weaken even more. "Well, that's my job—to prevent pretty female passengers from tripping and falling."

"Really?" Hailee returned his teasing remark with a smile and met his eyes. Their gazes locked for what seemed like minutes, and Hailee soon felt the heat of a blush creep onto her cheeks. She immediately averted her eyes and resumed scanning the crowd. "I...I'm actually looking for someone."

"Perhaps I can help. I haven't lived here quite a year yet, but I do know most of the folks in town."

Hailee turned and cast him a hopeful look. "I'm looking for a Reverend Nathaniel Adams."

"Reverend Nathaniel Adams?"

"Yes," said Hailee. "Do you know him? Or where I might find him?"

"You just did. I'm Reverend Nate Adams." The man smiled.

"Oh!" Hailee gasped. "I—I was expecting someone...someone else," she stammered.

"Someone else?"

"Yes...it was probably silly of me, but I expected you to be a bit older, maybe even a grandfather."

The reverend laughed heartily, but, rather than shame, a comforting warmth filled Hailee's heart.

"You wouldn't, by chance, be Miss Hailee Annigan, would you?"

"I am," Hailee said, suddenly relieved.

"Well, I have to admit, you're nothing like I expected, either." The reverend paused. "Forgive me, but I pictured a homely spinster."

"A spinster!" Hailee giggled. "I expect to have a few more years, at least, before being considered a spinster."

He chuckled. "I suppose I should formally introduce myself. I'm Reverend Maxwell Nathaniel Adams Junior, but everyone calls me Reverend Adams, or just Nate. Welcome to Pine Haven." He extended his hand toward her.

"Thank you. It's nice to be here," Hailee said, shaking his hand. "I'm Hailee Annigan."

"Well, Miss Annigan, let me carry your trunk, and I'll take you to the widow Marlen's house, where you will be staying." He hefted the trunk with apparent ease, even though it contained everything Hailee owned. "With any luck, I'll have you delivered to Widow Marlen's house before the folks of Pine Haven realize who you are. I had hoped you would have a chance to rest from your trip before everybody rushes to meet you."

"Thank you," Hailee said, falling into step beside Reverend Adams.

"Widow Marlen lives just down the road from the schoolhouse. I think you'll find that it's a nice place to stay."

Hailee nodded as they continued down the street, all the while praying she wouldn't stumble again. *Thank You, Lord, for helping me to find Reverend Adams so quickly!* she added. *My arrival in*

Pine Haven went even better than expected. Please, Father, go before me and guide me as I adjust to this latest undertaking.

CHAPTER SIX

Two days later, Nate traveled by wagon to Widow Marlen's in the late afternoon to escort Hailee to a welcome dinner at the Sawyer Ranch, the home of his aunt McKenzie and her husband, Zach. Aunt McKenzie had organized the event and invited several families, though not so many as to overwhelm the new schoolteacher.

Seconds after he knocked on the door, Widow Marlen opened it. "Reverend Adams! How nice to see you. Please, come in."

"Thank you, Mrs. Marlen." He stepped into the foyer. "I hope that you're getting along well with your new boarder."

"Oh, yes. Hailee is a dear. She's so considerate and agreeable." She moved to the bottom of the stairs. "Hailee? Reverend Adams is here!"

"Yes, Mrs. Marlen," came a faint reply. "I'll be right there."

Moments later, Nate heard a door close, and Miss Annigan appeared at the top of the stairs. Immediately, his breath caught in his throat. He'd found her to be beautiful when they'd met at the train station, but now, perhaps because she'd had time to rest and regain energy, she looked radiant, even in her simple frock. She was slender, yet with an athletic frame, as he'd learned when he'd held her briefly. Her dark blonde curls framed her oval face attractively, and her eyes, bluish-green in hue, reminded him of the ocean.

"Hello, Miss Annigan," he managed, trying not to stare as she descended the staircase.

"Hello, Reverend Adams," she replied with a smile.

"Are you ready to go? My aunt is delighted that you accepted her invitation." He offered his arm to her.

"Yes, thank you." She turned to Widow Marlen. "I'll see you later tonight, Mrs. Marlen."

"Are you sure you don't want to come along?" Nate asked. "It would be nice to have you there."

"I'm sure. I'm feeling a bit tired today, but you two have a pleasant evening and tell everyone I said hello."

"Of course," Nate said as he opened the door. "Watch your step," he said to Miss Annigan, hoping she wouldn't take offense at his teasing.

Thankfully, she grinned. "I've been trying hard to trip only when there is a true obstacle in the way."

Laughing, Nate assisted her into his buggy, then walked around to the other side and climbed in. "I hope that boarding with Widow Marlen will be suitable for you." He picked up the reins and prompted the horses forward.

"I have no doubt it will be," Miss Annigan replied. "She is such a kind and generous woman, and strong, too, considering that she lost her beloved husband after so many years of marriage."

"It has been difficult for her," Nate acknowledged. "When the school board began searching for a new teacher, they asked her to open her doors to a boarder, in hopes that the company would benefit her. The stipend she receives in exchange is a benefit, as well, since her husband didn't leave her a large inheritance."

Hailee nodded. "I don't think I could have asked for a nicer place to stay, and it's so close to the school." She looked around and seemed to be taking in her surroundings. "It's beautiful here. I had no idea what Pine Haven would be like, or how different it would be from Cincinnati."

Nate knew exactly how she felt. "I'm from Boston, so moving here was a significant change for me, as well. Yet I've found that there's no place I'd rather be. The sky seems never-ending, the summers are perfect, and most of the folks are friendly."

"Boston is enormous! You must have been shocked when you first arrived here."

"I was shocked, but also intrigued. I came here first as a young boy; I traveled with my grandmother to attend my aunt's wedding. Grandmother was almost scandalized by how 'rugged and wild' it was, but I couldn't wait to come back." Nate found it pleasantly easy to talk to Miss Annigan. And, while he'd met her only two days ago, it felt as if he'd known her for years. One thing was certain: he was thankful she wasn't an elderly spinster, and he wanted to know a lot more about her.

"I hope you won't be uncomfortable meeting a group of new people tonight," Nate said, glancing at her. She certainly looked confident and composed,

far from how he felt when he'd first come to Pine
Haven as the new pastor.

She smiled. "I guess I'm a little nervous, mainly
about meeting my students and their parents. I just
want to make a good impression. But everyone I've
met so far—you, Mrs. Marlen, and Mr. Victor at the
post office—has been extremely kind."

"Pretty soon, you'll know everybody in town.
You'll meet most of them in church on Sunday, but
after tonight, you'll at least recognize a few more
faces in the congregation. We've invited the school
board members and some of the townsfolk, including
Doc Orville and his wife, Diane; Sheriff Clyde Kinion
and his wife, Marie; Wayne Waterson, the town
blacksmith, and his wife, Wilma; Mr. Gerald Victor
and his wife, Geraldine; Fred and Lucille Granger,
who own and operate Granger Mercantile; Asa and
Rosemary O'Connell; and a few others.

"My family members will also be there, of
course. I think you'll get along well with them." Nate
paused for a moment. "Oddly, I've grown a lot closer
to Aunt McKenzie than I've ever been with my own
mother. After I came here for Aunt Kaydie's wedding,
she and I corresponded regularly, and she's the one
who told me that the pastor here had plans to retire
in a few years. Aunt Kaydie is soft-spoken and sweet;
she would do just about anything for anyone. They're
married to two of the most highly respected men in
Pine Haven, Zach Sawyer and Jonah Dickenson,
and they have five children between them—my cousins—four of whom will be your students. Chloe and
Bethany Ethel will easily be star pupils. As for the
twins, Clint and Tommy...prayer is in order." He gave
Miss Annigan a mischievous smile.

Her eyes grew large. "Are they troublesome?"

"Hmm. I think 'pranksters' better describes them," Nate replied. "They're the cutest little guys you ever saw, with red hair and freckled faces. Unfortunately, they make a great team; if there's mischief to be made, one of them is sure to take notice and include the other in his shenanigans." He glanced at her again and saw a flash of anxiety cross her face. "Don't worry, Miss Annigan," he added hastily. "You'll do just fine as the new schoolteacher."

"I hope so," she said. "While I've assisted other teachers, I've never had a classroom of my own, so this will be an adventure, in a manner of speaking."

"Just remember that I'm here if you need me. As a matter of fact, you'll never be short on support in Pine Haven."

"Thank you. I truly appreciate that."

"Do you have family in Cincinnati, Miss Annigan?" Nate asked.

"Please, call me Hailee. Miss Annigan sounds so...old."

Nate chuckled. "I'll call you Hailee if you'll agree to call me Nate."

"Agreed," said Hailee. "I have two younger brothers in Cincinnati, Philip and Reuben."

"Do your parents live there, as well?"

Hailee looked down at her hands.

"I'm sorry. I didn't mean to pry," Nate quickly said.

"No, that's all right," Hailee assured him. "My parents have passed on."

"I'm sorry to hear that."

"It was a long time ago. I was eleven when Pa died, thirteen when Ma died. My pa worked long hours in a factory, but he always had the energy to give me a ride on his shoulders. And my ma would read to us from the Bible and pray with us every night before bed. I will always miss them."

"Please accept my sympathies," said Nate, scrambling for words of comfort. Consoling those who grieved was the hardest part of his job.

"Thank you." Hailee sniffed. "Do you have family back in Boston?"

"My parents still live there, as do my grandparents. My grandfather has a law office there, and my father works for him. But I have no siblings, so I learned at an early age how to entertain myself."

"Was it difficult to make the decision to move to Pine Haven and leave them behind?"

Nate chuckled. "When I sensed God's call upon my life to be a man of the cloth, I knew it would be difficult for my parents to understand. But, for me, moving here wasn't difficult at all. It certainly helped, though, having aunts, uncles, and cousins here. I think I mentioned that I first came here to attend my aunt Kaydie's wedding?"

Hailee nodded.

"Well, I remember standing in the chapel after the ceremony and telling my grandmother that I was going to live here someday. She thought I was out of my mind, but I somehow knew that I would become a resident of Pine Haven one day. I think the feeling started even earlier, when the stagecoach rolled into town. How God orchestrated it all…now, that's a different story. I'll tell it quickly, because we're almost there."

Hailee looked up at the wooden arch that bore the name "Sawyer Ranch" as they rode beneath it, then turned expectant eyes back on him.

"My aunt McKenzie came to Pine Haven from Boston as a mail-order bride. She loves to tell the story of the first time she came to the ranch and saw that sign. I think she was in for a bit of a surprise."

"Your aunt was a mail-order bride?"

"She was. She came out here to marry Zach, but her primary motive was finding her sister, Kaydie, whose husband was abusive, and a lawbreaker, to boot. Praise God, it all turned out for the best. McKenzie fell in love with Zach, and after Kaydie's husband was killed by a sheriff, she found love with Jonah, a former ranch hand of Zach's."

Hailee shook her head. "More evidence that God sees us through whatever circumstances we're in, I guess."

"Yes, indeed." Nate noticed that several of the guests had already arrived, as evidenced by the cluster of wagons parked nearby. Tables had been set up beneath several of the large shade trees in the side yard and were spread with food, and a sign that read "Welcome to Pine Haven, Miss Annigan" had been mounted between two stakes.

"What a warm welcome!" Hailee exclaimed as Nate helped her out of the wagon.

"I'll make the introductions," Nate said, starting toward Aunt McKenzie and Uncle Zach, who stood near one of the tables, probably making final preparations. When they looked up and saw Nate approaching with Hailee, they grinned and came to meet them.

"Miss Annigan, meet McKenzie Sawyer and her husband, Zach."

"Nice to meet you," Hailee said, shaking their hands.

"We're so glad you're here, Miss Annigan," McKenzie said. "Please let us know if there's anything you need."

"Thank you. And, please, call me Hailee."

Nate scanned the group of children playing. "Their son, Davey, is over there near the trees," he said, pointing for Hailee's sake, "and over there is their daughter, nine-year-old Chloe."

Next, he led Hailee to the porch. "Over here, we have Kaydie and Jonah Dickenson. Jonah is a member of the school board."

"Welcome to Pine Haven," Aunt Kaydie said, beaming at Hailee.

"Their children are the twins I told you about— Clint and Tommy, who are seven. I don't see them right now. They're probably up to no good, though." He winked at Uncle Jonah. "They also have a ten-year-old daughter, Bethany Ethel; she's over there with Chloe."

As more guests arrived, Nate continued to make introductions. He was pleased that each person gave Hailee a warm welcome.

When the Grangers pulled up, he took a deep breath. "Last, but not least, Fred and Lucille Granger."

"Pleasure to meet you," said Fred, tipping his hat.

"Welcome, Miss Annigan!" Lucille gushed dramatically. "Yes, we're the Grangers, and we own Granger Mercantile, the best mercantile in town."

"It's the only mercantile in town," Fred whispered to Hailee.

Lucille narrowed her eyes at her husband, then turned to Hailee and smiled broadly. "Anyway, you be sure to let us know if there's anything we can order for you. I hear you come all the way from Ohio! At Granger Mercantile, we can order anything from anywhere in the United States, provided it's in our catalogue."

"Thank you, Mrs. Granger. I'll remember that," said Hailee.

"Oh, do call me Lucille. I haven't been called 'Mrs. Granger' since the day I married Fred, decades ago. We were walking out of the church to go to the potluck when I heard a lady say, 'Mrs. Granger! Mrs. Granger!' I had no idea I was being summoned; I simply thought that a Mrs. Granger was one of the guests. You see, Fred's mother had passed on some years before, so I knew it wasn't she who was being called. Anyway, the woman kept saying, 'Mrs. Granger! Mrs. Granger!' Finally, Fred asked me to please answer her, so that she wouldn't continue on and on. I came to my senses and realized Mrs. Morrison was talking to me! So, I turned around, and I said, 'Yes?' She proceeded to ask me how it felt to be Mrs. Granger. I told her I'd been Mrs. Granger for not quite five minutes, so I could not give her a detailed account as of yet." She stepped closer to Hailee and lowered her voice. "You see, just between us, Mrs. Morrison was one of those busybody types who liked to gossip."

"Very well, then," Hailee said with a smile. "Lucille it is."

Nate thought she was handling her first encounter with Lucille Granger rather well.

"You should also know that I am a longtime member of the school board, and that I was instrumental in hiring you."

"I can't begin to thank you for—"

"And another thing," Lucille cut in. "I—"

"Lucille, the girl has other people to meet," Fred grumbled.

"Oh, fiddlesticks!" Lucille rolled her eyes. "This is important. You see, Hailee—may I call you Hailee? I run another business besides the mercantile. It's a matchmaking service; I'm sure you'll hear of it soon enough, but it's called Lucille's Love Connections."

"A matchmaking service?" Hailee looked dumb-founded, and Nate did his best not to laugh.

"Yes. Reverend Adams may not have explained to you that his aunt McKenzie and uncle Zach were married all because of me. I wrote the advertisement Zach placed in several newspapers that ultimately brought his mail-order bride here to Pine Haven. And I can assist you, too, in finding the love of your life."

Nate cast a glance at Hailee. Sure enough, she was blushing. "I'll remember that, Lucille," she said.

"Yes, please do," Lucille urged her. Then, she held a finger to her lips. "Shh. Don't tell anyone, but I think I might convince Reverend Adams to be my next customer."

"Now, Lucille." Nate had heard her spiel too many times already. If she thought he was going to enlist her services, she had another think coming.

"I know, Reverend Adams, I know. Your work is for the Lord right now. But when you are ready to settle down and have a family, you just let me know. I'll be at the mercantile, the best mercantile in town."

Fred groaned. "It's the only—"

"We should let you move on," Lucille said, el-bowing her husband in the side. "It was nice meeting you, Hailee."

"It was a pleasure meeting you both, as well," Hailee said.

After the Grangers had walked away, Nate chuckled. "Oh, that Lucille. She's a rare breed, and we can thank the Lord for that. Her heart is in the right place, but she can be a bit...overwhelming, at times. She tried to talk my uncle Jonah into having her find a mail-order bride for him, too. And Mr. Victor from the post office? She was all set to write an advertisement for him when he fell in love with Lucille's cousin Geraldine, who was visiting from Wilmerville."

"She seems to be quite an interesting woman," Hailee affirmed with a giggle.

"You must be the new teacher!"

Nate turned and saw Rosemary hurry up to Hailee, her husband on her tail.

"Yes, I'm Hailee Annigan."

"Nice to meet you, Hailee. I'm Rosemary, and this is my husband, Asa."

"Rosemary and Asa have acted as adoptive grandparents to the Sawyer and Dickenson children, as well as to me," Nate explained.

"We are indeed blessed with so many 'grandchildren,'" Rosemary said.

"That we are," Asa agreed in his thick Irish brogue. "And how do you do?" He shook Hailee's hand.

"I'm very well, thank you," she replied. "I'm eager to make Pine Haven my home."

"This is a lovely place," Rosemary mused.

"It may take a bit of getting used to, coming from the city as you do," Asa said, "but don't forget that everyone in Pine Haven has moved here from somewhere else, and now we all call Montana home."

"Thank you for the reminder," Hailee said. "It's a comfort to realize that everyone else has been a newcomer, too, at some time."

Nate spotted his cousin Davey, standing nearby with his sweetheart, and motioned them over. "Hailee, I have to introduce you to my favorite cousin." As Davey approached, he said, "Davey, I'd like you to meet Pine Haven's new schoolteacher, Miss Annigan. Miss Annigan, this is my cousin, Davey Sawyer. He's McKenzie and Zach's son and Chloe's brother, to refresh your memory."

"Nice to meet you," Davey said, removing his hat. "This is Cassandra Waterson."

"Nice to meet you both," said Hailee.

"Davey and Cassandra are courting," Nate explained.

"Congratulations," said Hailee. "Your last name is familiar, Cassandra."

"I think you met my parents earlier. My pa, Wayne, is the blacksmith."

"Yes, you're right. And you look a lot like your mother."

It was true, Nate observed; like Wilma, Cassandra had bright hazel eyes and long black hair, though she let it fall over her shoulders instead of tying it up in a bun.

"That's what I've been told," Cassandra said. "And I consider it a compliment. Thank you."

"Davey was the first one to introduce me to the 'uncivilized activities' of the Montana Territory, as Grandmother would call them," Nate said, giving his cousin a good-natured slap on the back.

Davey grinned. "Let's just say Nate needed to do something other than attend tea parties with his ma."

Nate jabbed Davey playfully in the shoulder. "Thanks a lot!"

"See, he even talks like me now," Davey said with a chuckle.

"You have been an influence on me," Nate admitted, "though I won't say what type."

"How old were the two of you when you first met?" Hailee asked.

"Well, let's see...when I came for Aunt Kaydie's wedding, I was ten, and Davey...how old were you? Five? Six?"

"Six, I think," Davey said. "I remember you standing at the podium in the chapel and telling your grandmother that you would live here someday."

"Yes, to her utter dismay," Nate said, chuckling.

"She was dismayed, all right." Davey shook his head.

"We stayed in Pine Haven for a total of two days," Nate explained. "On the second day, Grandmother allowed Davey to give me a tour of the Sawyer Ranch. I was surprised that she would permit my younger cousin to show me around without an adult supervising, but I suppose she figured he would show me the corrals and the cattle stalls, and little else." Nate paused. "I remember it was unseasonably warm that day—abnormal for the last day of September. Davey suggested that we go swimming in the lake." Nate chuckled as he began to recount the day he became best friends with his cousin....

"I can't believe Grandmother let me show you 'round the ranch," Davey said with a grin.

"I can't believe she did, either. How old did you say you are?"

"I'm every bit of six years old." Davey puffed out his chest and dug his hands into the pockets of his overalls. "Did you know you're my first boy cousin? Ma told me about you an' all, and I couldn't wait to meet ya. I reckon it's nice having Bethany Ethel for a cousin, but she's just a baby, so she can't do anything fun. Not yet, anyway. Besides, she's a girl."

Nate studied his younger cousin. "I've never known any of my cousins," he mused.

"Well, now ya know me. Hey, I have an idea," said Davey, his eyes sparkling. "Let's me and you go swimmin'."

"Swimming?"

"Yeah! Haven't ya ever been swimmin'?"

"Yes, once or twice, I believe," said Nate.

"Good. Then, I won't have to jump in and save you from drownin' an' all."

"Where will we swim?"

"Down at the lake. It's not too far away."

"I'm not sure that's a good idea. Summer is over, and autumn is hardly the time to go swimming, don't you think?"

"Ah, don't worry none about that. It's a real nice sunny day, as far as I can tell."

Nate remained unsure about the whole thing. After all, what would Grandmother say? Wouldn't she have his hide if he did anything that she deemed unbecoming? On the other hand, what didn't she consider unbecoming? Maybe he should just go along with it and take advantage of the unseasonable warmth.

"If'n you don't come, you aren't gonna have any fun," said Davey.

"I suppose you're right."

"Good. Let's go. The swimmin' hole is right this way."

Nate followed Davey to the lake, all the while contemplating what to do. Grandmother hadn't specifically said that he couldn't go swimming, so what was the harm? He mentally listed off the things she had told him he couldn't do today: get muddy, wander too far away from the ranch, or ride the horses. No mention whatsoever about swimming!

"Here it is," said Davey, gesturing with a chubby arm. "Do ya see that there tree branch?"

Nate glanced at the tall tree on the edge of the water. Several of its branches extended over the water. "Yes."

"What we're gonna do is climb up on that little 'bankment over there by the tree, hang on to the tree branch, and swing out over the lake. When you're out over the water, far 'nough away from the bank, ya let go and make a big splash!"

"I don't know, Davey. Are you even supposed to be down here by yourself? I've never heard of a six-year-old swimming without supervision."

"I ain't swimmin' without super...whatever you said. You're here."

"Does your father know about this?"

"About what?"

"Does he know we're down here, and that you're going swimming?"

"Pa knows I like to swim, and he knows I'm a good swimmer, 'cause he's the one what taught me."

Nate still wasn't convinced. He studied his cousin once more. Davey looked strong enough to swim by himself; short and stout, he could probably put up a fair fight against Nate, who was thin and wiry. Not to mention that Davey seemed fearless, while Nate was wary of the unknown, mostly because he was never allowed to experience it. Deep down, he knew Grandmother would be none too pleased to find out he'd swum in a primitive swimming hole, with who knows what kinds of creatures living in the water. But if this little six-year-old was prepared to do it, Nate didn't want to look like a sissy, no matter what Grandmother would think.

"Come on, Nate! It'll be fun, I promise." Davey unbuttoned his overalls and stripped down to his long underwear. "It's hard to swim in these thick pants an' all," he explained. Then, Nate watched him scramble up the embankment and climb several lower branches to reach the long, thick branch that hung over the lake. Gripping the branch with his chubby hands, he clambered out and away from the bank. Still holding on to the branch, he slid his legs down so they were dangling. Then, he swung his legs several times before letting go with a loud yell. He made a huge splash when he hit the water, and then, moments later, he surfaced, laughing and cheering.

Nate watched with amusement. He'd never seen anything like it. The few times he had gone swimming had been at a friend's home. Yes, it had been in a lake, but there had been no swinging from trees. They had stepped slowly into the water and swum as dignified gentlemen. To Nate, flying through the air dressed in one's underwear was anything but dignified. Still, it did look like fun, and he realized how much he wanted to try it himself. He took off his outer layers of clothing, then carefully made his way along the embankment and up to the tree.

Treading water, Davey raised a fist in the air. "You can do it, Nate!" he shouted.

"Is the water cold?" Nate asked as he started his upward climb.

"Nope, it's great!"

Still, Nate shivered. His younger cousin was probably accustomed to cold water, and he fully expected it to shock his system. Yet, as he watched Davey splash around with a grin on his face, Nate resolved to join in the fun.

"Are you fixin' to stand there all day?" asked Davey.

Nate shook his head and kept climbing, his toes curling at the unfamiliar roughness of tree bark against his tender soles. With all of his strength, he reached up and gripped the tree branch, then swung forward, out toward the water.

But his hands started to slip, and before he could move out over the water, he lost his grip and fell, landing on his backside on the embankment. Wincing with pain, he struggled to his feet and looked over his shoulder. Sure enough, his backside was coated with mud. What would Grandmother say when she found out he'd ruined his expensive underwear?

"Um, you might want to try that again," Davey supplied. "You let go way too early. You're supposed to fall into the water, not on the bank!"

"Thanks for the commentary," Nate said with a scowl. Maybe this hadn't been such a good idea after all. But, now that he was already dirty, he figured he might as well give it another go.

He wiped his palms on his pant legs to dry them, hoping that would help his grip. Then, he climbed the tree once more and grabbed the branch with determination. Hand over hand, he moved out toward the water, leaving the bank behind.

"Now, swing a few times, and then let go!" Davey urged him.

Nate swung his legs once, twice, and then flung himself off, his eyes shut tight. He plunged into the water, then surfaced seconds later, gasping for air and paddling frantically with his arms and legs.

"Are ya drownin'?" Davey asked.

"No, I'm not drowning," Nate muttered. "I'm just trying to warm up. This water is rather chilly!"

"But wasn't that the best?" Davey asked, beaming.

"It was fun, yes. Are you sure you're supposed to be doing this all by yourself at your age?"

"I told ya, I'm old enough. Besides, I'm with an adult. Well, almost. You'll be an adult soon, right?"

"I'm far from an adult. I'm ten, soon to be eleven."

"Well, ya talk like you're an adult," Davey said, rolling his eyes.

"That's because I'm well-educated. Besides, people speak with more sophistication in the city than out here."

"Oh." Davey frowned. "I don't know nothin' 'bout the city. Ma keeps tryin' to teach me about city stuff an' how to be proper an' all, but for some reason, I'm just no good at learnin' that type of stuff. Oh, well." He grinned at Nate. "So, ya wanna try that again?"

"I suppose I could try it one more time." Nate swam to the shallow part of the lake and walked out, shivering in the autumn breeze.

"You've gotta have fun once in a while," Davey said, following behind him.

Nate nodded. Perhaps, Davey was right, despite his age and lack of education.

"Wait. Before we go again, we've gotta do the Cousin Code."

"What's the Cousin Code?"

"Just somethin' I made up. It'll go somethin' like this," he said, and then proceeded to reach over and slug Nate playfully in the shoulder.

"Ouch! That was the Cousin Code? Do you do that with Bethany Ethel?"

"No, it's a secret code, and it's just for boy cousins."

"All right," said Nate. He planted his fist playfully in Davey's shoulder. "The Cousin Code. I like that."

"Me, too. Okay, let's me and you jump in the swimmin' hole again," suggested Davey. "And, this time, have fun!"

So, the second time, and the third, and the next ten times after that, Nate allowed himself to enjoy swinging off the tree branch and dropping into the lake. He whooped and hollered like Davey did, to the point where his voice went hoarse. And whenever Nate hit the water, he tried to make the biggest splash possible. The two of them laughed harder than Nate had ever laughed, and he couldn't remember ever having more fun. This was turning out to be the best day of his life.

That is, until Grandmother appeared at the edge of the lake, her hands on her hips and her lips pursed together. "Maxwell Nathaniel Adams Junior!" she screeched. "What on earth do you think you are doing?"

"Uh, swimming?"

"I declare! I am fit to be tied, young man. I haven't seen such reckless behavior by a young gentleman since...since...I don't know when! Remove yourself *from that filthy water this instant and put your trousers back on immediately!"*

Nate shivered beneath the surface of the water. How had Grandmother found them?

"As for you, young man," Grandmother said, nodding toward Davey, "or, I should say, scalawag, you ought to know better than to bring your cousin out here. A swimming hole is no place for the future heir to the Worthington-Adams fortune!"

"Grandmother?" Davey interrupted her tirade.

"What is it?" Grandmother scowled at him.

"What's a scalawag?"

Nate closed his eyes and shook his head. "Wrong question, Davey," he muttered to himself. "Wrong question."

"That's about enough out of you, Davey Sawyer," said Grandmother....

By the time Nate finished telling the story, tears were running down his face from laughing so hard. Davey was bent over and clutching his stomach, and Hailee and Cassandra had joined in, both giggling.

"The look on Grandmother's face when she saw you in the swimming hole was priceless," Davey said.

"Was it ever!" said Nate. "It's exactly the same look my mother gets when she's frustrated with me, or with anyone else, for that matter. It's a wonder she could see, with her eyes narrowed like that!"

"Don't tell anyone," Davey said with lowered voice, "but I've seen Ma make the same face a time or two!"

"What about Aunt Kaydie?" Nate asked.

"Even Aunt Kaydie," Davey affirmed, "but in her mild, quiet manner, of course."

"I suppose it's a trait of all the Worthington women," Nate said, chuckling.

"I suppose so," Davey agreed.

"I sure had a heavy punishment from Grandmother after that episode."

"You're not the only one," said Davey. "Pa and I had a meeting in the barn, and it wasn't a pleasant one. The hour-and-a-half lecture wasn't the worst of it. After that, he let me know in no uncertain terms that six-year-olds weren't allowed to swim unless an adult—a real adult—was there with them."

"So, you two became best friends after that?" asked Hailee.

"We did," Nate said, "although we saw each other only one more time between that day and when I came back here as the reverend, and that was when Aunt McKenzie and Uncle Zach brought the family to Boston for Christmas. But we wrote to each other a lot, and we picked up right where we'd left off when I moved here last year."

Davey nodded. "The first thing I did was take Nate back out to the swimming hole. This time, Nate was a much better swimmer!"

"Thanks to that swimming hole," Nate said in a Southern accent, "my cousin 'n' me, why, we're two peas in a pod."

"This is why we don't let him hang around Uncle Jonah too much," said Davey. "He's startin' to talk like him, y'all."

"Uncle Jonah is from Mississippi," Nate explained to Hailee, who smiled and nodded.

"May I have your attention?" Uncle Zach raised his voice above the hum of conversations as he beckoned Hailee to come stand beside him.

When everyone quieted, Zach continued. "I know many of you have met her already, but I would like to formally present our new schoolteacher, Miss Hailee Annigan. She comes to us all the way from Cincinnati. Would you please join me in making her feel welcome?"

There was a hearty round of applause and several shouts of "Welcome, Miss Annigan!"

"We're glad you're here," Zach said, addressing Hailee. "If there's anything we can do to help you get settled, please let us know."

"Thank you," said Hailee.

Seeing that Zach's speech was over, the crowd dispersed, and people began seating themselves around the tables in the yard.

Nate stepped over to Hailee, who looked a bit lost. "Would you care to join me?" he asked her.

"I would, thank you. I still feel a little out of place."

Nate positioned his hand gently beneath Hailee's elbow and directed her to a table where several of his relatives were sitting, and they sat down. "What do you think so far?"

Hailee giggled. "I'm just praying I will remember everyone's name."

Nate chuckled. "It'll take some time, but, soon, it will seem as if you've lived here forever. Someone said that to me right after I'd moved here, and I didn't believe him. Now, though, I realize it's true. The people of Pine Haven are really just one big family."

"Nate?" Nate looked down the table and met Uncle Zach's gaze. "Would you lead us in a blessing?"

"Of course."

Nate waited for the crowd to quiet once more, and then he bowed his head. "Dear heavenly Father, we thank You for this day You have given us. Thank You for Miss Annigan, and for her bravery in coming to a new place to teach the children. Please help all of us to be an encouragement to her. We thank You for this food and ask that You would bless the hands that prepared it. In Jesus' name, amen."

After dinner, once everyone had said good-bye to Hailee, Nate drove her home. He could see that she was tired, and likely overwhelmed from having met so many people, but she conversed freely with him, as earlier, and he found himself feeling disappointed when they arrived at the widow Marlen's.

Nate helped her out of the wagon and accompanied her up the walkway, all the while wondering when he would see her again. As she worked to unlock the front door, he had an idea. "If you'd like, I could take you to the schoolhouse tomorrow and show you around. I know that school doesn't start for another two weeks, but it might be nice to use this time to arrange things the way you want them."

"Thank you, Rev—Nate. I would appreciate that very much," said Hailee. "And thank you for the lovely evening."

"You're welcome. Until tomorrow, Hailee."

"Until tomorrow," she said with a smile, then slipped inside and shut the door.

CHAPTER SEVEN

"Well, here it is," said Nate as he slowed the wagon to a stop in front of the schoolhouse the following afternoon. "Eleven or so years ago, the town organized a campaign to raise funds for a new building. The former schoolhouse was much too small for the growing population of children."

Hailee followed Nate across the yard to the staircase leading up to the front door. Filled with excitement to see the inside of the schoolhouse, Hailee misjudged the height of the first step. The toe of her boot caught on the wood, and she tumbled forward.

Nate caught her just in time to keep her from taking a dive into the stairs. With his arm encircling her waist to steady her, he helped her to her feet. "Watch out for that step. It's dangerous," he said with a grin.

Hailee giggled. Nate's handsome smile was enough to turn her insides to mush, let alone his strong arm still wrapped around her and his other hand on her back. She knew she should feel embarrassed, but "delighted" better described the sensation. "I...I'm rather clumsy, in case you hadn't noticed," she stammered.

"I hadn't noticed." Nate winked and gently released her.

"It's the oddest thing, really," Hailee continued, shifting her feet nervously. "I have no trouble when I run—which isn't often, mind you. But, if I'm walking, or doing the simplest, slowest of movements, I have the tendency to be anything but graceful, even if there's nothing to trip over at all. It's been a lifelong trait." She looked into Nate's eyes and read amusement. Her face must be the color of a ripened raspberry! "Oh, my. Here I am, rambling on and on. I fear, Rev—Nate, that if you spend much time with me at all, you'll find yourself rescuing me a time or two from the clutches of dangerous stairs."

"I'd be honored to come to your rescue," Nate chuckled.

"My hero!" Hailee regretted the word as soon as she'd said it. She looked down at her feet. "Thank you," she muttered.

"Let's see, now. Where were we before the stairs ambushed you?" Nate scratched his head. "Oh, yes. I was about to show you the schoolhouse."

His blue eyes twinkled, causing Hailee's heart to leap almost out of her chest as she followed him up the stairs to the door. When he unlocked it and pushed it open, she peeked inside and gasped. She hadn't known what to expect of the interior, yet this exceeded anything she might have imagined. While it was rustic and small, she hadn't seen a finer schoolhouse anywhere—perhaps because this one was hers.

She had stepped inside and was admiring the desks when a familiar voice broke the silence.

"Reverend Adams!" Lucille Granger burst through the door. "Oh, Reverend Adams! And Miss Annigan, how nice to see you."

"Yes, Lucille? What is it?" Nate asked.

"I was hoping I might borrow you for a moment."

"Could I meet you at the mercantile in five minutes?"

"It really can't wait," Lucille insisted.

"All right, then."

Hailee smiled to herself. How patient he was!

"Feel free to look around and familiarize yourself with the place," he told her. "I'll be right back."

"Thank you," said Hailee. She watched Nate follow Lucille out the door. Then, she turned and walked toward the front of the room, where she stepped up to the wooden platform. In the middle of it stood a wide, solid chestnut desk with finely turned legs. On one corner of the desk sat a kerosene lamp, and a thick, well-worn dictionary occupied the opposite corner. An attendance book—brand-new, from the looks of it—had been stacked atop a notebook, a slate, and a reading primer in the middle of the desk. She couldn't wait to use each of them.

Behind the desk was a matching wooden chair, which beckoned her to sit and daydream about the teaching adventure that awaited her. Hailee sat down and scooted the chair closer to the desk. Then, she opened the attendance book and pretended to do a roll call with an imaginary pencil. As she looked out over the classroom, she studied the three rows of desks, neatly aligned, with a slate at each place.

Next, Hailee turned around in her chair and looked at the blackboard, which hung on the wall. She stood up, selected a piece of chalk from the ledge beneath it, and, in large, cursive letters, wrote "Miss Annigan" in the top right-hand corner. In the middle of the blackboard, in even bigger letters, she scrawled the words "Good morning, class!" Stepping back, she assessed what she had written. How long had she dreamed of doing just that? For how many years had she dreamed of being a teacher with a classroom of her own?

Hailee noticed a United States map hanging in the corner. There were also three frames on the walls, two of them portraits of presidents George Washington and Abraham Lincoln, the third one empty, probably for displaying her teaching certificate.

Turning back to her desk, Hailee picked up the primer and stood in the front of the class to practice addressing her pupils. "Would you please take out your readers and turn to page fourteen?" She flipped through the pages of the reader, and, as she did, she remembered a time not so long ago....

"Hailee, Reverend P. L. Davidson is here, and he would like to meet with you," said Miss Fanshaw.

"Is everything all right?" It had been a year and a half since Hailee had been remanded to Headmaster Stewart for misbehaving. Yet, even when her shenanigans had been a regular occurrence, she had never been sent to see the founder of The Sanctuary of Promise, Reverend Davidson.

"Yes, everything is fine. There's nothing to worry about," Miss Fanshaw assured her. "Reverend Davidson is visiting today, and I believe he merely wants to ask you a few questions."

Hailee heaved a sigh of relief and followed Miss Fanshaw down the hall to the office Reverend Davidson used on his rare visits to the Sanctuary.

"Here we are," said Miss Fanshaw. She knocked on the door.

"Come in," said a deep voice from within.

Miss Fanshaw turned the knob, opened the door, and motioned for Hailee to enter.

She stepped inside and studied Reverend Davidson, who looked a lot older than the last time she'd seen him. His white hair was thinning, and, though he smiled broadly, he appeared frail. Thick glasses sat on the bridge of his nose, and the veins on his wrinkled hands were prominent. He was Hailee's ideal of a grandfather, since she'd never known either of hers.

"Miss Annigan." Reverend Davidson nodded. "And Miss Fanshaw." Hailee turned around and saw her teacher come in behind her. "Please, sit down, both of you." Reverend Davidson indicated the two chairs in front of his desk.

As Hailee sat down, she noticed Miss Torenz and Headmaster Stewart seated off to the side. Surely, Miss Fanshaw had been mistaken when she'd told her there was no need to fear!

"Hello, Hailee," said Reverend Davidson.

Hailee gulped. "Hello, Reverend Davidson."

"I believe you know everyone in the room, so I shall get right down to business."

Hailee nodded and shifted her feet nervously.

Yet Reverend Davidson's eyes twinkled. Perhaps her anxiety was unfounded. "You probably wonder why I asked to meet with you. I assure you, there's no reason for you to be concerned. Rather, I would like to discuss with you your graduation from The Sanctuary."

"My graduation?" Hailee looked at Miss Fanshaw.

"Yes, Hailee," her teacher explained. "You're reaching the age at which most of our residents complete their course of study here and move out into the world. You have excelled in your work, and we are pleased to say that we find you ready for the world outside The Sanctuary of Promise."

Hailee swallowed hard. She'd always known that the day would come when she would leave The Sanctuary, but she'd hoped to stay here for a few more years.

"Your years here have served you well," Reverend Davidson continued. "We have watched you turn your life around once you surrendered it to God. And you are one of our brightest pupils."

"Thank you, sir," Hailee managed to say. She had not expected to hear such affirming words. Still, she worried as to what she would do and where she would go after The Sanctuary.

Reverend Davidson must have noticed her panicked expression. "You have no need to worry, Hailee," he said with a chuckle. "We aren't about to shove you out of the nest without adequate preparation. I've spoken at length with Miss Fanshaw, who tells me that your dream is to become a teacher."

Hailee nodded. "Yes, sir."

"I admire your passion for wanting to help children. It is a passion I share. As you may know, Hailee, I am an orphan myself—an unfortunate situation, yet the Lord turned it into something positive by leading me to found The Sanctuary of Promise."

Hailee pondered that for a moment. She hadn't known that Reverend Davidson was an orphan. Was *it possible that God had plans for her that included the experience of having lost her parents?*

"Hailee, I would like to offer you the opportunity to gain teaching experience here at The Sanctuary. I've spoken with Miss Fanshaw, Miss Torenz, and two other teachers, all of whom have agreed to allow you to assist them with their teaching over the next year, as well as to instruct you in planning curriculum in such subjects as writing, arithmetic, history, and geography, so that you may be prepared to pass the exam and earn your teaching certificate. You will also have the opportunity to assist in leading Bible studies and teaching children to sew, cook, and master other useful tasks, which you yourself have been taught."

Hailee couldn't believe her ears. "I—I don't know what to say," she stammered.

"You don't have to decide right now," said Reverend Davidson. "I would like you to pray about this opportunity and then let me know sometime next week."

"Thank you," Hailee said, her eyes misting. What an opportunity!

"As I said, take it to the Lord in prayer and then let me know of your decision. You may discuss any questions you may have with Miss Fanshaw or Miss Torenz. Headmaster Stewart would be happy to sit down with you and discuss further details of what you can expect, if you'd like...."

"I'm sorry I took so long. Hailee?"

Hailee snapped to attention and looked up. Nate stood, facing her, on the other side of her desk. "Pardon me, Nate. I must have been deep in a daydream."

"A good daydream, I hope?"

Hailee blinked the tears out of her eyes, their presence a testimony to how strongly she'd felt the same emotions that had overwhelmed her on that important day. "Yes, it was a good daydream. How is Lucille?"

"She's fine. She needed me to lift a crate for her. It seems Fred is out of town, delivering some goods to the Kinnion family." Nate paused. "What do you think of the classroom?"

"It's wonderful."

"Please don't hesitate to rearrange or make alterations as you see fit. There's a credit line at the mercantile for any supplies you may need."

"Thank you. I appreciate your taking the time to show me the classroom so that I might know what to expect and how to prepare."

"My pleasure, Hailee. I'm so glad you're here. When I received your application for the teaching position, I couldn't believe someone from the city would want to come out here to teach."

Hailee smiled. "You were no more surprised than I was. I'd searched throughout Cincinnati for a teaching position, with the help of many friends, yet no schools seemed to be hiring. It was Dot, the woman with whom I boarded, who came across the newspaper advertisement for a teacher in Pine Haven, and she suggested that the rugged atmosphere might be a welcome change."

"We advertised in several local papers, mostly in Wilmerville, but also listed ads in several papers in Denver, Chicago, and Cincinnati. The response was far from overwhelming—I think we had four applicants—but yours stood out. I recall that in

Cincinnati, you spent a year helping the teachers at a home for orphans."

"Yes, that's right. The Sanctuary of Promise is a place for orphans and wayward juveniles. It does a wonderful job imparting subject knowledge and life skills to the children there. I was blessed with the opportunity to assist in teaching for one year. I had always hoped there would be a teaching position available there after I had earned my teaching certificate, but, as the founder was fond of saying, 'The teachers tend to stay indefinitely,' so there was not an opening."

Nate chuckled. "You must have been disappointed, but I have to say that I, for one, am glad there wasn't a teaching position available there." His eyes met Hailee's and held her gaze.

Hailee felt her face flush. Why was it that Nate had such an effect on her? "I'm glad, too," she agreed, "for it brought me to this lovely town."

"You worked somewhere else after The Sanctuary of Promise, if I remember correctly, but it wasn't a school."

"Yes, I worked at a textile factory—the same factory where my mother worked after my father died. I had been offered several jobs in other Ohio towns, but I wanted to stay in Cincinnati, in hopes of finding my...." Hailee stopped, the words stuck in her throat. The hours she'd worked in the factory had been long and grueling, and her earnings had accumulated slowly. Yet she'd persevered by dint of her determination to find her brothers and to save enough money to support them if, by some miracle, they were reunited.

"In case you found your...?"

Hailee cleared her throat. "Brothers. In case I found my brothers, Philip and Reuben."

"Your brothers? You told me they lived in Cincinnati," he reminded her gently.

Hailee sighed, wondering how much she should tell Nate. After all, she'd only just met him. "After our mother died, my brothers and I were separated. I posted notices throughout the city on a consistent basis, hoping they or someone who knew them would contact me. Yet no one ever did. I had a difficult time discerning whether it was the Lord's will for me to come to Pine Haven; if Philip or Reuben finally sees one of my postings, I'm two thousand miles away."

"I'm sorry. That must be so difficult."

"I pray daily that the Lord will reunite us, but sometimes it feels like a silly dream. I don't even know if they're still alive." She choked back tears.

"May I pray with you about that now, Hailee?"

"Yes, I would appreciate that." Hailee was overwhelmed by Nate's thoughtfulness. He'd known her for only a short time, yet he was already willing to pray with her about personal matters. Of course, that was his job, but knowing he cared meant a lot to her.

She closed her eyes as Nate began. "Heavenly Father, Your Word tells us in the Psalms that You are near to those who call upon You in truth. And we do just that today. Lord, You know of Hailee's desire to reunite with her beloved brothers, Philip and Reuben. We pray that You would keep her brothers safe and, if it's Your will, reunite them someday with their sister, Hailee. In Jesus' name, amen."

"Amen," Hailee echoed. "Thank you, Nate."

"Whenever you need someone to pray with you, please let me know."

Hailee smiled. "I can see why God called you into the ministry."

"Thank you. I pray I will always do it for His glory." Nate paused. "You know, Hailee, as I mentioned before, my aunt McKenzie came to Pine Haven with plans to find her sister Kaydie, and she finally did so thanks to an ad she placed in various newspapers. She had also hung notices in public places, such as the post office. From the stories Aunt McKenzie has told me, I think she figured she would come to Pine Haven, enlist Uncle Zach's help, and locate Aunt Kaydie in no time at all. Yet it was nowhere near that simple. Her search took a while, and I think there were many times when she was tempted to give up all hope of ever finding her sister—alive, especially. But what Aunt McKenzie didn't realize until later was that God had His hand on the entire situation, even when it looked hopeless. He hadn't abandoned Aunt Kaydie, nor had He forgotten about Aunt McKenzie's desire to find the person she most loved."

Nate looked Hailee in the eye, and she felt as if he could see her soul. "Never give up hope about finding your brothers. God hasn't forgotten about them, and He hasn't forgotten about you and your prayers to be reunited with them. He works in ways we can't comprehend, as the Bible says in Isaiah, chapter fifty-five, verses eight and nine: *'For my thoughts are not your thoughts, neither are your ways my ways, saith the* LORD. *For as the heavens are higher than the earth, so are my ways higher than your ways, and my thoughts than your thoughts.'* When He finally brought Aunt Kaydie to Pine Haven, it was in a way neither she nor Aunt McKenzie had envisioned. It was through a woman named Ethel, who brought

Aunt Kaydie into a relationship with Jesus Christ. So, don't give up hope, Hailee."

Hailee swallowed hard as fresh tears filled her eyes. Nate's words had touched her so deeply, comforting her, as well as giving her renewed faith that the Lord would indeed reunite her with Philip and Reuben. "Thank you, Nate. I needed to hear that."

She had been blessed beyond measure so many times in her life with people who cared for her. First, her parents, who had loved her dearly; then, Ella Fanshaw and Dot Pangbourn; and now, Nate.

Nate. Hailee looked up at him, his handsome face etched with compassion. And not only was he handsome, but he was also kind and caring, and he loved the Lord. What a treasured friend she had found.

In bed that night, Nate reflected on the conversation he'd had with Hailee about her brothers. It broke his heart to know she had been separated from them for so many years. Yet, he admired her for bravely moving across the country to teach in a town she had never visited. That couldn't have been easy. *Father, please let Hailee and her brothers be reunited in Your perfect timing*, he prayed. He would make it a point to add Hailee and her brothers to the list of people he prayed for daily.

Nate clasped his hands behind his head and stared up at the ceiling as his thoughts turned to how excited Hailee had been to see her classroom. Yet, she had been crying when he'd returned from helping Lucille. Had it been from despair over missing her brothers? From feelings of homesickness for Cincinnati? From being overwhelmed by the small, rustic schoolhouse? Surely, everything about Montana was much more primitive than anything Hailee had experienced in the city.

One thing was certain: he longed to spend more time with Hailee Annigan and get to know her even better. There was something about her that made him feel more at ease than he felt with anyone else.

CHAPTER EIGHT

At Granger Mercantile the next afternoon, Nate carried his purchases to the front of the store and set them on the counter. He half hoped to see Fred, but it was Lucille who came out of the office and greeted him.

"Well, good afternoon, Reverend Adams," she said with a bright smile.

"Good afternoon, Lucille," Nate replied. Lucille seemed especially exuberant today, and he immediately became wary of what she would say next.

Lucille remained silent for a few moments while she added up Nate's purchases. "I know that by now you've come to appreciate the fine customer service we offer at Granger Mercantile," she said as she loaded his items into a crate.

"Yes, you do have fine customer service here, Lucille." *All right, Lucille, I know you're up to something*, Nate mused.

"In fact, we at Granger Mercantile pride ourselves in offering the very best customer service in all of Pine Haven."

Nate merely smiled and nodded.

"You probably know that I have an equally renowned reputation for customer service at my other business, Lucille's Love Connections." Lucille waved a hand at the faded quilt on the mercantile wall, which was embroidered with the name of her matchmaking services. "Surely, you're aware of the successful matches I've arranged, not least of all the marriage of your aunt McKenzie and your uncle Zach."

Of course, Nate knew about Lucille's Love Connections. She'd been touting its benefits from the first time he'd met her.

"McKenzie and Zach were the first match I arranged, and the couples I brought together only multiplied from there. I also take credit for the marriage of Mr. Victor and my cousin Geraldine. After all, had it not been for my inviting Geraldine to visit Pine Haven, she never would have found wedded bliss. Plus, she is *my* cousin, after all." Lucille smiled, her cheeks rising so high that her small, beady eyes nearly disappeared beneath folds of skin.

"And then, of course, you have Keith and Lena Henderson, a fine young couple married more than four years now. They met at a barn dance at your uncle Jonah and aunt Kaydie's ranch. I take complete credit for their union, as well, for had I not tripped and fallen near the lemonade, neither Lena nor Keith would have needed to come to my aid, and they might never have met." Lucille's grin seemed to increase, if that were possible. "And, last but not least, there's Jim and Darleen Douglas. Darleen brought her famous stuffed chicken dumplings to the church potluck. Little did she know that she'd made Jim's favorite dish. I was the one who encouraged everyone to try Darleen's dumplings. Well, Jim tasted them and fell in love—with the dumplings and with Darleen! A finer couple Pine Haven has rarely seen. And, if I do say so, a finer matchmaker the State of Montana has never seen!"

Lucille paused and fluttered her eyelashes with a look of expectation. Nate refused to take the bait.

So, she said what he'd expected all along: "Reverend Adams, I believe it's time for another success story...yours."

Nate didn't know what to say. He'd run out of excuses.

Lucille leaned across the counter and eyed him. "You're a good-looking young fellow, if you don't mind my saying, so this shouldn't be too great of a challenge." She squatted down to reach something under the counter. Moments later, she stood again, holding a thick tablet and a pencil.

"Lucille...."

"Fiddlesticks, Reverend Adams. I know what you are going to say, and you needn't worry. While I do put a lot of time and effort into finding brides for the eligible bachelors of Pine Haven, I never demand compensation, even though I appreciate your concern that I be paid for a job well done. No, Reverend, payment is not necessary. The reward of watching poor, lonely bachelors find marital bliss is payment enough, and so I offer this service out of the kindness of my heart. After all, we are all called to make a difference in this world."

"Lucille—"

"So, Reverend, here are the details," Lucille interrupted him as she scribbled something in her notebook. "We can locate the love of your life in one of two different ways. One, I write up an advertisement for a mail-order bride. As you are probably aware, Zach Sawyer found McKenzie through this method. Two, I search throughout Pine Haven and, if necessary, the two neighboring towns, canvassing the eligible young women in order to find the perfect match to suggest to you. So, which will it be?"

"Uh...."

"Oh! Before you make your decision, let me get a closer look at you and record a physical description. It's of utmost importance to emphasize your attractive traits when seeking to provoke interest in potential spouses." Lucille reached up and gave Nate a pat on the head. "You do have nice, thick hair. That's a draw. You should see some of the eligible bachelors who have asked for my assistance and barely have a thread of hair on their heads! Not that hair is all-important, mind you, but it makes it difficult for me to put down the color of their hair when they have none! So, let's see...you have light-blond hair...yellowish, almost."

"Yellowish?"

"That's a much better description than what I had to write for your uncle Jonah. He can deny it as long as he likes, but he does have hair the color of a dark-orange pumpkin."

Dark-orange pumpkin, indeed! "I wasn't aware that you had a hand in Jonah and Kaydie's marriage."

"Oh, I didn't," said Lucille, "though I ought to get some credit. Whenever Jonah would stop by the mercantile, I made a point of talking about how beautiful Kaydie was." Lucille tilted her head with a pensive look, as if deep in thought. "I also suggested on more than one occasion that I could tell he had feelings for her," Lucille went on. "Poor fellow. I don't think Jonah realized how taken he was with her. So, even if I deserve no more than a shred of credit for their union, it's a substantial shred!" Lucille leaned over the counter and peered into Nate's eyes. "My, oh my, those eyes! How I wish my Fred had vivid, expressive eyes like yours. As it is, they've faded a touch over the years. But your eyes...they're captivating! A deep, dark blue, like the color of blueberries."

Nate resisted the urge to roll his "blueberry" eyes. For months, both Uncle Zach and Uncle Jonah had warned him that Lucille was bound to try to convince him to take advantage of her matchmaking service. At least it had happened later rather than sooner.

Nodding with satisfaction, Lucille scribbled something else in her tablet before looking up to study him again. "You have such nice, broad shoulders, too. As for your character traits, you are a strong man of God, courteous, charming, and...." Lucille looked up again and gave Nate the once-over. "Yes, you have an attractive build, indeed."

Nate felt his face grow warm. "Lucille, please don't take this the wrong way, but—"

"I only wish Fred had nice, broad shoulders. You see, the poor man has narrow, sloping shoulders, although I don't make mention of it. I don't want to hurt his feelings."

"That's gracious of you, Lucille."

"Now, Reverend, as far as your physical description is concerned, I'm stating only the truth. If you decide to place an advertisement in the newspaper, you must keep in mind that women like to know just what to expect. I heard about one woman in particular...." Lucille paused, looked left and right, and then motioned for Nate to lean in closer.

After he suppressed a sigh of frustration and obliged, she continued, her voice softened to a whisper. "I heard about one particular woman—Hillary, I believe she was called—from Wilmerville. She responded to an advertisement that went something like this: 'Tall, handsome man with dark hair, an amiable personality, and high social standing seeks beautiful woman for matrimony.' Well, Hillary, who was a beautiful woman with long, reddish hair, answered his advertisement. When they finally met, to her horror, she realized Abner Bates was not at all as he had described himself!" Lucille trembled. "Ugh! Abner was short, fat, bald, and poor. Not to mention that he was nearly always drunk, rarely bathed, and was missing most of his teeth! The few teeth he had were black and rotten. Can you believe that, Reverend?" Lucille reached for her handkerchief and dabbed at her cheeks. "I am devastated on Hillary's behalf. The lies she believed in the name of love! So, you see, Reverend Adams, we must describe you as accurately as possible."

Nate cleared his throat to cover the chuckle Lucille's tale had inspired. "Lucille, I'm not looking for a wife at this time. I've lived in Pine Haven for less than a year, and I'd prefer to get settled further before I begin courting anybody."

"Crumb cakes, Reverend! It's never too early to start searching for the woman God has planned for you. Besides, time goes so fast; one minute, you're young and full of energy, and the next minute, you're old and withered. Poor Mr. Victor nearly missed out on love because he waited so long to take a wife. I don't want that to happen to you."

"Really, Lucille, I think I can afford to delay looking for a wife for a few years, at least. I assure you, the day I decide to call on Lucille's Love Connections, you'll be the first to know."

"Is that a promise, Reverend Adams?"

Nate sighed. "Yes," he said. "If I decide to use a matchmaker, it will definitely be you.

"Hmm. Well, I suppose I could settle for that. But don't wait too long, Reverend. How old are you now?"

"Twenty-one."

"Twenty-one? Oh, my. Thirty is right around the corner! After that, you'll be forty, then fifty, then sixty, and then...oh, dear. Once you turn sixty, I'm afraid your chances have slimmed to almost nothing. I entreat you, Reverend Adams, not to delay this important search."

"I won't," Nate assured her. He gathered his purchases and headed for the door before Lucille could resume promoting her matchmaking services. "Thank you, Lucille. I'll see you at church on Sunday."

"I'll be there," Lucille called after him.

Nate walked out into the street and took a deep breath. He knew that Lucille had a good heart, and that she meant well, but the last thing Nate wanted was for her to find him a wife. He was still in the process of adjusting to his position as reverend, which was a considerable task.

"I think you'll find that Reverend Adams is a gifted preacher, especially for one so young," Widow Marlen said to Hailee as the two of them walked to church on Sunday.

Hailee smiled. "I'm looking forward to hearing his sermon."

When they climbed the steps to the church door, Nate was there to greet them. "Good morning, Hailee, Widow Marlen," he said, nodding.

"Good morning," they chorused in response. Hailee followed Widow Marlen down the aisle and into a pew. After she was seated, she turned around to take in the atmosphere of the small church. It was far from fancy, yet the warm, comforting feel put her in a worshipful mood.

Several other people shuffled into the building before Nate stepped up to the pulpit. "Good morning!" he began. "Before we start our service, I'd like to introduce you to the newest resident of Pine Haven, Miss Hailee Annigan." He smiled and gestured at Hailee, who felt the warmth of a blush on her cheeks at the dozens of eyes that seemed to stare at her. "Whether you've met the new schoolteacher or not, please join me in giving her a warm welcome."

A round of applause filled the tiny sanctuary. "Go ahead and stand, dear," Widow Marlen encouraged her.

Reluctantly, Hailee rose to her feet, nearly tripping over the bottom of her dress. She smiled and waved at the parishioners, all of whom grinned and waved back at her. As she quickly sat down again, she noticed an exception. Turning her head slightly, she looked out of the corner of her eye at the blonde woman across the aisle whose facial expression was far from pleasant. She scowled at Hailee for a few more seconds before turning her attention to the front of the church and smiling broadly.

"Pay her no mind," Widow Marlen whispered.

Hailee turned questioning eyes on the older woman.

"That's Etta Mae Nash, and she's probably just jealous."

Hailee nodded slowly. What possible reason could that woman have for being jealous of her? From what she could see, Etta Mae Nash had a rare beauty, and her clothes looked to be some of the finest Hailee had seen in Pine Haven. She couldn't imagine why Etta Mae might harbor ill-will toward her.

She didn't dwell on the issue further, for it was time to sing several hymns. Hailee stood with the rest of the congregation and joined her voice with theirs, resisting the urge to peek at Etta Mae and her evil eye.

After several songs, Nate climbed into the pulpit and invited everyone to sit. "Today, we're going to study the parable of the sower," he announced. "Please turn in your Bibles to Matthew, chapter thirteen. We'll read verses three through nine."

Hailee opened the Bible Dot had given her for Christmas last year. How she wished she'd been able to keep her mother's Bible! When she'd been caught by the police officer who had later taken her to The Sanctuary of Promise, she hadn't been permitted to retrieve any belongings from the vacant hotel where she'd lived. Months later, when she'd gone to visit with Miss Ella, nothing had been left to collect. That Bible had always been a cherished item, even when she'd felt far from God and wanted nothing to do with Him....

"Why can't we stay here, Hailee?" Philip asked, his lower lip trembling.

"Because the landlord, Mr. Shanks, would never allow that," said Hailee. She reached for the worn leather bag that had been her father's and began to load it with their meager belongings.

"Can't we just tell him we have nowhere else to go?" Reuben asked.

"We could, but he'd probably send us to some orphanage, and we'd be separated forever," Hailee explained. "Ma made me promise not to let us get separated."

"Then, where're we gonna go?" Philip wailed as tears began to trickle down his round cheeks.

"Oh, my sweet Philip," said Hailee. "Come here." She took her youngest brother in her arms. She loved him more than she could express. She'd cared for him when their pa had died in an accident at the factory, she'd cared for him when their ma had gone to work after that, and she would care for him now. It was almost like he was her own son. Hailee patted his soft, brown hair and kissed him on the cheek. "Everything's going to be all right. You'll see."

"Because God is taking care of us?" asked Philip.

Hailee gulped. Deep down, she believed that God had forgotten her family, but she couldn't let her brother know that. At six years of age, Philip needed protection from the harsh realities of life. He'd already endured too many of them. Besides, Philip loved the Bible story about baby Moses and how God had kept him safe when all the other male babies were being killed by Pharaoh. Hailee refused to tarnish that story in Philip's mind. It was better for him to believe God was protecting them.

"We'll be all right because I'm going to find a job," she said instead.

"Find a job?" Reuben scoffed. "Who's going to hire a thirteen-year-old girl?"

Hailee ignored his skepticism. "Yes, Reuben, I will find a job." While she loved Reuben, they had never gotten along extremely well. At eleven years of age, Reuben acted like he was the knower of all things, which irritated Hailee no end. Besides, she'd had more schooling than he.

"Where will we live?" Philip repeated, turning his worried eyes on Hailee.

"I found a place yesterday on Gardner Street. It's nothing fancy, but it'll do until I get a job and find us a more suitable home," she replied.

"I don't remember being on Gardner Street," Philip said.

"Lucky for you," sneered Reuben. "There's not much to remember, just a couple of shops and an old, abandoned hotel."

"Yes, and the hotel is where we'll stay until I find a job and save some money," said Hailee. She glared at Reuben, silently begging him not to destroy whatever small amount of hope Philip still had.

"I don't want to live there," Reuben groused.

"I know, and neither do I. But it's the only place I can think of where we can stay without being found, and I promised Ma we'd stay together. It'll be temporary, so, please, put your anger aside and be grateful we have somewhere to go."

"You sound like Ma," Reuben sneered. "I've never liked how you boss us around. Besides, it's your fault Pa died. If you hadn't asked for that new dress in the store window, Pa wouldn't have had to work late to earn the money to buy it."

"Reuben, please," Hailee begged him as tears filled her eyes. She already felt guilty enough.

"No, Hailee," Reuben persisted, his voice rising in volume. "Pa is dead because he worked late, night after night, to earn money for your new dress, and on one of those nights, the machine broke and killed him!"

"Reuben, please!"

Whimpering, Philip buried his face in Hailee's shoulder. "I want Ma!"

"I know, Philip, I know. So do I," Hailee sobbed. "So do I." She hugged him close and allowed herself to cry with him.

Reuben, meanwhile, stood to his feet and stomped into the other room.

Hailee wished that God hadn't deserted them, for then she could speak with Him about their pain and problems. But she knew it was futile. She no longer believed He loved her and her brothers, and she certainly didn't expect Him to help them. No, He'd had His chance to help them, first by protecting Pa, yet Pa was dead, and, second, by healing Ma when she'd fallen sick, yet He'd chosen not to. Hailee used the back of her hand to wipe the tears from her face. No, the Lord couldn't be counted on. The only person she could count on was herself. Still, it would make things easier if Reuben would cooperate.

"Reuben?" Hailee called out. "Can you come back here, please?" She didn't want to move and upset Philip, who was still curled up in her lap, whimpering quietly.

There was no sound from Reuben, yet Hailee knew he was in the adjoining room. After all, there was nowhere else to go in the two-room apartment. "Reuben, please?"

A few minutes later, Reuben entered the room, dragging his feet. "What?" he asked, scowling at her and Philip.

"I'm sorry, Reuben. I'm sorry for acting like a mother. Sometimes, I just can't help it; it's how I show concern. I know I'm not your mother, but I am your sister. Even when you and I don't see eye to eye, I still love you, Reuben, and I am trying to do what's best for all three of us. Can we put our differences aside and try to get along, for Philip's sake? You know he hates to see us fight!"

Reuben remained silent for a minute or so. Finally, he nodded begrudgingly.

"Good, then." Hailee sighed and gently wiped the tears from Philip's cheeks. "I've nearly finished packing everything. Take a look around, would you, Reuben, and make sure I haven't forgotten anything?"

Reuben glanced around the room, which had been almost empty for some time, since anything of value had been sold after Pa's death so that they could purchase food. "Did you get Ma's Bible?" Reuben asked.

"Yes," answered Hailee, patting the bulging leather bag. While she no longer shared her ma's faith, she never wanted to lose sight of the possession that had meant the most to her.

"Then, it looks like we have everything," said Reuben, checking under the bed.

"Good. We can go now." Hailee gently lifted Philip as she got to her feet. "Once we get outside, you can ride on my back. Reuben, would you please carry the bag?"

Reuben nodded, picked it up, and led the way out of the apartment....

Hailee was roused from her reverie by the sound of Nate's voice. She listened and followed along as he read the thirteenth chapter of Matthew.

> *"'Behold, a sower went forth to sow; and when he sowed, some seeds fell by the way side, and the fowls came and devoured them up: some fell upon stony places, where they had not much earth: and forthwith they sprung up, because they had no deepness of earth: and when the sun was up, they were scorched; and because they had no root, they withered away. And some fell among thorns; and the thorns sprung up, and choked them: but other fell into good ground, and brought forth fruit, some an hundredfold, some sixtyfold, some thirtyfold. Who hath ears to hear, let him hear.'*

"This passage depicts four types of people and the different ways they respond to the Word of God," Nate began, then started to analyze the traits of each type of person. "The third person, represented by the thorny ground, hears the Word and embraces it with delight. Unfortunately, when hard times come, this person turns from God."

Hailee felt a jab in her heart as Nate expounded upon his description. *I have been like thorny ground, Father,* Hailee confessed silently. *When Ma and Pa taught me about Your Word when I was a young girl,*

I embraced it. I longed to hear Ma read the Bible each night and to hear Pa tell of how much You love us. I loved to hear them sing hymns at church, and I begged them, along with Philip and Reuben, to tell the story of baby Moses again and again. But then, so much happened, Lord, and I turned from You. I gave up on You. Hailee reached for her handkerchief and dabbed at the tears that trickled out from the corners of her eyes. When she felt Widow Marlen reach over and give her hand a squeeze, she hoped no one else had noticed she was crying. *Father, forgive me for giving up on You. I recognize the error of my ways. Thank You for bringing me back to You at The Sanctuary. Please plant the seed of Your Word in my heart so that it will never be uprooted, so that my faith will remain steadfast, no matter what troubles may come.* Hailee sat with her eyes shut and felt the Lord's peace wash over her. Never again would she turn from the One who loved her so much.

When the service was over, Nate greeted the parishioners as they exited the church. When Hailee and Widow Marlen arrived at the door, he invited Hailee to stand with him, so that he could introduce her to anyone she may not have met.

"That's an excellent idea," Widow Marlen told Hailee. "I'll wait for you in the churchyard."

Hailee nodded and took her place next to Nate. After his touching sermon and the tumult of emotions she'd experienced, she welcomed the opportunity to participate in something as lighthearted as meeting new people. Widow Marlen was right; Nate was a gifted speaker who captivated his listeners with the words God had put in his heart.

After about five minutes of introductions, Hailee's cheeks were sore from smiling. Among the final few parishioners who trickled out of the church, she noticed the sour-faced blonde approaching with an older woman—her mother, perhaps?

"What a nice service," the older woman said to Nate.

"Thank you, Mrs. Nash," he replied, nodding. "How is Mr. Nash?"

"Oh, he's fine, just fine. As I've said before—and I hope you won't be offended, Reverend—Anders is far too busy these days to attend church."

"Of course. Please tell him I wish him well. Have you and Etta Mae met Miss Annigan?"

"No, I don't believe we have," the woman replied. "Anders serves on the school board, as you know, but we were unable to attend the dinner at the Sawyer Ranch. A pity, but we had more important matters to tend to." She nodded at Hailee. "Welcome to Pine Haven," she said. "I am Rowena Nash, and this is my daughter, Etta Mae"—she turned back to Nate— "who, by the way, Reverend, has not had the fortune of joining you for a picnic by the lake. Summer is drawing to a close, you know!"

Nate cleared his throat. "Etta Mae, this is Miss Annigan." Clearly, he wasn't comfortable addressing Rowena's not-so-subtle hint.

Hailee smiled at Etta Mae, whose expression remained impassive as she scanned Hailee from head to toe. She said nothing but merely nodded.

"Hello, Mrs. Nash," Hailee said, looking at her mother.

"Mother, we need to go," said Etta Mae. "So long, Reverend Adams. I look forward to seeing you soon." With a wave of a gloved hand, she followed her mother down the steps and into the churchyard.

"Please excuse them," Nate said quietly. "The Nashes are a prominent family in Pine Haven, and I pray for them daily—especially Anders." He paused. "Would you care to go for a walk?"

"That would be nice," Hailee replied. "I'll tell Widow Marlen that I will meet her at home."

A strange fluttering sensation moved through her stomach as she walked back to Nate after talking with Widow Marlen. Yet it wasn't from nervousness, for, oddly, she felt more comfortable with Nate than with almost anyone else, even though she'd known him but a few days.

As they started down the main street, nearly deserted at this hour, Hailee admired the peaceful setting. Nate began pointing to the various buildings and telling her who owned each business. When they reached the post office, Nate gestured to a bench. "Would you like to sit down? I saw that something in my sermon seemed to upset you, and I thought you might like to talk about it."

He had seen her crying? She wondered who else had noticed. Yet she didn't regret the sense of conviction she'd felt nor the moment she'd shared with the Lord.

"I don't mean to pry," he added, "and I don't want to embarrass you, but I was concerned."

"It was something you said in your sermon," Hailee acknowledged as she lowered herself onto the bench.

Nate sat down beside her. "You don't have to tell me about it if you don't want to."

Hailee turned to face Nate. His blue eyes showed concern, and she desperately wanted to tell him everything—where she'd come from, the mistakes she'd made, the years she'd spent at The Sanctuary of Promise prior to becoming a teacher there. Yet she knew it wouldn't be wise to bare all those details. He seemed to like her, and she wanted it to stay that way. Knowing much more about her past would surely change his mind. Besides, there was no sense in jeopardizing her new job when she hadn't even taught one lesson.

"I don't mean to pry, Hailee," Nate repeated.

"I don't mind," Hailee assured him. "It's just that it felt as though you were talking about me when you described the 'thorny ground' person who embraces the Lord, only to turn away from Him in times of hardship."

"I think we're all tempted to wonder if the Lord is there when things get really tough."

"Have you ever felt that way?"

"Yes, many times," Nate admitted.

"Several years ago, I thought that the Lord had abandoned me. I know now that He never left me. I'm the one who left Him."

"Thankfully, God never turns His back on us, even when we've abandoned and rejected Him. His mercy is never ending, and He longs for us to trust Him completely."

Sniffling, Hailee nodded.

"And I hope you know that you can come to me at any time about anything. I'm not God, but I do have a lot of practice with forgiveness and consolation," Nate added. "You don't need to worry about what I might think of you."

"Thank you, Nate." Hailee blinked back her tears. *Yes, you may be there for me now, but if you knew the real me, you would send me back to Cincinnati.*

"I mean that, Hailee," Nate said, as if he'd read the doubt in her mind. "But now, we can talk about something else, if you'd like. There's a barn dance at my aunt Kaydie and uncle Jonah's on Saturday night, and I would be honored if you would come with me."

"A barn dance?" Hailee repeated, surprised by the turn their conversation had taken.

"Yes. It's a tradition they've started to mark the end of summer, and it's a lot of fun, from what I hear."

Hailee began to giggle. "I don't think you really want me to go to a barn dance with you."

"Why is that?"

"Have you forgotten how clumsy I am?"

Nate shook his head. "That doesn't concern me in the least."

"All right, then. If you're sure you don't mind dancing with me and my two left feet, I'll go." Hailee felt excited already.

"I'll pick you up at six o'clock, then," said Nate.

CHAPTER NINE

That night, after she'd finished reading from her Bible, Hailee sat at the small desk in her bedroom at Widow Marlen's and reflected on her first Sunday in Pine Haven. First, she had attended church and been convicted during Nate's sermon. Next, she'd made the acquaintance of many people, yet those who stood out were the rude Nash women. After that, she'd enjoyed a walk with Nate and accepted his invitation to the barn dance next Saturday. She realized it was the time she'd spent with the handsome reverend she cherished the most, and it was difficult to think of anything besides the barn dance and the opportunity it would afford her to get to know him better.

Yes, with the exception of Etta Mae's unfriendly behavior, everyone in Pine Haven had welcomed her with open arms. "Thank You, Lord, for the kind people of Pine Haven," she prayed. Then, a disturbing thought occurred to her. What if the fine folks of Pine Haven somehow discovered the truth about her past? What if they knew she'd lived in the streets, stealing food and committing other crimes? She would no longer be so welcome.

Hailee climbed into bed and pulled the sheets up to her chin as she remembered how, over the first several weeks, that they'd lived in the vacant hotel, she'd done everything to make the abandoned hotel feel like home for her brothers. Almost every day, she'd gone hunting for a job. While she'd found a few odd jobs to perform for petty cash, she hadn't been able to secure a permanent position. Their meager funds quickly ran out, and it had broken Hailee's heart to have to resort to more desperate measures to provide for her brothers and herself....

"Excuse me, sir?" Hailee said, shyly approaching the man who owned a dry goods store several blocks from Gardner Street. He was her only hope, since the previous twenty-three places she'd sought employment had turned her away.

"Yeah? What can I do for you, little missy?"

"Sir, I was wondering if you could use some help sweeping your store. I need to support my brothers, you see, and—"

"Sorry," the man said, looking her up and down, "I don't need any help."

"Please, sir. I'd gladly take food as my payment."

"I told you, I don't need any help, not from you, and not from any other vagrant. Now, get out of here!" He shooed her away and shut the door.

Dejected and low on hope, Hailee shuffled back to the abandoned hotel.

"I'm hungry," Philip whined when she walked through the door.

"I know, honey," said Hailee. "Reuben should be home soon. Maybe he's found something." He'd started searching for a job the previous week, when they'd begun to worry about Hailee's prospects of finding a job.

She sat down in a chair and propped her feet up on a wooden crate. Blisters lined the edges of her heels, the result of her having walked miles and miles throughout the city wearing shoes that were too small for her.

Several minutes later, Reuben came in. "Any luck?" Hailee asked him.

"No," Reuben grumbled. "Nobody wants to hire a vagabond boy who hasn't bathed in weeks."

Hailee sighed. "I don't know what to do. We're almost out of money."

"I'm so hungry that my tummy is talking," Philip moaned.

Hailee's heart broke. She hadn't expected it to be this difficult. "I'll tell you what, Philip," she said. "I'll go right now and find us something to eat." She gave him a hug. "Reuben, you watch Philip. I'll be back soon."

"Where are you going?" asked Reuben, following her to the door.

"To get us something to eat."

"But we have hardly any money left. You said so, yourself."

"Don't worry," Hailee assured him.

"What're you gonna do?"

Hailee looked over at Philip, who played quietly on the floor. Then, she returned her gaze to Reuben and lowered her voice to a whisper. "Please don't tell Philip, because he's too little and won't understand."

"Go on," said Reuben.

"If I can't find any food in the garbage cans outside the nearby eateries, then I'm going to grab something without being noticed."

"What?" Reuben hissed. "You know stealing is wrong, Hailee. What would Ma say?"

"Look, Reuben. Ma isn't here. Pa isn't here. There's no one to help us, so I have to do what I have to do. Besides, I'll pay them back whenever I can afford to. It'll be just a little bit of food."

"But what if you get caught?"

"I won't." Hailee forced determination into her voice to hide the fear she felt.

"How do you know?" Reuben whispered.

"What're you talking 'bout?" Philip called to them.

"Just a minute, Philip. This is big kid talk," Hailee replied. Then, to Reuben, she whispered, "I just know, that's how." Why did Reuben always have to argue?

Reuben folded his arms across his chest. "That's not good enough."

"Well then, I won't get caught, because I'm quick. I was the fastest runner at our school, remember? And Pa always said I run like the wind."

"Okay, okay," Reuben conceded. "Just make sure you run like a tornado."

"I have to go now. Keep an eye on Philip," Hailee told him again. Then, she grabbed her worn leather shoulder bag and slipped out the door....

The first time Hailee had stolen, the item had been a loaf of bread. She'd stuffed it inside the leather bag while the store owner had his back turned, then snuck out the door and walked as nonchalantly as she could past the front window. When she'd rounded the corner into the alley, she'd taken off running as fast as she could toward Gardner Street. Fingers crossed that she wouldn't trip and fall, Hailee had continued her sprint until she'd reached the hotel and disappeared inside.

She'd paused outside their door to catch her breath before entering. Reuben had been less than grateful, saying, "All you brought us is a loaf of bread?" yet he'd finally thanked her and said he was glad she hadn't been caught. Hailee had broken the loaf into three pieces, making sure hers was the smallest, and shared it with her hungry brothers.

From that day forward, stealing had gotten only easier for her. To protect her conscience, Hailee had likened herself to a mother bird, flying off to collect food for her babies, who waited with open beaks at home in their nest. She winced at the thought of their empty stomachs, and her determination to keep them nourished soon eliminated any feelings of compunction.

After several weeks, Hailee no longer feared getting caught. She developed a specific strategy for each store from which she stole and made sure to target a wide array, even if it meant walking for hours to reach them, to avoid falling into a pattern that might generate suspicion. She must have gotten too comfortable with her routine, though, for on one fateful day, she was caught red-handed....

Once her sack was stuffed with as many apples as it could hold, Hailee turned and started for the door. She'd almost reached it when she heard a male voice shout, "Stop that girl!"

Hailee shoved her way through the door and began to run, but it was too late. She felt a strong hand grab her arm and yank her to a stop. Wincing in pain, Hailee turned and looked up into the eyes of a tall man dressed in a fine suit. Without a moment's hesitation, she kicked him in the shin.

He immediately let go of her and grabbed his leg, and Hailee spun around and sprinted off, never slowing her pace till she reached the hotel. Gasping for breath, she stumbled inside and collapsed on the floor. "I just got caught," she answered Reuben's questioning look, "but I escaped. Whew, that was close."

"Maybe I should do it," Reuben suggested.

"You!" Hailee studied her brother. Reuben was not a fast runner, and, while he had a quick wit, he lacked street smarts and common sense. Sending him in her stead would be too risky. "That's all right, Reub, but you did give me an idea. Can I borrow your other pair of pants?"

"What do you want with my pants?"

"I think the store owners are getting wise to me. Even though I've started stealing from other dry goods stores farther away, I think they're still on the lookout for a skinny girl with long, blonde hair and a faded dress. Suppose I disguise my appearance—"

"And pretend you're a boy?"

"Yes."

"I must admit, you are a genius, Hailee."

Hailee beamed. It was the first compliment she'd heard from Reuben in a long time. They had recently started to get along better, and that brought her joy. "I'll cut my hair, too," she added.

"Are you sure?"

"I don't think they'll believe I'm a boy with these blonde curls." Hailee twisted a tight ringlet around her finger.

"Do you want to do it now?"

"Sure."

They searched several rooms before finding a pair of scissors in an old desk. After making sure Philip was otherwise occupied, Reuben went to retrieve his other pants, while Hailee stood in front of a mirror and started cutting. Thick tendrils of blonde covered the floor at her feet, but she refused to look down, knowing she would probably cry to see all of the hair she no longer had.

Reuben looked on, pointing out spots she'd missed, as she continued cutting, until her hair was no longer than her ears. Then, she took the handheld mirror Pa had given her for her eighth birthday, turned around, and used the mirror to check the back of her head. Hailee gasped, suddenly overcome with regret. She'd always loved her hair; it was like Ma's, thick and blonde and beautiful. Now, the majority of it was gone, replaced by a horrifyingly crooked haircut. She looked down at the floor now and couldn't tear her eyes away from the hair that was piled there. Tears sprang to her eyes. She shouldn't have taken such a drastic measure.

Just then, Philip walked into the room and gasped. "What happened to your hair?"

Hailee rubbed her eyes and smiled. "I needed a haircut," she said simply.

"But I liked your hair. It looked like Ma's."

"Come here, sweet Philip." Taking her brother in her arms, Hailee gave him a big hug. "Do you know how much I love you?"

"As much as this?" Philip extended his arms in opposite directions.

"Even more than that," Hailee whispered.

"More than that?"

"Yes. I love you more than all the trees and flowers and rocks in the world."

Philip giggled. "Ma always said that."

"It was true," Hailee affirmed. "And do you know what? This afternoon, I'm going to get us something good to eat."

Philip grinned. "You mean, like pie or cake?"

"Something like that."

"I can't wait!"

"Now, you be a good boy for Reuben and work on your penmanship. When I get back, I'll help you with some addition."

"What's 'dition?"

"It's something you do with numbers, and I bet you'll be so good at it."

Philip giggled. "As good as Pa?"

"I bet so." Pa had been an intelligent, loving man, and she saw so much of him in Philip. "I need to go now." She kissed Philip on his button nose, then went to change into Reuben's clothes.

When she emerged, Philip burst out laughing. "Hailee, why are you dressed like Reuben?"

"He let me borrow his clothes because it's getting colder outside," Hailee explained, hating to lie to her little brother.

"Oh."

"I'll be back soon." With that, Hailee left in search of pie, cake, or other sweets. As she walked along, she thought about how busy and full her days had become. In the mornings, she went "hunting for food," *as she called it. She liked the way that sounded; it was almost as if she were one of the early settlers, maybe a Pilgrim, and she needed to scavenge for every meal. When she returned home, she spent some of the afternoon instructing Reuben and Philip in the subjects they would have learned at school. Her favorite subjects to teach were reading, arithmetic, and history. Although she had no books at her disposal, she had an excellent memory, and everything she'd learned, she imparted to her brothers. Hailee had been one of the smartest pupils in her class, and she yearned to share that knowledge.*

After that, Hailee would sometimes go "hunting for food" again, and then, before they went to bed, she would tell her brothers the baby Moses story. Reuben had tired of hearing it and often decided to go to bed, instead, but Philip never tired of hearing his favorite Bible story. Yet Hailee refused to read from the Bible. God had abandoned her, and so she had no use for the words found in His Book.

Hailee turned and glanced at her reflection in a store window. She certainly looked the part. Proud of herself for being so convincing, she dug her hands into her pockets, as she had seen Reuben do. Even though she had a feminine face, her new haircut and scruffy clothes should allow her to easily pass as a boy. She looked down at her chest. Fortunately, she hadn't developed any noticeable curves, so that made it even easier. Unless someone recognized her face, no one would be the wiser....

For the next six months, Hailee had started each day by "hunting for food." When her hair had grown longer, she'd ditched the disguise, for she'd feared that her male persona might have become familiar to certain shopkeepers. She'd managed to escape every time, though there had been a few close calls, and she'd become adept at talking her way out of most any predicament. She'd always come home with food for her brothers, and she'd continued their daily schooling.

That is, until the day she'd gotten caught and couldn't go home. Hailee closed her eyes. Yes, the past from which she had come was dotted with crime and behavior she wasn't the least bit proud of. She had changed, true, but that didn't mean she would feel comfortable if any of her newfound friends in Pine Haven learned about her past.

CHAPTER TEN

True to his promise, Nate arrived at six o'clock on Saturday evening to take Hailee to the barn dance. She had been nervous all day thinking about it. For one, she couldn't dance. She'd never been taught and had never once attended a dance. Moreover, lately, her mind had been filled more and more with thoughts of Nate, which always made her heart race.

"Good evening, Hailee," Nate said when she opened the door. He offered her his arm.

What a gentleman! "Good evening, Nate." She took his arm and allowed him to lead her to the buggy.

"You look beautiful tonight, Hailee," Nate said as he helped her to climb in.

"Thank you," Hailee replied. She owned few dresses and was glad she'd saved her favorite dress— a blue floral pattern—for this special occasion. "Did you attend many dances when you lived in Boston?" she asked him as he prompted the horse forward.

"I did, though they were never as enjoyable as a barn dance. My mother made sure I was present at every social event I was invited to while I was at home on holiday from boarding school."

"Your parents must be so proud of you for moving out here to pastor a church!"

Nate chuckled. "Not exactly. Far from it, in fact. You see, my grandfather founded one of the most respected law firms in Boston, where my father is a partner. My parents wanted me to attend law school, become an attorney, and join the family practice."

"How did you decide to become a reverend instead?" Hailee asked.

"Well, it certainly wasn't the obvious choice. My family attended church, but it was to fulfill a social obligation, not to engage in genuine worship. For years, I didn't have a relationship with the Lord, and I'm sad to say my parents still don't know Him. I've prayed for years that they will someday come to accept Jesus Christ as their Lord and Savior."

Hailee was quiet for a moment, not wanting to sound nosy. Soon, though, she asked, "When did you come to know the Lord?"

"When I was seventeen, Vance, another student at my boarding school, invited me to go to church with him. I didn't know Vance very well; he lived at home, since his house was near the school. Anyway, I went to church with Vance's family and learned the truth about Jesus and what He did for me on the cross. It was as if my ears had suddenly been opened. I still remember sitting there in the sanctuary and hearing the gospel message for the first time. I'm humbled that the Lord drew me to Him. He could have allowed me to continue on as I had been doing, never realizing what was really important in life."

Hailee was amazed at Nate's story. "And now, you're a man of God who leads others to Christ," she mused.

"Only God could have opened the door for me to do that. My parents kept insisting I follow their plans for my future. Throughout my years at boarding school, law school loomed like a dark cloud in my future. I think my parents realized, deep down, that I would take another path, even before they found out I would choose seminary. After all, I had changed since becoming a Christian, and so had my priorities." Nate paused. "My family puts a lot of emphasis on making money and belonging to the right social circles. When I gave my life to Christ, my priorities became reading my Bible, praying, and learning as much as I could about God and His truths. My parents couldn't understand it. Mother even made arrangements for me to court her best friend's daughter, since a marriage between us would secure our families' financial futures for generations to come."

"I imagine your parents didn't take it too well when they discovered your new set of priorities," Hailee commented.

"Not at all," said Nate. "Father kept telling me I needed to spend less time in the Bible and more time learning the law. I just couldn't bring myself to study those law books. I spoke to Vance about it—we had become close friends by this point—and he suggested I pray about my future and place it in the Lord's hands. At first, I thought Vance's suggestion was crazy. Why would I give my future to the One who already knew what my future held? But I did as Vance said, and, before I knew it, the Lord placed in my heart the desire to become a reverend.

I finally talked my parents into allowing me to attend seminary instead of law school. I don't know what disturbed them more: the idea of my becoming a man of the cloth, or the thought of my moving to Pine Haven." Nate chuckled.

"They didn't like Pine Haven?" From what she knew of the town, she couldn't imagine anyone not liking it, although she remembered Nate saying that his grandmother hadn't.

"They find this area too 'primitive.' Compared to Boston, it is, I guess. Yet from the moment I came to Pine Haven eleven years ago for Aunt Kaydie's wedding, I knew I would live here someday. I prayed about it and asked God to bring me back, if it was His will. He answered my prayer in ways I never would have imagined. Reverend Eugene's position became available, and here I am. I was surprised when I was offered the position, since I was fresh out of seminary and had never really preached before." Nate chuckled. "But, as Aunt McKenzie likes to remind me, 'With men this is impossible; but with God all things are possible.'"

"I've proven that verse in my own life, as well," Hailee said. "I never imagined that the school board of Pine Haven would hire someone who had never taught in her own classroom."

"I, for one, was happy you applied for the position," Nate said. "I know that the school board considered each applicant prayerfully, and you were the individual they felt God leading them to hire."

"I feel so blessed to be here," Hailee remarked. "And I never would have guessed that you'd had no prior preaching experience. Your sermons are profound and well planned, and you deliver them so smoothly."

"Thank you, Hailee. I see that you understand the importance of complimenting me, since I had a hand in hiring you." Nate winked at her.

"Well, of course!" Hailee teased back. "It would be a shame to lose my teaching position before I've even begun."

"True, true," Nate affirmed. "See that you continue to make only laudatory remarks about my sermons for as long as you wish to retain your job."

"I know for a fact that I will endure—I mean, enjoy—all of your sermons," Hailee said, giggling.

Nate chuckled. "Very funny, Miss Annigan. I never knew that the woman we'd hired would be so witty!"

"Why, thank you!"

Nate deepened his voice in mock seriousness to say, "Just keep in mind that we hired you to teach serious subjects and proper manners, not silliness."

"If that's so, Reverend Adams, then I fear you may have hired the wrong woman, perhaps an aging spinster with thick spectacles and a crotchety demeanor. For you are sorely mistaken if you believe for one minute that's what I intend to be."

"Ah, Miss Annigan, I know you aren't such a woman. For one, you don't have thick glasses."

Both of them burst out laughing, their voices ringing through the trees that lined the drive to the Dickenson Ranch. Hailee couldn't believe how comfortable she felt with Nate. She was glad he'd invited her to the barn dance and thankful she'd been brave enough to agree to come. Hoping Nate wouldn't notice, Hailee stole a glance at his handsome profile. Unusual feelings welled up inside of her whenever she was with him, and she wondered if she might be falling in love.

"Here we are," Nate said as he slowed the wagon to a stop. When they were parked in a line of wagons, he came around and helped her out. Then, he offered her his arm, and they started toward the barn. So many people were gathered there, it looked as if the entire town was in attendance.

As they came closer, a group of fiddlers began tuning their instruments, and couples started lining up on the makeshift dance floor. Hailee had never seen anything like it before.

"Would you like to dance, or would you like to watch for a few songs?" Nate asked.

"I...I guess I'd prefer watching for a while, if that's okay," Hailee replied. "I've never really danced before."

"That's fine," Nate replied. "I'll get us some lemonade, and we can sit right here."

"That would be nice," Hailee said, lowering herself onto the bench he'd indicated.

Moments later, Nate returned, carrying two glasses of pale liquid. He handed one to her.

"Thank you." She accepted the glass and took a sip. The flavor took her back to the birthday party where she'd first tasted the beverage. It had been at the home of her friend Clara. She remembered playing in the backyard...dancing, spinning...and colliding with Clara, causing them both to tumble into the dirt. Clara's dress had been ruined, and she'd never invited Hailee to another party. Oh, why had she accepted Nate's invitation to this dance? It could end only in disaster!

"Hailee? Are you feeling all right? You look awfully pale."

Hailee snapped out of her reverie and stared at Nate. "I'm not sure I should dance at all. I'm so sorry, Nate."

"Nonsense! You'll be just fine."

"You don't know how clumsy I am or how prone I am to cause accidents."

Nate only grinned. "Okay, then. Would you like to step outside for some fresh air?"

Hailee thought for a moment, then nodded. The dancing was mesmerizing and intimidating at the same time, and she was eager to get away from it for a time. She stood up and followed Nate out of the barn and up a small hill.

He turned around to face her. "Now then, let's teach you how to dance."

"What? Oh, Nate, I don't think that's a good idea—"

"Please at least try, Hailee. No one can see you here, so you need not worry what anyone thinks."

"But, what if I fall, or—"

"You aren't half as clumsy as you think you are. Come on; I'll show you the dance they just did inside." Nate held out his hand.

Reluctantly, Hailee placed her right hand in his, then watched, both intrigued and delighted, as he bowed. "May I have the honor of dancing with you this evening?" he asked.

"Y-yes, I suppose so." Hailee stifled a giggle.

Next, Nate moved closer to Hailee and put his left arm around her waist. She felt her cheeks grow hot, and she had to remind herself to breathe. "Nate—"

"Here, now we go in a square with our feet, counting the steps, like this."

Hailee followed Nate's lead. "I don't know..." she said, fearing she would trip over her feet any second and make a complete fool of herself in front of Nate.

"You're doing fine. Just continue to follow my lead."

Hailee managed to follow along without stumbling for a few more minutes, ever aware of Nate's hand holding hers and his other hand on her waist. The feelings that fluttered within her were so new and unexpected, and she wanted to close her eyes and savor his closeness. Yet she thought better of it, knowing that if she closed her eyes, she would surely lose her balance.

"Are you ready to go inside and dance with everybody else?" Nate asked.

"Inside? I—I'm not sure. Can we practice a bit longer?"

"Sure." Nate continued counting the steps.

Hailee paid close attention so as not to trip. She actually found herself enjoying the dancing lesson—until she moved forward and stepped squarely on Nate's foot.

"Ouch!"

"Oh, my! I'm so sorry!" Hailee released Nate's hand and took a step back, horrified. *Now you've done it, Hailee*, she thought. *You've made a complete fool of yourself!* "Nate, are you all right?"

"I think I may have a few broken toes," Nate said, then proceeded to hobble around in circles while moaning, "Oh, my aching foot!" He paused and leaned down to examine his foot. "Did you happen to notice if Doc Orville was in attendance?"

"You wait right here. I'll go fetch him," Hailee assured him. *Nate will never dance with you again!* she lamented.

Nate stood and placed his hand gently on her arm. "I'm fine, Hailee. I was only teasing you."

"Oh! Thank goodness. I warned you about my clumsiness."

"And here, I thought I was safe because there aren't any stairs for you to go up or down," Nate teased. "But honestly, Hailee, I'm fine. I barely felt a thing."

"I'm sorry, Nate. I'm just too awkward and unpolished to dance before an audience."

"You'll do fine, Hailee. You aren't the first person to step on a partner's foot, and you certainly won't be the last. I apologize for teasing you."

"If you're sure you're all right...."

"I'm sure. See?" Nate walked in a circle without limping. "No harm done. Are you convinced?"

"Yes, but what if we go inside, and I step on your foot again, or trip, or—"

"You'll be fine. Just one dance, and I'll quit pestering you." Nate grinned boyishly at her.

"Are you guys gonna stay out here all night?"

Hailee whirled around at the youthful voice.

"Hi there, Clint, Tommy," Nate said, then turned to Hailee. "You remember these two, right? They're Aunt Kaydie and Uncle Jonah's."

"Of course! Hello, you two."

Nate turned back to the twins. "No, boys. We're going in now to dance."

"Good thing," Tommy said, "'cause there ain't no music out here."

"Isn't any music," Nate corrected him.

"That, too," Clint said.

"Maybe you should step in and teach English from time to time," Hailee teased.

"Hmm...I'll have to think about it," Nate replied with a grin. "Come on. Let's dance."

✺

Nate felt a twinge of nervousness as he led Hailee into the barn. He wasn't worried about her tripping or looking silly but what others might assume when they saw them together. He was attracted to Hailee, of course, but he wasn't sure he was ready to make that fact public, especially since he wanted to get to know her a lot better.

Thankfully, when they joined in the dance, everyone else seemed focused on themselves and their partners. Hailee did remarkably well and tripped only a handful of times, which prompted laughter instead of tears.

After several dances, Nate needed a break, and it looked as if Hailee could use one, as well. "I don't know about you, but I could go for another lemonade," he told her.

"That sounds wonderful. All of this dancing has certainly made me thirsty!" Hailee replied, following him to a stack of hay bales on the edge of the dance floor.

"That wasn't so bad, was it?" Nate said with a grin as Hailee sat down.

"No, you're right. That was actually a lot of fun!" She fanned herself with her hand. "It helped that I had a good teacher. Thank you for convincing me to try dancing."

"My pleasure," Nate replied.

Hailee giggled. When she looked up, their eyes locked, and, for a moment, Nate felt powerless to tear his gaze away. Everything else in the room faded away, out of focus. *Wake up, Nate!* he urged himself. "I'll go fetch us some lemonade," he finally said.

Hailee looked away and nodded. "Thank you."

Nate wove through the crowd and made his way to the table of refreshments. While he waited his turn, he saw Aunt McKenzie and Uncle Zach moving toward the dance floor.

"Aren't you going to ask your lovely wife to dance, Fred?" Aunt McKenzie asked as she passed the Grangers.

Fred furrowed his brow. "Who?"

"Your lovely wife—aren't you going to ask her to dance?"

"My lovely wife?" Fred looked even more confused.

"Good grief!" Lucille exclaimed. "Remember me, your lovely wife?"

"Oh, you. Sorry about that, Lucille. Would you care to dance?" Fred asked, extending his hand to her.

"I suppose so," Lucille replied.

Nate shook his head and chuckled to himself as he picked up the pitcher of lemonade and filled two cups. The Grangers were an odd couple, but they'd been happily married for several decades. That was something Nate wanted for himself someday, and he couldn't help but wonder if he'd found the woman with whom he hoped to spend the rest of his life.

Nate picked up the cups of lemonade and turned around—and found himself face-to-face with Rowena Nash and Etta Mae.

"Why, Reverend Adams, what a pleasant surprise!" Rowena exclaimed.

Nate suspected that Etta Mae's mother was far from surprised to see him. "Good evening, Mrs. Nash, Etta Mae," he said, nodding politely.

"My daughter looks absolutely ravishing tonight, doesn't she?" Rowena gushed. "We ordered her gown

from one of the finest dressmakers in Chicago so
that she would be utterly stunning when you asked
her to dance tonight."

Nate smiled, hoisting the cups of lemonade in
hopes that the two women would realize they had in-
tercepted his mission and excuse him. But he knew
the possibility was highly unlikely. Rowena Nash
seemed determined to marry her daughter off to no
one but him, and he had only a hint of why. The
reputation of the Adamses of Boston had managed
to reach her ears, and she had mentioned more than
once how she hoped he would return there someday
to pastor a large, prosperous church and raise a family. That she wanted her daughter to be the mother of
his children had been more than clear.

"Have you been enjoying yourself, Etta Mae?"
Nate asked her, trying to be polite.

"Oh, yes, Reverend Adams." Etta Mae batted her
eyelashes at him.

Had he not been a well-bred man versed in the
odd ways of young women, he might have thought
she had an eye condition. However, he had attended
many a dance in Boston and had seen countless in-
stances of the "fluttering eye syndrome," as he called
it. Of everything he'd left behind in Boston, the man-
nerisms of wealthy young women searching for a
suitable mate were truly what he missed the least.
He'd grown up with girls who'd been shallow and self-
serving, and if they'd paid him special attention, it
had been because of his family's wealth and the prospect of living a life of luxury as his wife. Nate was
beginning to realize that he hadn't escaped that type
of woman by moving to Pine Haven, for gold diggers
could be found in every state of the Union. Yet he was

determined to find a woman who loved him for who he was, not for his family's wealth and reputation.

Rowena cleared her throat. "Etta Mae would *really* enjoy herself if a certain someone would ask her to dance."

Etta Mae continued to blink her eyelashes at him. "She's absolutely right."

"Well, it was nice speaking with both of you," Nate said, hoping his feigned obliviousness would fool them. "If you'll excuse me, I need to deliver this lemonade to Miss Annigan."

"Please, Reverend, allow me!" Rowena exclaimed, grabbing both cups out of Nate's grasp.

"Mrs. Nash—"

"It's no trouble, I assure you. Now, go along, you two, and enjoy yourselves."

With that, Rowena turned and marched off toward Hailee, leaving Nate alone with Etta Mae. He supposed it couldn't hurt to dance with her for one song—and just one song—so as not to offend her.

So, he held out his hand and bowed to Etta Mae. Instantly, she took his hand in a viselike grip and yanked him toward the dance floor. He could only pray Hailee wasn't paying attention.

Hailee was looking around, trying to locate Nate, when Rowena Nash stepped into her line of vision. "Hello, Miss Annigan. Reverend Adams asked me to bring you this." She thrust a cup of lemonade toward her.

"Oh! Thank you, Mrs. Nash," she said as she took it from her.

"You're quite welcome." Rowena lowered herself onto the bale of hay next to Hailee. "It was the least I could do, considering how anxious the good reverend seemed to dance with Etta Mae."

Hailee managed a smile, though it felt as if she'd been hit in the stomach. As she took a sip of lemonade, she peered over the rim of the cup at the dance floor, where she spotted the two of them amid the other couples. Etta Mae moved with the grace and poise of an experienced dancer, and she and Nate made a handsome pair, much to Hailee's dismay.

"What do you think of Etta Mae's dress?" Rowena whispered.

"It's lovely."

"Well, it's more than lovely! We had it shipped all the way from Chicago. The leg-of-mutton sleeves are the latest fashion across the country." She paused and looked Hailee up and down. "I'm surprised that you aren't wearing something more fashionable. You are from the city, are you not?"

"Cincinnati, yes."

"Well, I guess I'm surprised to see you dressed in plain calico. Surely, you have something finer you'll want to wear when you start teaching in the fall."

Hailee didn't know what to say. She glanced down at her dress. It was one of her favorites, and she'd sewn it herself with fabric Dot had given her for her birthday last year. She'd never thought it to be unsuitable in any way.

"Oh, would you just look at them?" Rowena beamed in the direction of the dance floor. "Don't those two make a lovely couple? It's as if they were made for each other."

They certainly looked like they were made to dance together. Etta Mae matched Nate's movements, step for step. No wonder Nate was eager to dance with her! And not only was she graceful, but she was the picture of beauty, too. Her long cascade of hair flowed and bounced with every twirl, her flawless skin glowed in the dim candlelight, and her exquisite gown enhanced her shapely figure.

Hailee reached up and tucked an unruly curl behind her ear. Her own dark blonde hair had a mind of its own, something she hadn't been bothered by until this moment.

"Well, I'd best be on my way," said Rowena, interrupting Hailee's thoughts. "I have so many folks to see!" With a wave of her hand, she stood up and glided off, leaving Hailee alone with her envy.

Nate glanced over at Hailee, sitting alone again on the hay bale. He wished more than anything that the song would end. However, the musicians had gotten quite zealous and kept playing the chorus over and over again.

"Reverend Adams?"

Nate returned his gaze to his dance partner. "Yes, Etta Mae?"

Just then, the music ended, giving Nate the perfect opportunity to excuse himself. Fortunately, it wouldn't be proper for her to ask him for another dance. It wasn't that she was unattractive; she was beautiful. And it wasn't that she couldn't dance; she had more grace than most people he knew. But her determination to marry him made him want to keep his distance.

"Well, thank you, Etta Mae," he said. "I hope you enjoy the rest of your evening."

"Thank you," Etta Mae squeaked. She stared at Nate as he backed away.

He turned around and made a beeline for Hailee but noticed that she was no longer seated on the hay bale where he'd left her. Where could she have gone? Outside, perhaps. Nate proceeded to the door, stepped out, and looked left and then right.

There was Hailee, seated on a large, flat rock to the right, her back to him.

"Hailee?"

She jolted and looked up at him.

"Sorry if I startled you." He walked over and sat down beside her. "Would you care to join me for another dance?"

"I think I need some more fresh air, if that's okay," Hailee said. "It's so lovely out here, so calm and peaceful. And I've never seen a more colorful sunset."

"I felt the same way when I first came here," Nate said. "In fact, I can't really recall ever seeing a sunset in Boston. I'm not sure if that's because I was usually surrounded by tall buildings, or if I simply didn't take the time to marvel at one of God's most amazing creations."

"I didn't notice it much in Cincinnati, either," Hailee admitted.

Nate leaned back and looked up at the sky, where the stars had started to twinkle. "Out here in the wide open, we have no choice but to notice the sunset and the stars."

Hailee nodded but said nothing. She seemed to be lost in thought.

"Hailee, are you all right?"

"I'm fine."

"You seem...I don't know. A bit upset, perhaps."

"It was just something Mrs. Nash said."

He'd seen Mrs. Nash talking to Hailee while he was dancing with Etta Mae. He should have known she would badger her. "Hailee, I'm sorry if she said something hurtful. You shouldn't pay her any heed."

Hailee sighed. "You're right."

Without thinking, Nate reached over and gently placed his hand on top of Hailee's. It seemed like the natural thing to do. Besides, he wanted to comfort her and keep her from being discouraged.

When Hailee flinched slightly, Nate pulled his hand away. "Sorry," he said. "I didn't mean to make you feel uncomfortable."

"You—you didn't," she stammered.

Nate turned to face Hailee, his eyes searching hers.

"Aren't ya ever gonna go dance?" a voice behind them asked.

Nate and Hailee both turned their heads.

"Well, if it isn't my two little cousins, spying again." Nate grinned at Tommy and Clint.

"We ain't spyin'," Clint insisted. "We're playin' cowboys an' Indians."

"We thought all the 'dults were supposed to be dancin'," Tommy said.

"O' course, we could use another cowboy out here," Clint suggested, his eyes hopeful.

Nate chuckled. "I think we'll pass, but thanks, boys." He stood to his feet, then reached for Hailee's hand and helped her up. "Unless, of course, you'd rather stay out here and play with Tommy and Clint...."

Hailee giggled. "Another time, perhaps."

"Davey likes to play cowboys an' Indians with us," Clint said matter-of-factly. "He's real convincin', too."

"That's nice of him," said Nate.

"So, whaddya say?" Tommy asked.

"I think I'll ask this lovely lady for another dance," Nate said.

Hailee blushed and stared at the ground.

"May I have another dance?" Nate asked, tilting his head to catch her eye.

"Eww! 'Dults can be so strange!" Tommy declared. "Come on, Clint. Let's go rescue the wagon train o' settlers!" The two boys raced toward the house and disappeared around the corner.

Nate held out his hand. "Shall we?"

Hailee smiled as his fingers clasped hers. With his other hand, he touched the small of her back and held her gently at arm's length. Then, he matched his steps with hers, moving to the rhythm of the faint strains of music drifting out from the barn.

That night, Hailee went to bed with every intention of sleeping—such a full day from which to recover! But, as usual, her mind was far from ready for slumber. She couldn't believe how much she'd enjoyed dancing and how, even being so close to Nate, she hadn't felt concerned about tripping or looking foolish. In fact, she thought she might dance every day, if it would mean being with Nate. He produced feelings within her she'd never experienced before, and now, lying wide awake in bed, she finally recognized those feelings as love.

CHAPTER ELEVEN

*O*n the first day of school, Hailee stood in the doorway of the schoolhouse and greeted each student as he or she entered the classroom. She hoped to do as good a job as the previous teacher, Miss Schreibeis. According to Nate, Miss Schreibeis had taught in Pine Haven for thirteen years. She'd loved children and had a gift for making them feel special. She'd also been an excellent educator, ever patient in her instruction and discipline. At the conclusion of the previous term, she'd gotten married and moved with her husband to Wyoming.

Hers would be a tough act to follow, Hailee knew. But Nate had encouraged her, saying, "There's room in the hearts of the children of Pine Haven for more than one excellent teacher, Hailee."

When the students had taken their seats, Hailee walked to the front of the room and faced them with her biggest smile. "Welcome, everyone. My name is Miss Annigan," she said, indicating the blackboard, where she'd written her name in chalk, "and I am the new schoolteacher. I look forward to getting to know each of you. I have met several of you before, but let's go around the room and introduce ourselves, anyway. Please give your first and last name." She turned to Bethany Ethel Dickenson, who was seated in the front row to her right. "We'll start with you."

"Bethany Ethel Dickenson." The girl smiled back at her, and Hailee was struck by how closely she resembled her mother, Kaydie, with her long, blonde hair and petite figure.

"Hello, Bethany Ethel." She beamed. "Next?"

"Chloe Sawyer," said Chloe, seated next to Bethany Ethel. She was tall and thin, with dark hair like her father's and piercing green eyes like her mother's.

The introductions continued, with each pupil giving his or her name. When it was the Dickenson twins' turn, the seven-year-olds smirked and chorused, "We are Clint and Tommy Dickenson."

"Yes, thank you," Hailee said. "Now, who is who?" When she'd first met them, she'd tried to pinpoint a unique feature on one or both of them to help her to tell them apart. But they were as identical as they came, both of them stout and husky with gray eyes, carrot-colored hair, and freckled cheeks.

"I'm Clint," said one.

"Hello, Clint," Hailee said.

"No, you're not Clint," the other insisted. "*I'm* Clint."

"No, siree! *I'm* Clint."

The argument escalated as the boys started a wrestling match of sorts.

"Boys! Boys, please!" Hailee walked briskly toward them, her hands on her hips.

They stopped immediately and faced forward, each one wearing a mischievous grin. If she didn't know better, Hailee would say that the "fight" had been an act. Either way, she was less than amused.

"Now, which one of you is Clint, and which one is Tommy?" she asked, keeping her voice firm.

"Neither of us," one of them said. "You must be thinkin' of some other someones."

The students began to howl. It seemed that Hailee had no choice but to play along. She furrowed her brow and scratched her head. "You two do look very familiar," she began. "I believe I met you not too long ago, at a barn dance at the Dickenson Ranch."

"Oh!" one of the twins said. "In that case, my name is Bethany Ethel."

"It is not," interjected the real Bethany Ethel. "Just wait till Ma and Pa find out about this!"

"All right, boys." Hailee put her hands on her hips. "Enough playing. Tell me who's who, please."

"I'm Tommy," one boy said, pointing to himself. "And he is Clint."

"Don't lie, Clint. I'm Tommy, and you're Clint."

Hailee sighed and said a quick prayer. With the likes of Clint and Tommy Dickenson in her classroom, it would be a very long first year of teaching.

Yet Hailee acknowledged that, for a while, she had been anything but the perfect student....

Hailee sneaked up the stairs to the top floor with really no purpose other than to be nosy. It was her fourteenth day of school at The Sanctuary of Promise (she'd kept track), and she had mixed feelings about the place that was supposed to change her life and prepare her for a bright future.

One of the girls in her sewing class had told Hailee that the top floor was reserved for the group of unmarried female teachers who lived at The Sanctuary. Hailee was growing fond of some of her teachers, especially Miss Fanshaw. Her care and concern seemed genuine, and, so far, Hailee had kept the promise she'd made to Miss Fanshaw not to try to escape again. Hailee also liked Miss Torenz, the petite, elderly teacher who wore thick glasses. But there was one teacher she strongly disliked: Miss Badger, whose personality and appearance fit her name perfectly, in Hailee's opinion. She was forever pestering her students to do their arithmetic, the subject she taught and seemed to love more than anything else in the world, and her long, narrow nose and dark, beady eyes reminded Hailee of the badger she'd seen once while on a picnic with her family.

Miss Badger grew easily frustrated and was prone to throwing tantrums whenever her students failed to understand her instruction. With her infamous wooden ruler, she would tap her desk furiously and snarl, "Now, pupils! Pay attention!" In a word, Miss Badger was mean. How she had managed to secure employment at a Christian organization such as The Sanctuary of Promise was beyond Hailee. Perhaps it was because Miss Badger was highly intelligent, borderline genius, when it came to arithmetic. However, not many of the students respected her, although the few she favored held her in high regard. Hailee could tell that her feelings of dislike for Miss Badger were mutual. It seemed to her as if the teacher sought out every opportunity to embarrass her in front of her classmates and make it clear that she was among her least favorite students.

Having reached the top floor, Hailee moved stealthily down the hall, keeping her back against the wall. When she came to a corner, she peeked around to make sure no one was coming. Then, convinced she was alone, she moved sideways around the bend and down the next hall on her quest to find the staff living quarters.

The first door she passed was closed, as were the three that followed. But the fifth door on the left-hand side was open wide, and Hailee could hear the sounds of high-pitched opera singing coming from inside:

> "I would love you all the day.
> Ev'ry night would kiss and play,
> If with me you'd fondly stray
> Over the hills and far away.
> Over the hills and far away."

Doing her best to stifle a giggle, Hailee crept closer to the doorway and peeked inside. The singer was none other than Miss Badger! Her back was turned, but Hailee recognized her large, boxy figure. As she belted out the notes, she waved her arms dramatically, as if she were performing at the theater. Yet there was something different about her.... Hailee gasped. Miss Badger's hair! Instead of the pile of rich, red curls she usually wore pinned atop her head, her hair was thin and mousy, and it had been cut short.

Miss Badger stopped singing and looked around. Quickly, Hailee jumped back and hid just outside the door, hoping she hadn't been seen. Moments later, the singing resumed. Hailee breathed a sigh of relief and cautiously stepped into the doorway again, crouching as low as she could. She surveyed the living quarters, her gaze falling on a bed and a bureau across the room, and, along the wall to her left, a parlor chair. On top of the chair was—could it be?—a red wig! This was better than anything she'd expected to find. And she couldn't resist the opportunity to seize it. Casting a glance at Miss Badger to make sure she was still caught up in her singing, Hailee inched toward the chair, snatched the wig, and crawled back out of the room, while Miss Badger kept up her vocal cacophony.

With the wig concealed under her dress, Hailee snuck back downstairs and into the room she shared with four other girls. There, she gathered her materials for her classes that day, which included arithmetic. She couldn't wait to see the look on Miss Badger's face when the wig came flying through the air toward her in the middle of class. Or, perhaps Hailee should hold it for ransom, in exchange for a promise from Miss Badger to show her more kindness. Hailee shrugged and stuffed the wig into her bag. She would decide later how to reveal it to her teacher.

Throughout her morning classes, Hailee could hardly contain her excitement about going to arithmetic class. When at last it was time for the subject she usually dreaded, she walked down the hall with a bounce in her step toward Miss Badger's classroom.

After the students were seated, Miss Badger stormed into the room, a silk scarf tied over her head. It was all Hailee could do to keep from giggling, because she alone knew why her head was covered.

Click, click, click went the chalk as Miss Badger scrawled a series of atrociously complex math problems on the blackboard. Whether a redhead or a mousy brunette, she showed no mercy in her expectations of her students.

When Miss Badger finally turned around, it looked to Hailee as if she'd been crying. Immediately, her heart sank. What had she done? She hadn't meant to cause her teacher real distress.

"It disturbs me greatly to have to call upon you, my pupils, to help me solve a mystery that has plunged me into utter despondency." Miss Badger closed her eyes and took several deep breaths, then looked at her students once more. "You see, I'm not really a redhead." She proceeded to untie her scarf. As she removed it and revealed her brownish-gray hair, a wave of gasps and murmurs arose from Hailee's classmates. "I always wanted red hair," she continued, "so I purchased a wig several years ago from the man who supplied the acting guild of which I was a member. You may have attended one of our performances here in Cincinnati... but I digress. I grew so accustomed to that wig and received so many compliments that I began to feel insecure without it." Miss Badger sighed and pressed a hand to her heart. "Woe is me! As I was preparing for class this morning, I discovered that my wig was gone."

The more emotional Miss Badger became, the guiltier Hailee felt for stealing her wig. Maybe she could sneak it back to her room after class. Yes, that was it. She'd be none the wiser as to where it had gone for the day.

Seconds later, though, Miss Badger's voice changed as she yelled, "Now, tell me, you contemptuous students, who took my wig? I mean it—somebody had better tell me NOW!" She had gone from soft and whiny to loud and belligerent.

Hailee gulped, now feeling a little scared. There was no telling what Miss Badger would do to her if she found out she was the culprit.

"*I said, tell me who took my wig!*" Miss Badger's eyes looked as if they might bulge out of their sockets. She began tapping on her desk with her wooden ruler, so violently that Hailee feared it might snap in two.

Several of the younger pupils began to cry, and Hailee was half tempted to join them. Just then, Kathleen Sorenson, a goody-goody who'd never been exceptionally nice to Hailee, raised her hand. "Excuse me, Miss Badger?"

"Yes?"

Kathleen pointed a finger as she stammered, "Is—is that your—your w-wig, Miss Badger?"

Hailee followed Kathleen's finger and looked down at her bag. Her stomach sank, for there were several telltale red curls poking through the opening. She thought she'd shoved the wig beneath all of her books! Eyes wide with terror, she met the steely gaze of Miss Badger, who marched briskly toward her.

Hailee cowered as Miss Badger grabbed her bag and yanked out the wig. "Hailee Annigan! What is the meaning of this?"

Hailee called upon her skill of deceit to cover up the theft. "I—I took your wig, Miss Badger, because... because I thought it was so beautiful, and—"

Pain shot through her ear as Miss Badger pinched and pulled on it. Wincing, Hailee stood up and followed her out of the classroom and down the hall, straight to the headmaster's office.

As punishment, Hailee had been required to do extra kitchen duties. She had also received another Scripture verse from Miss Fanshaw—Matthew 7:12, "Therefore all things whatsoever ye would that men should do to you, do ye even so to them"—*and been asked to write a lengthy essay on the Golden Rule.*

The rest of day one went as well as could have been expected. As much as Hailee enjoyed having her own classroom, she was grateful when it was time to send the students home.

"See you tomorrow!" she called after them as they scattered through the school yard.

After she'd finished a few tasks in the class-room, Hailee gathered her bag and prepared to go home. On the porch, she closed the door and locked it. When she turned around, she was delighted to see Nate approaching, a beautiful bouquet of flowers in his hand.

"Hello, Miss Annigan," Nate said with a wink as he handed her the flowers.

"Nate, what a nice surprise!" She inhaled the sweet fragrance. "These are beautiful."

"Genuine Montana wildflowers. I found them yesterday at the Sawyer Ranch."

Hailee studied the bouquet of mostly purple-colored flowers. "I've never seen such delicate blooms."

"Those are called harebells. They remind me of a church I attended in Boston—my friend Vance's church," Nate said. "It was the most beautiful church I'd ever seen, and it had a belfry with three bells. When I saw these flowers swaying gently in the breeze, I couldn't help but pick a few. They looked so peaceful and serene, the way I felt at Vance's church."

"It sounds lovely."

"It was. The church my family attended was lovely, too, but this one was small and modest, yet somehow even more beautiful. I think I felt that way about it because I always sensed the Lord's presence so strongly there."

Hailee smiled. "Thank you for the flowers."

"You're welcome." Nate offered her his arm. "May I walk you home? I'm eager to hear all about your first day of school."

Walking Hailee home from school became a daily ritual, one Nate looked forward to more and more each day. He enjoyed their pleasant conversations. Plus, he told himself, he was keeping up on the local children, as any upstanding school board member would do.

Three weeks into the school year, Hailee seemed to be more comfortable with her students, and, according to Nate's cousins, she was doing an excellent job.

"How was your day?" he asked her on a Thursday afternoon as they linked arms and started across the school yard.

"Oh, it was fine, thank you!" Hailee replied. "We've been working hard to prepare for the annual spelling bee next Friday, and I think the children are just about ready."

Nate chuckled. "In the mercantile yesterday, Lucille was raving about the intelligent pupils of Pine Haven. She invited every person who walked through the door to the spelling bee."

Hailee gave him a knowing smile. "Thank goodness for Lucille! However would we publicize important events without her help?"

"All I know is, she consistently delivers the news faster than the local newspaper."

"And she takes great pride in that, I'm sure."

"So, you think the students are ready for the spelling bee?"

"I do, especially my star pupils—your cousins Chloe and Bethany Ethel, to name a few."

"And what about your not-so-star pupils?" Nate asked.

"Now, now. I try not to use negative words to describe my students," Hailee teased.

"Okay, then, I'll ask you directly: what about Tommy and Clint?"

She smiled. "I'm happy to report that while I'm not too confident Tommy and Clint will advance to the final round of the spelling bee, I do know that since their parents threatened to cancel their family fishing trips on Sundays if they get into mischief, the twins' behavior has improved significantly."

"Uncle Jonah mentioned that to me last weekend," Nate recalled. "Their weekly fishing trips are a big deal, so it's no wonder the twins are shaping up."

Hailee nodded. "This has been their calmest week yet. They didn't start a wrestling match during story time or even stand on their chairs and make monkey sounds in the middle of the arithmetic lesson!"

Nate laughed. "That's good to hear." He directed Hailee to a large rock facing the river, where they'd often stopped to sit.

"For a while, I wasn't sure if I was cut out to teach those troublemaking twins," Hailee confessed as she sat down. "But, now, their mischief is almost endearing—when it doesn't distract the rest of the students."

"You're an excellent teacher, Hailee," Nate said as he sat down beside her. "I knew you would do fine, even with two 'troublemaking twins' in your class."

"Thank you for the vote of confidence. I guess I can relate to them, because—promise not to tell anyone?—there was a time when I was quite the troublemaker, myself."

"You?" Nate chuckled. "I figured you to be the straight-A student who raised her hand to answer every question."

Hailee giggled. "I did end up being a good student, but I also did plenty of things I'm none too proud of."

"Haven't we all?"

"Do you mean to tell me you weren't the perfect student, either?"

Nate grinned. "Oh, there was a time or two when I gave the teacher some grief."

Hailee feigned shock. "Care to share?"

"Sure…if you will."

"It's a deal, but you go first."

"All right. When I was in the fourth grade, my friends and I came up with a plan to take revenge against two boys in our class, Marshall and Hiram. Those two were forever tattling on my friends and me and just about everyone else in our class. They were the teacher's pets and two of the most annoying kids I'd ever met."

"You sought revenge?" teased Hailee.

"Yes. Keep in mind, though, this was long before I knew what the Lord says about revenge." Nate grinned. "I was wiry and small for my age, so it was decided that I should be the one to crawl under the desks and tie Marshall and Hiram's shoelaces together. They were none the wiser, since they were busy trying to be the first ones to complete the writing assignment. Nearly everyone else in the class knew about the prank, and they were on our side, since all of us had been victims of Marshall and Hiram's tattling. When the teacher rang the bell for recess, the two stood up, still oblivious to the fact that their shoes were connected. They weren't on their feet for long, and they ended up having to cut the laces to separate themselves, since I'd done such a grand job with the double knot!"

Hailee raised her eyebrows. "That sounds like quite the scheme!"

"Now it's your turn," Nate said, grinning.

Hailee hesitated a moment. "I'm not proud of this—in fact, I felt remorseful shortly after doing it—but I once sneaked into the living quarters of my least favorite teacher, Miss Badger, and stole her wig."

"You stole a teacher's wig? That was no small act of bravery, I'm sure."

"That was long before I knew what the Lord says about stealing," said Hailee. "On my second-to-last day at The Sanctuary of Promise, I apologized to her and asked her to forgive me."

"And did she?"

Hailee nodded. "It had been three years since I'd pulled that shenanigan, and, in that time, Miss Badger's spirit had softened greatly. She not only forgave me but also opened up about her past, telling me how a man to whom she'd been betrothed had changed his mind at the last minute and jilted her, and also how she'd come to teach at The Sanctuary after losing her job in a local theatrical troupe. She said she'd finally realized that all those hardships were working toward something better for her, and she encouraged me, albeit jokingly, that all of the stunts I'd pulled as a student would better prepare me to handle the difficult children when I had a classroom of my own."

Nate winked at Hailee. "It sounds like those experiences are working for your good, even though I never doubted you would do just fine as the new schoolteacher."

Hailee blushed. "I'm just thankful to God for the work He did in me during my years at The Sanctuary of Promise. It was a blessing to be able to leave my mischief and misdeeds behind and to become one of the very people who helped that transformation to occur. If it hadn't been for my patient, loving teachers, I never would have become a teacher, myself."

"And I'm thankful to God for bringing you to Pine Haven for your first teaching job." Tentatively, Nate reached out and took Hailee's hand in his.

To his delight, she didn't resist but intertwined her fingers with his. He gently rubbed the back of her hand with his thumb. "I am truly glad you came here, Hailee," he said quietly, almost whispering.

"I'm glad, too," Hailee whispered.

Nate looked over at her, and their eyes connected for a moment of intensity before she averted her gaze and blushed again. He was struck anew by her beauty.

"Did you have a good day?" Hailee asked after several moments of silence.

Nate cleared his throat. "I did. It was a busy day, with several visits. Tomorrow, I'll start preparing my sermon for Sunday."

Hailee nodded. "Have you chosen a theme for your message?"

"I was thinking of spending some time in the book of First Kings for the next few weeks and studying the chapters on the prophet Elijah."

"That sounds interesting. You are a gifted speaker, Nate."

"Only by God's grace," he responded. "I never expected the Lord to use me in this way. But then, we rarely know ahead of time the calling He's placed on our lives."

"That's true. I never expected to be a teacher, even when I'd begun to dream about being one."

"And I certainly never expected to be sitting here by the river in Pine Haven, Montana, holding hands with the town's finest schoolteacher—and the most beautiful."

Hailee giggled. "And I never expected to be sitting here, holding hands with the town's finest pastor."

"What a pair we make," Nate said.

"And to think that we both grew up in the city, only to leave it behind for the 'uncivilized West.'"

Nate chuckled. "God certainly has a way of opening doors in unexpected places."

CHAPTER TWELVE

The following weekend, Hailee sat down at the desk in her room, opened a drawer, and took out a piece of stationery and a pen. Then, she began her letter to Ella.

My dearest Ella,

I hope this letter finds you well. I have been teaching for about one month so far, and I have an entirely new appreciation for you and all of the teachers at The Sanctuary! I have a wonderful group of students to teach, though there are two particularly trying pupils: seven-year-old twins Tommy and Clint Dickenson. They are among the cutest youngsters I've ever seen, yet they seem to thrive on mischief and throw daily challenges in my direction. I am reminded of Galatians 6:7: "For whatsoever a man soweth, that shall he also reap." Please accept yet another apology for the trouble

I caused you during my first year at The Sanctuary. Perhaps, in time, Tommy and Clint will be among my star pupils. Such a turn of events would be a miracle, indeed!

I have enjoyed getting to know the citizens of Pine Haven, all of whom have welcomed me with warmth and friendliness. There is one person in particular of whom I have grown quite fond—the pastor of Pine Haven Chapel, Reverend Nathaniel Adams (better known as Nate). I am beginning to better understand your feelings for Officer Ulmer. Nate is kind, caring, and thoughtful, not to mention unusually handsome. God has given him the gift of preaching, and I never tire of listening to the wisdom he imparts at church on Sunday mornings. (I also never tire of watching him. He has the bluest eyes you've ever seen and strong, muscular shoulders, despite his slender frame.) Nate walks me home from school almost every day, and he taught me to dance, as well, at a barn dance last month. Have you ever heard of such an event? They seem to be quite popular here. You would have been proud of me, Ella, for I didn't trip over my own feet, as I am wont to do.

I hope that you will meet Nate someday. I know that the two of you would get along famously. The only thing that continues to nag at my heart is the fear of what he would do if he were to find out about my shameful past. After all, Nate is a man of the cloth, and the things I have done, while

I know the Lord has forgiven them, would surely repulse him beyond reconciliation. He seems desirous of courting me, and I should like that very much, though I hope not to presume too much. Oh, merciful heavens! Here I am, rambling on about utter foolishness. I am grateful that I may tell you about this, Ella. Whatever would I do without your friendship?

Please pray that I would muster boldness to be honest with Nate and tell him the truth about my past. Also pray that my words will fall on merciful ears.

Please say hello to the other teachers and to Officer Ulmer. I look forward to hearing from you as soon as you are able to write back!

With much love,
Hailee

Hailee folded the letter and placed it in an envelope. If she hurried, she could make it to the post office before it closed.

"Mrs. Marlen, I'm heading to the post office," she announced as she descended the staircase. "Is there anything I can get for you while I'm out?" She rounded the corner into the sitting room.

Widow Marlen was sitting in an upholstered chair with a book on her lap. She looked up from the book she was reading. "I can't think of anything, dear. But do tell Mr. Victor and Geraldine hello for me, please."

Hailee nodded. "Of course. I'll be back soon." She stepped out into the late afternoon sunshine and took a deep breath. How fresh the mountain air smelled! She was beginning to grow attached to this small, western town and its residents. Hailee strode along the boardwalk, smiling and greeting everyone she passed by name. "Thank You, Lord, for bringing me here," she prayed under her breath. "The only thing that would improve my situation would be to have Philip and Reuben here, but I know that You have heard my cries and that You have our best interests at heart."

Moments later, she entered the post office. "Hello, Mr. Victor," she greeted the man behind the counter.

"Well, good afternoon, Hailee. What a pleasant surprise. How are you?"

"Very well, thank you. I need to mail this letter, please." She handed Mr. Victor the envelope containing Ella's letter.

"That will be two cents."

Hailee reached into her change purse, fished out two pennies, and set them on the counter. "Widow Marlen sends her greetings to you and Geraldine."

"Thank you. How is she?"

"She's fair, though I know she still grieves the loss of her husband."

"I'm glad you're living with her now, Hailee. I know she appreciates your companionship." Mr. Victor affixed a postage stamp to the envelope and placed it in the bin behind him. "Everything is going well at the school, I hope?"

Hailee nodded. "I think I'm finally beginning to settle in. I enjoy the students, especially."

"All of them?" Mr. Victor said with a wink.

Hailee giggled. "Word travels fast in this town!"

"Well, it comes as no surprise that Jonah Dickenson's boys are giving you a hard time. That's what they're known for doing."

"It is much different being on the other side of the desk," Hailee admitted.

"I'm sure you'll handle them just fine." He winked again. "Oh, I almost forgot! I have a letter for you."

Her heart soared at the news, for she loved receiving mail. Maybe it was another letter from Ella Fanshaw or Dot Pangbourn, both of whom had sent her one note already.

"Here you are," said Mr. Victor, handing her an envelope.

Hailee looked down at the return address in the left-hand corner. *Philip Annigan Llewellyn, Cheviot, Ohio.* Her heart stopped.

"Hailee, are you all right?"

She blinked and looked up at him. "Yes, I—I'm fine, Mr. Victor."

"Not bad news, I hope."

"No. Not bad news."

"Very well, then. Have a good day, Hailee."

"Thank you, Mr. Victor. You do the same." Hailee wasn't sure how she'd make it back to Widow Marlen's house. Her mind was a fog of joy and relief. Could it be that her years of dreaming were about to become reality?

She stumbled over to a bench and plopped down, unable to contain her excitement any longer. She read the return address once more to make sure she hadn't been mistaken. Still, it bore her brother's name, albeit with a new last name, and the town of Cheviot, Ohio. She closed her eyes for a quick, silent prayer of thanksgiving. Then, she tore open the envelope, yanked out the folded sheet of paper, and spread it out on her lap.

Dear Hailee,

I can't believe I have found you! I saw your posting at the train station when we went there to see my aunt and uncle off to Minnesota.

I am eleven now. I was adopted by Jean and Lyle Llewellyn, and we live on a farm in Cheviot, Ohio. I have a dog named Leopold who knows lots of tricks. I have taught him to shake hands, fetch, and roll over. I also have a pet rabbit. I never did think of a good name for her, though, so we just call her "Rabbit."

I go to school, and my favorite subjects are writing and arithmetic. I think that's because you did a good job of teaching me when I was younger. I really like to write. I wrote a story about a boy and his adventures that won the class award for Best Composition Piece.

How are you? What are you doing in Montana? Did you get adopted, too? Have you heard from Reuben? I have not. We were separated that day you didn't return to the hotel, and I have always wondered what happened to you. But I knew you wouldn't have left us on purpose. I'm just glad you are all right. I wish I knew what happened to Reuben.

Ma says we can save our money and take a trip to come see you. She's real nice, and so is my pa. He is teaching me all about farming so that someday, if I want, I can take over the farm. I think I would like to farm and also write for the Cheviot Weekly Newspaper.

Please write back soon. I love you and miss you.

Your brother,
Philip

Hailee reread the letter three times, then carefully folded it up again and slid it back inside the envelope. She slumped down on the bench, overwhelmed by gratitude to the One who'd made it all possible. Tears fell down her face and soaked the collar of her dress. *Thank You, Father, that Philip has found me.* Clutching the letter to her chest, Hailee stood up and headed toward the chapel. She wanted to share the news with Nate.

When Hailee entered the church, she found Nate at his desk, working on Sunday's sermon.

He looked up when she entered his office. "Hailee! Are you all right?"

She tried to speak but couldn't answer. Instead, she burst into tears.

Nate jumped up from his desk and came to her side, placing a hand on her shoulder. "Hailee, what's wrong?"

"N-nothing's wrong," she managed. "I—I just received a letter from my—my—"

She handed him the envelope as another sob escaped her throat.

Nate peered at the envelope. "Philip Annigan? That's your brother!"

Hailee nodded, wiping her eyes.

"So, he's found you! Is he all right?"

"Yes." Hailee sniffled. "He was adopted, and he lives with a family in Cheviot, Ohio."

"That's wonderful news!" Nate exclaimed. "I can only imagine how overwhelmed you must feel, after so many years of praying, and now, to know that your brother is alive and well...."

"I know. I can't believe Philip found me. He said he saw a notice I'd posted at the train station."

"What a blessing." Nate gave her shoulder a squeeze. "Does he know where your other brother is?"

Hailee shook her head. "He asked if I had heard from Reuben. Maybe he was adopted, too." She paused and thought for a moment, still trying to let this new reality sink in. "At first, when I saw Philip's name on the envelope, I couldn't believe it. I only wish he'd found me before I left Cincinnati."

Nate leaned closer and met her gaze. "Hailee, if you want, I will make arrangements for you to travel back to Cincinnati for a visit. I'm sure we could find someone to fill in at the school during your absence."

Hailee thought for a moment and then smiled. "That's thoughtful of you, Nate, and a very tempting offer. I have a sense, though, that I should stay here for the time being, however hard that may be."

"Are you sure? It would be no problem at all to order you a train ticket. I know how eager you must be to see your brother."

"Thank you, Nate. Your offer means more to me than you can imagine. But I've waited five years to hear from my brothers, and I'm sure I can wait a little longer to see Philip. Besides, he mentioned that he and his new family are thinking of coming here for a visit."

"If that's how you feel," Nate said, gently enfolding her in his arms. "If you change your mind, be sure to let me know."

Hailee nodded and rested her head on his shoulder. For now, all she wanted was to relish the fact that her brother had found her and to rest peacefully in Nate's arms.

That night, Hailee sat down at the desk in her room to write a letter to Philip. Three times she crumpled up the piece of paper and began again on a fresh page, and still her tears of joy at hearing from her youngest brother soiled the paper and caused her writing to smear. Yet, finally, her fifth attempt captured the words of her heart.

My dearest Philip,

What a wonderful answer to five years of prayer! I praise the Lord that you saw my posting at the train station. How I had longed to hear from you! You are so precious to me, and I have missed you terribly.

I am thankful to hear that you are doing well. I'm especially glad that you love to write. You would make a fine reporter for the Cheviot Weekly Newspaper. I miss those days when I taught you. You always were a smart boy.

It's wonderful that you were adopted by a nice family. I look forward to meeting them.

I am a teacher in Pine Haven, Montana. Pine Haven is very small but full of nice

people who have given me an exceptionally warm welcome. I have eighteen pupils
and have made many friends among the
townsfolk.

Philip, I feel I must tell you the truth about
why I did not return to you and Reuben that
day. I was arrested for stealing food and
was taken to The Sanctuary of Promise,
where I spent the next three years. I was
desperate to find you and Reuben, and my
teachers routinely searched for you, but
to no avail. Yet I never gave up hope that I
would find you both again someday.

I have not heard from Reuben, either, and
I pray he is well.

Know that you are always in my thoughts
and that I pray for you daily. I love you and
miss you.

With much love and affection,
Hailee

CHAPTER THIRTEEN

Two weeks later, on a sunny Saturday afternoon, Nate came to Widow Marlen's to take Hailee on a picnic by the lake. When they reached their destination, Nate helped Hailee out of the wagon, then reached for the large picnic basket. They selected a spot on a small hill overlooking the lake, but Hailee was eager to get her feet wet.

"Race you to the lake!" Hailee shouted after Nate had set down the picnic basket.

Nate cast her a quizzical look and then raised his eyebrows. "Are you sure you're up for the challenge? You've never seen me in action."

Laughing, Hailee bent over and untied her boots. She had always been more agile when barefoot, especially since she'd been shoeless during the days when running from angry storekeepers had been the norm.

"I think I'll leave my boots on," Nate said. "They may be a bit heavy and cumbersome, but I'm not accustomed to moving without them."

"Suit yourself," said Hailee. She got into the runner's stance she'd practiced for years. Immediately, her mind traveled back to an especially exciting race she had participated in at The Sanctuary of Promise....

"Everybody take your mark," Miss Fanshaw said.

Hailee joined the other students on the starting line. She was one of only two girls who had elected to participate in the running relay. A lot of the girls considered it unladylike, while others simply didn't think they could compete with the boys. But Hailee knew better. She loved to run, and she was fast. Today, she planned to win the race and show everyone just how speedy she was.

"Everybody ready?" Miss Fanshaw asked. "On your marks, get set, go!"

Hailee bolted ahead, her legs picking up speed with every step. Out of the corner of her eye, she saw Jacob Ingram, her biggest competitor, closing in on her lead. Focusing on the finish line, Hailee pushed herself even harder, her legs pumping faster than ever.

Jacob might have beat her before, but not today. A thrill of triumph rushed through her as she broke through the ribbon....

"Hailee?"

"I beg your pardon," Hailee said, jolted out of her reverie by Nate's voice. "I was just remembering a relay I ran in a few years ago."

"So, you say you're an experienced relay contestant?"

Hailee laughed. "I don't know about 'experienced.' I've just always enjoyed running."

"Did you win that relay you were daydreaming about?"

"I did," said Hailee. "The boy who finished second was right beside me, but I was the one who broke the ribbon."

"I'll have you know, Miss Annigan, that I'm not too bad a runner, myself."

"We'll have to see about that, Reverend Adams," Hailee teased. "What should we use as the finish line?"

Nate gazed toward the lake. "How about that large rock?"

"Perfect." Hailee positioned her body toward the finish line and hoisted the hem of her dress with one hand.

"All right, then," said Nate. "Shall I give the commands?"

"Please do!"

"On your mark, get set, go!"

Hailee flew like the wind toward the large boulder. The soft grass felt good beneath her feet. She stole a quick glance aside and realized she and Nate were neck and neck, so she pushed herself harder, pumping her free arm and legs as fast as she could. *For mercy's sake, I haven't done this for so long!* she thought to herself. *I'm out of practice!* As they came nearer and nearer to the finish line, Hailee pushed herself harder and harder.

Racing toward the lake, Nate had to fight the temptation to hang back and watch Hailee rather than keep his eyes on the path in front of him. She was quite the sight, with her long, blonde hair flowing behind her and her delicate facial features steeled in a look of sheer determination. She was quick, he'd give her that, and, for a moment, he considered doing the gentlemanly thing and allowing her to win. But he thought better of it. Hailee seemed to enjoy true competition as much as he did, and what fun was a victory gained from a handicap?

They both reached the finish line at exactly the same time. Hailee sat down on the boulder, laughing uncontrollably and gasping for breath. "That was... so...much...fun!"

Nate collapsed in the grass beside the rock. "That was fun," he agreed, willing his lungs to take in air.

"We'll...have to...do that again," Hailee said. "As...a tiebreaker."

Nate chuckled. "We can't let it go down in history that Nate Adams and Hailee Annigan tied in a footrace, now, can we?"

Hailee shook her head. "That simply wouldn't do."

"I never realized how competitive you are," Nate observed. "But I like it," he quickly added.

"What's the sense in racing if you don't do it to win?" Hailee retorted.

"Good question." Nate chuckled, getting to his feet. "Well, I think I'm ready for lunch. I'll go fetch the picnic basket."

Hailee nodded and stood. "Those sandwiches Widow Marlen made do sound mighty appealing after that brisk run."

Nate started to turn, but his eyes stopped on Hailee, unable to look away. Her cheeks were still flushed from exertion, and several blonde tendrils that had come loose from their comb curled up and away from her face in a way that he found irresistible. He reached up and tucked several strands of stray hair behind her ear. "You are beautiful, you know, even after a vigorous run."

Hailee held her breath and closed her eyes for a moment. Then, she opened them again and held Nate's gaze. He was mesmerized. "I—I suppose I should go fetch the picnic basket," he repeated. But he couldn't move. He didn't want to tear his eyes away from this amazing woman God had brought into his life.

Hailee nodded mechanically but never broke eye contact. So, Nate leaned his head closer to her. Cupping Hailee's chin in one hand, he moved closer yet, then wrapped his other hand around her shoulder and drew her nearer still.

When Hailee closed her eyes, Nate brought his lips to hers.

Hailee welcomed Nate's kiss and indulged in it. As soon as he leaned away, she wanted desperately for him to kiss her again. Nothing compared to the feel of his arms around her and the sensation of his lips on hers.

If Nate knew the person you used to be and the things you used to do, he wouldn't be kissing you, sneered a voice in her head. *As a matter of fact, he'd want nothing to do with you.*

At the thought, Hailee pulled away and looked down.

"What's wrong, Hailee?" Nate asked with concern in his voice.

"Nothing," she muttered. She felt bad for not being honest with the man who had won her heart, but she didn't want to talk about her past right now.

"Hailee, if something's wrong—"

"It's nothing, Nate." Surely, if he knew she'd been a thief, a liar, and the worst of troublemakers, he would drop his affection for her. After all, he was a man of the cloth, a righteous and honest man, a man the townsfolk looked up to and respected. It wouldn't do for him to court a woman with a past like hers.

Nate stared at her, looking hurt and confused. Yet Hailee could not bring herself to explain. Not yet, at least.

Moments later, Nate turned and headed toward the picnic basket. His broad shoulders slumped slightly, and his walk was slow and plodding. Hailee's heart broke. She had hurt him, had made him feel rejected, and why? To protect herself from rejection. She bit her lower lip, determined not to cry. She had been such a fool to think someone like Nate would ever be interested in someone like her. She was an orphan who had resided in both a jail cell and a home for wayward juveniles. For a considerable part of her life, she'd been convinced that God had abandoned her, when, in fact, she had abandoned Him. Moreover, Nate came from a well-to-do family with a fine reputation to protect. No, there was no way a romance could bud and flourish between Nate and herself. Hailee only regretted that she hadn't realized this sooner, so as not to lead Nate along and make him believe she considered him more than just a friend.

Nate took his time fetching the picnic basket. He needed to sort out what had just happened, yet he felt confused beyond hope. He'd been so sure that Hailee felt the same way about him as he did her. He'd thought for certain she'd wanted him to kiss her. After all, hadn't they been spending almost all of their free time together? Nate gulped. Of course, just because he was fond of her didn't mean she was fond of him. Perhaps he had misread her. *Lord, I don't know how Hailee feels about me, but You know how much I care for her,* he prayed. *Please, help us to be honest with each other and to overcome this sudden awkwardness that's arisen between us.*

Nate carried the basket back to their spot beside the lake and set it on the boulder. Silently, he removed the cloth napkin covering the contents and spread it on the boulder as a tablecloth. Then, he took out the two sandwiches and arranged them on the cloth.

Without a word, Hailee reached for a sandwich and placed it in her lap. Then, she folded her hands and bowed her head.

Nate did the same. Usually, he would pray aloud, but Hailee's eyes were closed, and it appeared she was saying her own prayer. So, he did, as well, though he didn't feel completely sincere. *Dear heavenly Father, thank You for this food and the hands that prepared it. Thank You, too, for this beautiful day You have blessed us with. Please help us to live our lives for Your glory. In Jesus' name, amen.*

When he had finished, he opened his eyes and took a bite of his sandwich.

"Widow Marlen made apple pie, as well," Hailee finally said, breaking the uncomfortable silence.

Nate nodded. "She's a good cook. When I first arrived in Pine Haven, she invited me to her house for dinner a couple of times."

"I really admire her," said Hailee. "She's become like a grandmother to me."

"I think a lot of people in Pine Haven think of her in that way." Nate hoped the small talk would ease the tense situation. Yet a knot remained in his stomach—as well as in his heart. "I'm glad it all worked out for you to stay with her." He studied Hailee as she ate her sandwich. If he couldn't have her love, he would have to try being content with her friendship. After all, he enjoyed spending time with her, more than with anyone else.

"I'm glad it worked out, too," said Hailee.

Nate saw a troubled look in her eyes. He may not have known her for very long, but he knew her enough to understand that she was sensitive. From her reactions to hearing Rowena Nash's unkind words and receiving a long-awaited letter from Philip to being determined to see her students learn and succeed, even tutoring several of them on her own time, she was deeply affected by the opinions and well-being of other people. What was it that bothered her so? What was it about *him* that bothered her? He thought about asking her but decided against it. He'd experienced enough confusion this afternoon and suspected that any explanation would only add to his befuddlement.

At church on Sunday, Hailee resolved to listen attentively to Nate's sermon but avoid his eyes. She couldn't handle the shame she would feel at meeting his gaze. Not only had she made a complete and utter fool of herself, but she had already fallen in love with him, when she should have kept him at arm's length.

As a hymn was sung, Hailee's mind wandered, and her troubled thoughts resurfaced. *Nate, you're too good for someone like me. If you knew the things I've done, even though I no longer do them, I doubt you would be able to look at me in the same way. You've never been wayward or recalcitrant, while I have an entire list of sins and wrongdoings that would bring you shame to be associated with me. I'm sorry that I allowed myself to fall in love with you and failed to discourage your affections earlier. To court me would only bring you heartache....*

Hailee's mind flooded with memories of the first time she met Nate, of the barn dance, and of after-school strolls. While the thought of him finding out about her past had never left her mind, it had found its way into the far recesses of her thoughts—overshadowed by the love that she was sure was growing between them.

As she had so many times in the past week, Hailee began to imagine the two of them discussing the misunderstanding that had occurred during their picnic and why she couldn't afford to encourage his interest in her. She'd played out the scenario in her mind so many times that she had memorized it. Yet Hailee had yet to voice the script she'd stored in her mind. It had been eight days since she'd last spoken to Nate. And he'd kept his distance, too. There had been no more walks after school and no more surprise visits at Widow Marlen's house.

"Please follow along in your Bibles as I read from the nineteenth chapter of First Kings." Nate's voice caught Hailee's attention and pulled her out of her reverie. She opened her Bible and found the passage, preparing to learn. After all, she was in church to grow in her faith, not to daydream and rehash events over which she had no control.

"Let's read about the prophet Elijah, starting with verse four: *'But he himself went a day's journey into the wilderness, and came and sat down under a juniper tree: and he requested for himself that he might die; and said, It is enough; now, O LORD, take away my life; for I am not better than my fathers.'*" Nate paused and looked up before continuing. "Even the prophet Elijah, who had been used by God with great results, experienced times of discouragement. Elijah was a man of faith, a man of courage, a man of obedience. Yet when Jezebel threatened his life, Elijah decided he'd had enough. He was afraid and prayed that the Lord would take his very life. Elijah pitied himself and sought an end to his fear, frustration, and despair. Like Elijah, all of us have felt the burden of discouragement weigh heavily on our shoulders...."

As Nate spoke, Hailee couldn't help admiring his powerful voice and strong conviction. He had a true gift for reaching others with the Word of God. He was never condemning, never judgmental. Instead, Nate read directly from the source of truth—the Bible— and preached straight from his heart.

Suddenly, Hailee felt a stab of guilt for causing Nate such discouragement when she'd pulled away from him. Yet she, too, was discouraged, feeling powerless to do anything about his discouragement. It was something the Lord alone could mend.

After the service, Nate stood outside at the doorway to the church, shaking hands with the parishioners, as he did every Sunday. It had been difficult to focus on his sermon, and he silently asked God to forgive him for focusing on something other than bringing His message to the congregation.

"Hello, Reverend Adams!" exclaimed Rowena Nash as she approached him, Etta Mae by her side.

Nate snapped to attention and nodded. "Mrs. Nash, Etta Mae."

"Excellent sermon," Rowena said. "We would be honored if you would join us for dinner tonight."

"You're very kind to offer, Mrs. Nash, but I have a standing engagement this evening."

Etta Mae's eyes grew large, and she exchanged a nervous glance with her mother.

Rowena looked back at Nate and pasted on a smile. "Would it be unbecoming of me to inquire as to with whom you plan to dine?"

"No, not at all. I've been invited to the Sawyer Ranch to have dinner with my uncle Zach, my aunt McKenzie, and my cousins."

"Oh," said Etta Mae, pressing her lips together in a pout.

"Another time, then," Rowena said.

"Perhaps." Nate smiled. "Have a pleasant day!" He wasn't going to make any promises. If only he could find a polite way to tell Etta Mae that he wasn't interested in her.

Nate continued to greet the congregants and shake hands with them. Out of the corner of his eye, he saw Hailee at the end of the line, her attention focused everywhere but on him. His heart sank, and he was half tempted to run to her and ask what he'd done to upset her. Had he misinterpreted her feelings for him, as he'd suspected earlier?

"What do you think about that, Reverend Adams?"

Nate shook his head and blinked when he realized the Grangers were standing before him. "I'm sorry, Lucille. What were you saying?"

"What was I saying? I'm surprised at you, Reverend! You're usually such an attentive listener."

"Forgive me, Lucille. My mind was elsewhere. Please, tell me what you wanted to say. I'm listening now."

Lucille reached up and fingered her large pink hat. "Oh, Reverend Adams!"

"Yes, Lucille?" Nate felt his patience waning. He wanted to speak with Hailee, but if Lucille continued like this, he feared she might slip out without talking to him.

"Well, I...I just wondered if you thought I could pass for a society woman of Boston, what with this fine ornament of fashion on my head." She beamed up at him, causing every wrinkle on her face to deepen.

"I beg your pardon?"

"Oh, Reverend Adams, if I were thirty years younger and hadn't yet met Fred...." Lucille blushed.

What is she trying to say?

"Doesn't this hat make my face glow?" Lucille touched the brim of her elaborate, oversized hat, while craning her neck to the side, as if that were necessary to balance the heavy headpiece with its ornate beadwork and pair of pink feathers sticking out like off-centered goat horns. "When I ordered this hat from the catalogue, I thought to myself, *Lucille, you have arrived!* Of course, when it arrived, Fred didn't agree with me. He said to me, he said, 'Now, Lucille, a hat like that is just a bunch of hogwash!' Can you believe it, Reverend—Fred saying such a thing? I was horrified. I told him, I said, 'Now, you listen here, Fred Granger. This is a tea hat, and I will not heed such inconsiderate words!" Lucille stopped to catch her breath.

Nate glanced at Lucille's husband, who stood nearby.

"Come on, Lucille," Fred said, rolling his eyes. "Reverend Adams has better things to do than listen to you talk about that ridiculous hat. It's bad enough you bought the thing, but to wear it to church and discuss it with the reverend?"

"I removed it while we were inside," Lucille reminded him. "Now, kindly hush so I can finish telling Reverend Adams my story." Lucille put a finger to her chin. "Now, where was I? Oh, yes. I was telling you about Fred's reaction. Well, pay no mind to Fred's reaction, Reverend. This is the type of hat all the women in the cities are wearing. And to think that I, Lucille Granger, am in possession of such a hat!" She fanned herself with her hand.

"It is...exquisite," Nate managed.

Fred shook his head. "I've had my eye nearly poked out by those darn feathers at least a dozen times. I'm not sure I'd call it 'exquisite.' A pain in the behind, maybe."

"Oh, hush!" Lucille scowled at her husband, then turned to Nate. "You're a refined man with good taste. Surely, you understand the important position of fancy hats in a woman's wardrobe."

"Yes. Uh, Lucille...." Nate eyed the people lined up behind the Grangers. Hailee was still among them.

"I pestered Mr. Victor almost to death asking him every day for a month if my order from the Montgomery Ward Wish Book had arrived. He assured me I would be the second person to know—he'd be the first, of course. So, I waited and waited. Finally, the order arrived. I barely made it back to the mercantile before ripping the box open to try it on. Lo and behold, I do believe this hat has made a new woman out of me!"

Fred muttered something under his breath, and Lucille jabbed him in the ribs. "Now, tell me, Reverend, did you feel like you were back in Boston when you laid eyes on me wearing this hat?"

"It does look like something the women of Boston might wear," Nate acknowledged. He would agree with almost anything Lucille said, as long as it helped move her through the line.

"Very well, then. See, Fred? I told you so."

"Hogwash," muttered Fred.

"Have a pleasant afternoon, Lucille and Fred," Nate said, hoping they would take the hint.

"And you do the same, Reverend," said Lucille.

Once the Grangers had left, Nate greeted several parishioners before Hailee stepped toward the door. "Hello, Hailee."

"Nate." She nodded.

"It's good to see you here today."

"Likewise."

"Hailee—"

"I must be going. I promised Widow Marlen I would have lunch with her today."

"All right." Nate watched Hailee walk out of the church. Regret hit him like a jab in the stomach, and he knew without a doubt that he didn't want to watch Hailee Annigan walk out of his life.

After dinner that night, Nate asked Uncle Zach if he could speak with him in private.

Uncle Zach agreed and suggested they go out to the barn.

"So, what's on your mind?" he asked, leaning back against a stall.

"I need some advice."

Uncle Zach chuckled. "I sure wish Davey or Chloe would say that to me sometime. They seem to think I give too much advice, unasked for."

Nate grinned. He had found more than just an uncle in McKenzie's husband; he'd also found a friend. "I think that's your job as a father."

"I suppose. So, what kind of advice do you need?"

"It has to do with...um...Hailee Annigan."

His uncle nodded. "Go on."

"I'm not sure if you've noticed, but I...we...uh...." Nate shifted his weight from one foot to the other. "I really like her, Uncle Zach. More than like her, really. I...I have feelings for her that I've never felt for any other woman."

"I'll admit that I have noticed the attention you've been paying her." Uncle Zach smiled. "I've also noticed that she cares for you, too."

Nate sighed. "That's what I thought, until last week, when we went on a picnic and it became clear

that Hailee doesn't have the same feelings for me
that I have for her."

"She said that to you?"

"Well, no, not directly. But it seemed obvious,
the way she pulled away after I—" Nate cleared his
throat, feeling embarrassed. "After I kissed her," he
mumbled.

"I take it she didn't identify what was troubling
her?"

"No, she didn't. Yet I can't think of anything I
might have done to upset her. So, it seems to me that
she simply doesn't feel the same way...."

"Hmm. Your situation reminds me of a disagree-
ment McKenzie and I had the other day," Uncle Zach
murmured.

Nate was taken aback. He'd never seen his aunt
and uncle disagree about anything.

"I won't go into details," Uncle Zach went on,
"but she and I had formed enough faulty assumptions to fill a horse corral. We had misread each other's motives, even though we knew better and should
have sat down and talked about the situation. We
don't argue often, but I can tell you that this was one
of the biggest conflicts we've ever had."

"And you resolved it?"

"We did, after some serious discussion. You see,
Nate, even after all of these years of being married,
we still misunderstand and misinterpret each other's
intentions at times."

"So, you think I might be incorrect to assume
that Hailee doesn't feel the same way about me as I
feel about her?"

"I have no way of knowing, Nate, and neither do you." Uncle Zach put his hand on Nate's

shoulder. "The assumptions we make about others' motives are usually wrong because we don't have all the facts. And the only way you'll get the facts is by sitting down with Hailee and talking with her. It's a form of judging when we draw conclusions based on the actions of others but don't know the whole story. I came to that realization during my argument with McKenzie, and it convicted me to apologize and make sure we were honest with each other."

"That makes sense," Nate said. "I never thought about it that way."

Uncle Zach nodded. "I was also convicted by John eight, verse thirty-two."

"'*And ye shall know the truth, and the truth shall make you free.*'"

"Exactly. Only by sitting down and talking to Hailee will you know the reason behind her actions. Tell her that you care about her and desire to bridge this distance between you."

"I tried to talk to her after church this morning, but she rushed off."

"Talk to her in private, Nate. I'm sure she didn't feel like discussing anything on the steps of the church. Ask her if she'd like to join you for a walk after school."

"We used to walk together after school almost every day." Nate sighed. "I've missed our walks."

"Ask God to give you the words to say and to open Hailee's heart to hear them. McKenzie and I will pray for the same things, as well."

"Thank you, Uncle Zach. This helps a lot."

"Of course, Nate. You know I'm here for you."

"I appreciate that."

"And, remember, nothing worthwhile in life comes easy. If you care about Hailee the way you say you do, don't back down and let these words go unspoken. Pray for a solution and then act as God guides you toward it."

When he went home later that evening, Nate thought and prayed long into the night about what his uncle had said. "Lord, please give me the opportunity to speak to Hailee and guide my words. Father, I rely on Your help to resolve this matter according to Your will...."

CHAPTER FOURTEEN

On Thursday afternoon, when the last pupil left the schoolhouse, Nate approached the building and climbed the steps. Twelve days had passed since his picnic with Hailee, since the awkward tension had arisen between them. In that time, Nate had prayed almost hourly for the words to say. He needed to share his heart with Hailee and find out what was on hers—the sooner, the better.

When he knocked on the doorframe of the open door, Hailee glanced up from her desk, a look of surprise on her face. "Hello, Nate," she said as she stood.

"Hello, Hailee. Would you care to go for a walk?"

She looked down at a stack of books on her desk and reached out to straighten them. After another moment of silence, she looked at him again. "I think I'd like that."

Nate sighed with relief. *That's a start*, he thought. He waited for Hailee to go through the doorway, then followed her down the steps and into the sunshine. "The leaves on some of the trees have started turning," Nate observed as she briefly stepped back up to close the door. "Fall will be here before long." He cringed. Could he think of nothing better to talk about than the weather?

Hailee nodded and looped her arm through his. Silence prevailed as they started down the street. After several blocks, Nate gently steered them toward a picturesque grove of trees by the river. "Hailee, I think we should talk. And not about the weather."

Hailee nodded and bit her lip.

Nate took a step closer and looked her in the eye. "I'm sorry I kissed you, Hailee."

Her gaze steady, she replied, without hesitating, "I'm *not* sorry you kissed me, Nate."

"You're not?"

"No."

"But, the way you pulled back...I figured you were angry with me."

"No, Nate. That wasn't it at all." Hailee sighed. "I'm sorry for the way I've been acting. I never meant for things to get so complicated between us."

Nate cleared his throat. He remembered Uncle Zach's words: *"Nothing worthwhile in life comes easy."* There was no better proof of the veracity of that statement than the marriage of Zach and McKenzie, or even Jonah and Kaydie. Both relationships had been far from easy at first, but the Lord had been at work in them all along, and, in the end, they recognized that they were meant to be.

Nate looked at Hailee. Whatever it took, he would fight for the love that had started to blossom between them. Too much of his heart was already invested. "I care about you, Hailee. A lot."

"I care about you, too, Nate."

"I guess...." Nate paused, waiting for the right words to say. "I guess I just assumed that you thought of me as more than just a friend."

A tear trickled down Hailee's cheek. He hadn't meant to make her cry!

"Hailee, please don't cry."

"It's just that I...." She fell silent.

"What is it?"

"It's just that...you don't understand."

"Then, make me understand, Hailee. I want to understand."

She closed her eyes and shook her head.

"Do you have a beau back in Cincinnati?" The way she'd distanced herself since the picnic would make sense if her heart belonged to another.

"Oh, mercy, no!" Hailee's eyes were wide open now. "No, of course not."

"That's good. For me, I mean." Nate felt like a fool. "Please, Hailee. Whatever it is, you can tell me."

Hailee met his eyes. Hers were tinged with pain. But why?

"Please, Hailee."

She stole a peek to her left and right, then looked at him again.

"I alone am listening," Nate assured her, taking her hands in his.

"Nate, I...I've done some things I'm not at all proud of."

Nate stared at her in disbelief. This was about her past? A part of him felt relieved. He'd thought that the problem was her feelings for him—or the lack thereof. "Hailee, we've all done things we aren't proud of."

She shook her head again, fresh tears welling in her eyes. "I haven't been honest and forthright with you. I...I used to steal and lie. I caused trouble and was seldom honest."

"My sweet, beautiful Hailee. Is that what this is all about?" He released her hands and wrapped his arms around the woman who had captured his heart. "Sweet Hailee. We all have done things we shouldn't have done."

"But I...I didn't want y-you...to...." Sobbing now, Hailee collapsed in Nate's arms. He held her strongly, gently.

"You didn't want me to think less of you, is that it?" he whispered.

Hailee nodded.

"Oh, Hailee." He covered her hair with tiny kisses and pulled her even closer to him. "Nothing, and I mean nothing, could change the way I feel about you."

"But you're a man of the cloth, and I've done terrible things. I've deliberately tricked people, and—"

"Do you still deliberately trick people?" Nate kept his voice soft and gentle.

"No," she whispered.

"Do you still lie and steal and cause trouble?"

"No. At least, I try not to, but I did lie to you when I told you nothing was wrong."

Nate closed his eyes. *Father, please guide me and give me the words to say.* He stepped back and held Hailee at arm's length. "Remember what the apostle Paul wrote in Romans? *'For all have sinned, and come short of the glory of God.'*"

Hailee looked down and kicked a stray pebble with her toe. Then, she met his eyes again. "But you are a pastor from a prominent family. Associating with me could tarnish your reputation."

Nate chuckled warmly. "First of all, you could never tarnish my reputation. Second, my family's wealth and status don't matter to me. I am not my parents or my grandparents, and my life is here in Pine Haven; it's no longer in Boston. Third, and most important, do you think I've never sinned, Hailee? Do you think I never operate outside of the Holy Spirit's leading? If so, you couldn't be more wrong. I still make mistakes every day. There are many things I've done in the past that I'm not at all proud of." He paused. "One particular sin haunted me for years, and, while I know God has forgiven me for it, I'm still working toward forgiving myself, by God's grace. Would you like me to tell you about it?"

Hailee nodded and listened as he told her a story from his past. Nate's voice shook as he recalled the day he wished he could forget....

Nate climbed into his buggy with his three closest friends, Hank, Orin, and Carl. "Where should we go?" Hank asked.

"Wherever it is, let's do something adventurous," Orin suggested.

"Want to go swimming down at White Springs Pond?" Carl asked.

"Nah. We always do that," said Orin. "And it isn't adventurous."

"Let's drive around for a while till we think of something," Hank suggested.

Nate nodded. He needed to release some tension, having just completed a major exam at school. He started the horses with a click of his tongue.

The four drove around for a while and talked, mostly about their classes. "Mr. Flynn's tests are far too difficult," Carl stated.

Hank sneered. "That's because you never study."

"I do, too," Carl insisted.

"Well, you could learn a thing or two from Nate," Hank went on. "He always scores the highest on all the tests."

"My father already has my future all planned out," Nate groused, "and it isn't at all what I want to do. If I were really smart, I'd fail out of my classes so that law school would not be an option."

"Let's head out toward the country," suggested Orin. "There's bound to be something fun to do there. It's too boring here in the city."

Nate steered the buggy toward the outskirts of town. It had been some time since he'd left the city. Maybe a change of scenery would do them all some good.

"Hey, check it out!" Hank pointed off to the right.

Nate followed Hank's finger and spotted a spindly man wearing a tattered hat. He stood behind a wagon and appeared to be lifting a crate into it. "It looks as if he's having some trouble." Nate pulled his buggy to a stop on the side of the road. "Can we help you, sir?" he called out.

"We didn't set out to be Good Samaritans," Orin grumbled.

Nate shrugged and climbed down from the buggy. What was the harm in helping someone? Like him, his friends didn't really know how it felt to be in need, and they probably didn't know how it felt to help someone in need.

"Yes, uh, please, help me!" the man grunted.

Right away, Nate noticed his accent, which, along with his fair complexion and blond hair, indicated he was probably Scandinavian.

"Let's do something adventurous instead," Orin whispered, coming up behind Nate.

"Like what?" asked Hank, joining them.

"Like, not help him?" Carl said.

Nate turned to his friends. "Why can't we just help him? We'll be on our way soon enough."

"Why can't we just help him?" Orin mimicked him in singsong. "Give us a break, Nate. You're always interrupting our fun by helping people. I reckon if we continue hanging around you, we'll never have any adventures at all."

"What do you have in mind, Orin?" Hank asked, the excitement rising in his voice.

"You, there!" the man shouted. "Can you help me lift this?"

Nate watched as the man attempted to lift a heavy crate and place it back into the wagon, from which it had evidently fallen. He took a step forward.

Orin caught Nate by the shoulder. "Not so fast, Good Samaritan," he said. "Let's do something different for a change."

Nate rolled his eyes. Orin spoke as if he himself was in the business of helping others and had suddenly decided he didn't feel like it. Yet in the two years he'd known Orin, Nate couldn't recall a time when he had helped anyone but himself.

"I mean it, Nate," Orin jeered. "Get back here."

Nate rolled his eyes and stepped into the huddle his friends had formed.

Always the instigator, Orin laid out his plan with precision. "Nate, you and Carl will take the buggy. I'll drive this man's wagon. Hank, you'll ride with me."

"What?" Nate had no idea where this was going.

"You heard me," said Orin. "Here's your chance to prove to me that we should keep spending time with you."

Nate gulped. These three were his closest friends, and he would be hard-pressed to replace them, since he was extremely shy and didn't make friends easily. Orin, Hank, and Carl were from Worchester, each of them from a wealthy family. Orin's father was a physician, Hank's was a politician, and Carl's was the president of the prestigious First Bank of Worcester.

"Why are we taking the man's wagon?" Carl asked.

"Because, you ninny, it'll be fun to see his face," Orin replied. "Besides, have any of you ever driven a wagon before?"

"No," the other three chorused.

"Wagons are for poor folk," Hank added.

"That's right," said Orin. "I've never driven a wagon. Now is my chance. We'll drive it as fast as those horses can go—that is, if Nate isn't going to be a coward."

Nate sighed. He hated making decisions, mostly because, for the sixteen years of his life, all of his decisions had been made for him. It seemed that the same thing would happen now, since everybody else agreed with Orin's plan. "What will you do with the wagon after you've gone for a ride?" Nate asked.

"Who cares?" said Carl. "The point is to have some fun."

"You think too much," Orin told him. "Now, is everyone ready?"

Hank and Carl nodded eagerly.

"What about you, Good Samaritan?"

"I'm ready," Nate replied, trying to mask the hesitation in his voice.

Orin glanced over at the man and chuckled. "From the looks of that guy, we don't need to worry about him defending himself."

Nate stared at Orin. At six feet four inches, and weighing probably 260 pounds, he was big for his age. Nate had no doubt he could overpower the man on his own, without the assistance of his three friends.

"Let's go," said Hank. "I'm ready for some adventure."

"Hey, you don't reckon we could race, do you?" Carl asked. "That would be much more adventurous than simply stealing the wagon."

"That's exactly what I was thinking," said Orin. "We'll race—you and Nate in the buggy, me and Hank in the wagon. Let's say that the losers have to treat the winners to ice cream."

"Agreed," Hank and Carl said.

"Vill you please help me?" the man asked. Nate saw that he had set down the crate and was approaching them.

"Sure," said Orin. "You need help lifting that crate into your wagon? Come on, Hank." The two of them jogged past the man toward the wagon and hoisted the crate onto the wagon bed.

"Thank you!" the man exclaimed. "I can't tell you how grateful I am."

"We like helping people, don't we?" Orin said, nudging Hank in the side.

"Yeah, we do," Hank agreed.

"Vell then, I must be on my vay," said the man.

"There's just one problem," said Orin. "We need your wagon."

"My vagon?"

"Yes, your 'vagon,'" Orin said, mocking his accent.

"But, vhy?"

"Come on, everyone. Let's have us an adventure!" Orin shouted.

Before the man could react, Carl climbed into Nate's buggy, while Orin scrambled into the wagon. "Come on, Nate!" Carl yelled.

Nate hesitated, then jumped up beside him.

"Ready? Set? Go!" Orin shouted.

"Vait! Please, vait! You can't take my vagon!" the man shouted after them.

"I don't want to do this," said Nate.

"Too late, Good Samaritan!" yelled Orin. "Let's see who's the faster driver!"

"You see, Hailee, we all have at least one thing we fear is unpardonable."

Hailee blinked at him. "Did you ever see the man again?"

"Yes, a year later," said Nate. He remembered the day as if it were yesterday....

Nate followed Vance out of church after the service. It had been only a couple of weeks since Nate had accepted Jesus Christ as his Lord and Savior, and already God was working on his heart in noticeable ways. "Vance, there's something I have to do," Nate told his friend.

"Are you all right?"

"I will be. There's just something I need to make right."

"My mother's dinner invitation still stands, if you're able to come."

"I'll be there."

"Good. I'll see you then." Vance turned and headed up the street.

Nate stood still for a moment, then lifted his face toward heaven. "Lord, will You please give me the courage to do what You're calling me to do?" he prayed. "Please soften the heart of the man I must visit." With that, Nate started down the street in the opposite direction. He should have done this a long time ago, but it had taken a nudge from God to prompt him to action.

Nate had managed to find out the name of the man whose wagon he and his friends had stolen. He was a Swedish immigrant by the name of Hans Anfinson, and he lived with his family four miles outside of town. "Lord, let him be at home," Nate prayed as he climbed into the buggy he had borrowed from his parents and urged the horse toward the Anfinsons' farm. If Mr. Anfinson was not at home, Nate would just have to wait until he returned. This was something he needed to do as soon as possible. The Holy Spirit had convicted him about the wrong he had done, and he was determined to make it right.

When Nate reached the Anfinsons', he gulped at the tiny, makeshift home. He'd known that the family was not well-to-do, but he hadn't realized how impoverished they were. Their dwelling had half a roof, tall weeds had overtaken what had once been a garden, and hole-ridden garments hung from a thinning rope strung between two trees. A thin, sickly-looking cow stood in a corral on one side of the house. "Lord, if only I had known…please, Father, forgive me." In his heart, Nate knew that his heavenly Father had heard his confession and had forgiven him. Yet it was impossible for him to feel at peace, faced with what lay before him.

Clutching a thin brown envelope, Nate started toward the front door. "Whatcha doin' mister?" a little voice asked.

Nate turned and saw a skinny boy who looked about six years old standing in the yard. He had the same blond hair as the man Nate sought, so he figured he must be his son. "I've come to see your pa," he replied.

"Pa's not well," said the boy.

"Has he taken ill?"

"He fell off the roof while he was tryin' to fix it and broke his leg. He hasn't felt good since."

Nate shook his head. If he were handier at fixing things, he'd return the next day and make the roof as good as new. But he wasn't handy. He'd never learned how to work with his hands, and anytime something had broken, someone else had fixed it for him. The exception was this situation, which Nate needed to mend himself.

Just then, Nate remembered a man from church named Chet who had refurbished some of the pews. Perhaps Nate could hire him to fix this man's roof.

"Didja want to see Pa?" the boy asked.

"Yes, I do."

"You can follow me, then." The boy turned and walked toward the house. "Ma?" he called as he opened the door. "There's somebody here to see Pa."

Mrs. Anfinson came to the door, a baby perched on her hip. "Vat is it that you vant?" she asked, furrowing her brow. "Ve don't need vhatever it is that you sell."

"I'm not here to sell you anything, Mrs. Anfinson. My name is Nate Adams, and I was wondering if I might speak with your husband."

"Vhat business do you have vith him?"

"It's...uh, confidential."

"Confidential?"

"Private," Nate clarified. "I need to talk to him about something in private."

"My husband is not vell."

"Your son told me, and I'm sorry."

"Are you sure you are not trying to sell us something?" Mrs. Anfinson narrowed her eyes at Nate.

"You have my word," Nate assured her. He looked at the baby she held, who stared at him with a curious expression.

"I think you should come back another day," Mrs. Anfinson said, adjusting the baby on her hip.

"Ma'am, please, I need to speak with your husband. It will take only a minute."

"He is not vell."

"I know that." Nate prayed for patience. "But what I have to say to him might help him feel a little better."

"Are you a doctor?" Mrs. Anfinson asked.

"No."

"Then, who are you?"

"I am a student."

"Vhat vould a student vant vith my husband?"

"Just to speak with him."

Poor Mrs. Anfinson still looked concerned. She had large circles under her blue eyes, and Nate figured her to be about thirty, though she probably felt much older, judging by her apparent fatigue. Her dress was faded, and there was a small hole in one shoulder, which was causing the material to unravel there.

Two little girls appeared in the doorway. They looked like they were twins. "We're hungry, Mama," one said.

Nate stared at the girls. They couldn't be any older than four. *Lord, please, show me how to help this family,* he prayed silently.

"All vight, you can come in, but for a short time only." Mrs. Anfinson ushered Nate inside. "I'll go see if he is awake." She plodded down the hallway and peeked inside a doorway. "Hans? Are you avake?" she asked gently.

"I am," was the feeble-sounding reply.

"There is someone here to see you."

"Send them avay. I'm not expecting company."

"He said he needs only a minute to speak vith you, and he is not a salesman."

"All right," sighed Hans.

Mrs. Anfinson came back and motioned for Nate to go down the hall. "I time you," she told him. "You have five minutes. That is all."

Nate nodded, wondering how Mrs. Anfinson would time him. She no more had a watch than she had a bolt of fabric to sew a new dress.

When Nate stepped into the room, Hans narrowed his eyes at him. "Vhat is it you vant?"

"I need just a moment of your time, Mr. Anfinson."

"Who are you?"

"My name is Nate Adams. You can call me Nate."

"All right, then. You can call me Hans."

Nate studied the man whom he'd wronged so terribly. His face was worn and weary-looking, and his body was frailer than Nate had remembered. He lay on the bed in obvious pain.

"Please, sit down." Hans pointed to the lone chair at the nearby table.

Nate scooted the chair closer to the bed.

"Vhy is it you look familiar to me?" Hans asked.

Nate shuddered. "What I am about to say will likely disturb you at first, Hans. But, please, let me say my piece."

"Vhy vould it disturb me?"

"Well, it's because I'm one of the boys who stole your wagon several years ago."

"Get out!" Hans shouted. "Get out now!"

"Hans, please, listen to me."

"No. It is your fault my son almost died!"

Nate could feel his legs shake. "Hans, I came here today to apologize—"

"I don't care about your apologies!"

"What we did was wrong. I realize that now. In fact, I knew it then, but I was too afraid of losing some of the only friends I had if I refused to participate in their scheme. I've changed since that day. I've become a Christian."

Hans had quieted. "Go on."

"It was wrong of us to steal from you, and the Lord laid it on my heart to seek you out and ask for forgiveness. I should have helped you that day, not made your life more difficult."

"I valked all the vay home that day, without the medicine I had purchased for my son. No one vould help me find my vagon and horses. Finally, my horses came back to me, but no vagon; I never saw it again. My son needed that medicine and almost died. If our neighbor had not gone to town...."

"I am so sorry, Hans. I didn't know."

"Vhat do you mean? So, you think it is all right to steal from a man if his son vasn't sick?"

"No, that's not it at all. I just…." Nate paused. "I can't change the past, Hans. I can change only what I do with it."

"I had food in that crate, too. Ve do not have much food, but I had saved up to buy some flour and sugar. It vas all gone vhen you stole my vagon."

"Again, sir, I am terribly sorry."

"You should be sorry," Hans muttered. "I cannot feed my family in good times, let alone vhen my vagon is stolen. You should be ashamed."

"I am. I have come to give you this." Nate handed Hans the thin brown envelope. "Please take it."

"I don't vant your charity."

"It's not charity," Nate insisted. "It's payment."

"Payment? For vhat? I not do vork for you."

"It's payment for the wagon we took."

Hans opened the envelope and peered inside. "Did you steal this money, too?"

"No, sir. I worked to earn some of it, and the rest is from my allowance. I'm also going to have a man come to fix your roof. His name is Chet, and he attends my church."

"Vhy you do this?"

"Because I need to right a wrong."

Tears had formed in the corners of Hans's eyes, and he fingered the money. "This is enough to feed my family for the vinter."

"Yes, Hans, it is. And enough to have a doctor come to look at your leg."

Hans nodded, tears streaming down his face. "Thank you."

"You're welcome," said Nate. "I'd better be going now. Your wife told me I had only five minutes to speak with you. I suppose that time is up by now."

Hans leaned forward and placed a hand on Nate's arm. "I forgive you."

Nate blinked back his own tears and nodded before walking toward the door, filled with gratitude to God....

"So, Hailee, I've also done things I'm not at all proud of. Sure, I gave Hans some money for his troubles, but I never could have given back what was truly stolen from him. In a sense, we robbed him of hope and of faith in mankind. But I've changed, and I don't worry about being judged for my past misdeeds, by men or by God. And you shouldn't, either. I didn't know you back when you did the things you're ashamed of. But that doesn't matter. The woman I know—the woman I adore—is the one standing before me now."

Hailee blushed. "I...I care about you, too, Nate. And I enjoy spending time with you."

"And I with you."

"I wish things could be the way they were between us."

"I do, too."

Hailee giggled. "It seems we agree on at least several counts."

"I suppose we do." Nate stepped forward and took her face in his hands. "Will you forgive me for jumping to conclusions? Can we put all of this behind us?"

"Yes, of course. I'm sorry, too."

Nate smiled and dropped his hands to her upper arms. "I suppose it would be too forward of me to ask the prettiest girl in town if I could have another chance at kissing her."

"Why, Reverend Adams!" Hailee said with mock indignation. Then, she winked and whispered, "I suppose I could grant that request."

Nate laughed as he pulled her closer. He kissed her on the forehead before allowing his lips to travel down her face and greet her mouth. With gentleness, passion, and love all combined into one, Nate kissed her.

Thankfully, Hailee didn't pull away. If anything, she seemed more passionate than he, as if she wished the moment would never end. He knew he did.

CHAPTER FIFTEEN

How was your day?" Nate asked Hailee when he greeted her at school the following afternoon.

"It went well," she said, locking the door behind her. "Tommy and Clint got into trouble only twice!"

Nate laughed. "They're making progress, I suppose." He held out his arm. "I'd like to take you for a drive today, if that would be all right."

Pleasantly surprised by his proposal, Hailee nodded eagerly. "Friday afternoons are the perfect time for leisurely drives."

At the end of the walkway, Nate assisted her into his buggy, then climbed in beside her and prompted the horses forward. "I have something I've been meaning to ask you."

She felt her heart rate double. "Yes?"

"I was wondering if I might have the pleasure of courting you, Hailee."

She drew in a breath quickly and held it. Even though she'd been hoping for this, expecting it, she hadn't been prepared for his question at that moment. "I—I don't know what to say."

"You could make me a happy man and say yes."

"Yes! Yes, of course."

"Good. For a second there, I was a bit concerned."

"I'm sorry, Nate. I was simply surprised." She'd also thought she might have been dreaming. She gave her arms a little shake, just to be sure.

"Are you all right?" Nate asked.

Hailee giggled. "I just wanted to make sure I wasn't dreaming."

Nate threw back his head in a round of hearty laughter. "No one else makes me laugh like you."

She shrugged. "Some things just seem too good to be true!" Yet she could feel a blush creeping into her cheeks. She'd never been courted before. At The Sanctuary of Promise, courting had been forbidden, and she'd been too young, anyway. And when she'd started teaching there, her work had kept her busy, leaving her no time for matters of the heart. She'd regretted it then, but now she was thankful. She wouldn't have wanted to miss out on Nate.

"I suppose we haven't known each other for very long, but there's something about you, Hailee, that makes me feel as though I've known you for years. You're...different, somehow."

"Different?" She sent him a teasing smile.

"I meant that in a good way," Nate added, his eyes twinkling. "You must know that I've grown quite fond of you."

Hailee giggled. "And I of you, Reverend."

"Just think. Today, we are celebrating our first day of courtship. I knew the minute I woke up this morning that today was going to be an exceptionally good day."

Hailee reached over and placed her hand gently on Nate's arm. She was consumed with feelings of excitement and anticipation for what the future held. For the first time, she understood what her dear friend and mentor Ella Fanshaw had meant when she'd discussed matters of the heart and her relationship with Officer Ulmer. Ella had said she was so filled with nervous excitement that she thought her stomach would never be settled. Yes, for the first time, Hailee knew just what Ella had meant.

After taking Hailee back to Widow Marlen's, Nate stopped at the post office, thankful he'd arrived before closing time. Mr. Victor handed him a single piece of mail, and Nate had no need for the return address to know who had sent it. The ornately decorated envelope could have come from none other than his mother.

Standing outside the post office, Nate tore open the envelope, unfolded the expensive stationery, and let his eyes traverse the page of familiar script.

Dearest Nate,

We hope this letter finds you well. Your father and I are in good health. I am pleased to announce that your father just prevailed in Stanley v. Melton. He so wished you could have been here to see him argue the case. He has reserved Mr. Jones's old office for you for when you return to practice law. I trust that you will not disappoint him.

I also wanted to let you know that your father and I are planning to visit Pine Haven. We have long been curious about this place

*where my sisters live and finally decided
to find out what all the fuss was about. We
are scheduled to arrive on September 20.*

*Please greet Aunt McKenzie and Aunt
Kaydence for us.*

With love,
Mother

Nate refolded the letter and slid it back inside the
envelope. Just then, his heart stopped. *September 20
is tomorrow!* How could it be that his parents would
arrive in Pine Haven the following day?

His thoughts were interrupted by a commotion.
He looked up and saw a crowd gathering in front
of Granger Mercantile. Stuffing the letter into his
pocket, Nate crossed the street and approached the
group. He could see Sheriff Clyde Kinion standing on
the boardwalk at the front, and it looked as if he was
about to address them.

"Fellow citizens of Pine Haven," he began, then
paused. When everyone had quieted down, he continued. "Thank you for taking a moment out of your
day to listen to the very important news I am about
to share." Sheriff Clyde cleared his throat. "Just minutes ago, I received a telegram from Sheriff Harmon
in Wilmerville, where two convicted felons by the
names of Eustace Hayes and Rolf Northrop have escaped from jail."

A swell of gasps and murmurs arose from the
crowd.

"Please, allow me to finish," Sheriff Clyde spoke
above the din. When it was again quiet, he continued. "I don't want to cause anyone undue alarm. At
this time, there is no reason to assume that Hayes

and Northrop are anywhere near Pine Haven. I tell you this only as a precaution. Sometimes, we here in Pine Haven get a little complacent because there isn't a whole lot happening by way of criminal activity in our town. That being said, I do need to let you know that these two men are armed and dangerous. If you come into contact with them, do not try to apprehend them."

"Sheriff Clyde?" It was Uncle Jonah who spoke.

"Yes, Mr. Dickenson?"

"Are you able to tell us the crimes they committed that landed them in prison?"

"That I do know." Sheriff Clyde paused, looking hesitant.

"Well?" Jonah and several others demanded.

The sheriff pursed his lips. Then, he said quietly, "They are wanted for murder."

This time, a frenzy of gasps and shrieks arose from the crowd, and Sheriff Clyde raised his hand, trying to quiet them. "Again, I tell you there is no reason—no reason at all—to believe that Eustace Hayes and Rolf Northrop would be heading this way. There is nothing for them in Pine Haven." Sheriff Clyde scanned the crowd. "Reverend Nate, would you mind leading us in prayer?"

"I would be honored, Sheriff." Nate smiled at those who turned around to face him. "Would you all join me in prayer?" Nate folded his hands and bowed his head. "Lord, we ask for Your protection over the citizens of Pine Haven. Please give the authorities wisdom and guidance as they seek to locate these dangerous men. Thank You for blessing us and keeping us safe. In Jesus' name, amen."

After that, the crowd dispersed, but the chatter continued. Nate made his way toward the church, where he planned to continue writing his sermon for the service on Sunday. After that, he would stop at Widow Marlen's and tell Hailee about the news Sheriff Clyde had shared, as well as to let her know that his parents were coming tomorrow. A mixture of excitement and apprehension crowded his mind as he wondered how his parents would react to meeting her. He could only pray that they would treat her with kindness and respect.

On Saturday morning, Hailee finished braiding her long blonde hair and took one final look at her appearance in the mirror on the wall. Her nerves were a jumble, both from the disturbing information Nate had relayed yesterday about two murderers on the loose and from the thought of meeting Nate's parents for the first time. They were due to arrive on the morning train, and he'd invited her to join them for a picnic this afternoon.

"Lord, please calm my mind and settle my thoughts," Hailee prayed as she finished getting ready. "To know that two men have escaped from a nearby jail is disturbing enough, and I ask that You would enable them to be recaptured and that You would keep the citizens of Pine Haven safe in the meantime." She took a deep breath. "And, Lord, You know how nervous I am to meet Nate's parents. I worry they won't approve of me, since I come from a family of neither reputation nor wealth. Please bless our time together today. It's in Your name that I pray, amen."

She smiled at her reflection, feeling a new sense of confidence. Surely, Mr. and Mrs. Adams would approve of the woman their son was courting. A thrill rushed through her at the very word, *courting.* Just when she'd feared she would not have a future with the man she loved, the Lord had turned things around, and now he was her beau. How unbelievably blessed she was!

Nate went to the train station to meet his parents. When they stepped off the train, they looked exactly as he'd remembered them. His mother, Peyton, had her long, dark hair tied up in a fancy coiffure and wore a fashionable gown of turquoise satin with leg-of-mutton sleeves; his father, Maxwell, sported a fine tailored suit on his thin frame. "Mother and Father!" Nate called, rushing over to greet them. "Welcome to Pine Haven." He took his mother's hands in his.

She smiled, almost warmly. "Thank you, Nate. It's wonderful to see you." Her smile turned into a disapproving frown. "This village, however...."

"How was your trip?" Nate preferred not to hear how primitive she found Pine Haven to be.

"Oh, rather long and tedious, I'm afraid. As we traveled further west, I continued to ask myself, *Where are all the buildings? The homes? The people?* All we saw was mile after mile of fields and trees. A more dismal sight I've never seen! We passed the occasional cluster of cattle and several herds of deer and wild horses...so very uncivilized." She glanced around, shaking her head. "And have you ever seen such drab little homes?"

"Now that we're here, I still wonder what all the excitement is about," Nate's father put in.

Nate sighed. "Pine Haven is vastly different from Boston, I know. But, please, don't judge it until you've gotten to know some of the people. They're all fine citizens, I assure you."

His mother scrunched up her nose. "So far, I've seen no one who matches that description. Well, except for you, of course."

His father chuckled drily. "I'm afraid we may be looking for some time."

Nate ignored their comments. "My buggy is right over there," he said, pointing. "I thought you might like to stay with me."

"With you?" Mother raised her eyebrows.

"Yes. My home is just down the street, on the edge of town."

Nate and his parents walked to the buggy, trailed by the steward who hauled their luggage.

"I'm glad you decided to come for a visit," Nate said as they set off toward his house. "Aunt McKenzie and Aunt Kaydie will be thrilled to see you."

"They should be. It's been years since they moved all the way out here."

"The folks here don't seem to mind looking dowdy," Father remarked. He pulled out his gold pocket watch and glanced at it.

"The pace of life here is much more relaxed than in Boston," Nate explained. "People here are working folks. Most of them are ranchers. Over to your right is my church."

"Your church?" His father furrowed his brow.

Nate chuckled. "The church where I am the reverend," he clarified.

"Your congregation must be small," his mother mused.

"It is, but it's been growing over the past couple of months." Nate gestured to the other side of the road.

"Over there is the schoolhouse. This afternoon, I'll introduce you to the new schoolteacher, Miss Hailee Annigan. She also happens to be my sweetheart."

"I beg your pardon?" his mother screeched. "Am I to understand that you are courting this person?"

"Yes, Mother. I know you'll like her. She's beautiful, intelligent, and kind."

"Well, I suppose those qualities are important," she conceded. "Still, what about our plans for you in Boston? Does this Hailee Annigan plan to follow you back to Massachusetts once you come to your senses?"

"Mother, please don't start with your plans for my future. I would like us to have a pleasant afternoon." *Lord, please help me to control my tongue when I'm tempted to lash out at my mother*, he prayed silently. *Grant me wisdom, gentleness, and self-control.*

"Here we are. This is my home." Nate stopped the horses in front of the two-story whitewashed building. He thought his parents would appreciate the railed porch, which reminded him vaguely of the fine porch that wrapped around the front of their home in Boston. The large cottonwood tree in the front yard and the flowers surrounding it looked nice, too, he thought.

"This?"

"Yes, Father. I purchased it shortly after moving here. It's close to the church, which is nice, as I enjoy walking to work every day. It has been a blessing to me—one of countless blessings the Lord has bestowed on me since my arrival in Pine Haven."

His father appeared mildly interested, so Nate continued. "There are twelve acres out back, two of which are fenced in. There's the corral where I keep the horses," he said, pointing, "and, to the right, the barn and garden. It's a small ranch, which is fine with me, since my duties at the church don't leave me a lot of time to work outside. Still, it's better than any ranch I could have imagined, and Uncle Zach and Uncle Jonah have been teaching me how to maintain it."

"I really have heard enough for now," Mother said, rubbing her temples. "Your father and I need to go inside and rest for a bit. It's been a long trip."

"Of course," Nate said. "You can rest for a few hours, and then, whenever you're ready, I'd like to take you on a picnic lunch."

After getting his parents settled in the extra bedroom, Nate went to the kitchen to prepare their lunch, praying all the while. *Lord, thank You for bringing my parents here safely. I ask that You would make our visit enjoyable and soften my parents' hearts toward Hailee when they meet her this afternoon. Finally, Lord, I pray that someday, somehow, You would soften the hearts of my parents toward You and draw them to Yourself, no matter what it takes.*

CHAPTER SIXTEEN

"Hailee, dear?" Widow Marlen called up from downstairs. "Reverend Adams is here!"

Hailee's stomach flipped. "Thank you," she replied. "I'll be right down."

With a final glimpse at her reflection, Hailee turned and left her room. As she descended the stairs, she prayed once more for composure as she met Nate's parents.

"Hello, Hailee." Nate greeted her at the bottom of the stairs. "You look lovely." He kissed her hand.

"Thank you, Nate. I feel far from calm, though. In fact, I can't remember the last time I felt this nervous!"

"It'll be all right," he assured her as they left the house.

Hailee nodded but felt a swirl of anxiety in her stomach at the sight of the nicely dressed couple seated in the buggy.

"Mother and Father, I'd like you to meet Hailee Annigan," Nate said when they reached the buggy. "Hailee, this is my mother, Peyton Worthington Adams, and my father, Maxwell Adams."

Hailee smiled weakly at each of them. "Nice to meet you both."

"Likewise," said Maxwell, tipping his hat.

"Yes, nice to make your acquaintance," said Peyton.

Nate helped Hailee into the buggy and then climbed up beside her. He turned around to face his parents. "We'll take you to a beautiful spot by the river where we can picnic," he told them.

"That sounds delightful," Peyton said.

They rode along in silence, and Hailee was thankful. She was much too nervous for conversation, and Nate didn't seem inclined to talk, either. She closed her eyes and prayed, instead.

Several minutes later, Nate stopped the buggy beneath a grove of trees and climbed down. After helping Hailee from the buggy, he reached for the large picnic basket and the quilt and led his parents to a prime location next to the soothing rush of the river.

"Would you care for some lunch?" he asked.

"That would be fine, son," said Maxwell.

Hailee spread out the quilt Nate had brought and then helped him unload the picnic basket. When all four of them were seated, Nate cleared his throat. "Let's ask the Lord to bless this meal."

His parents exchanged a nervous glance, then closed their eyes and bowed their heads. Hailee did the same as Nate prayed, "Heavenly Father, we thank You for bringing Mother and Father here to Pine Haven. What a blessing it is to spend time with them. Please bless this food You have provided and watch over us for the duration of our visit. In Jesus' name, amen."

Maxwell and Peyton cleared their throats, looking uncomfortable. Hailee supposed they weren't accustomed to hearing their son pray.

After Nate had distributed their sandwiches, they ate without speaking for a few minutes, until Peyton broke the silence.

"So, Hailee, are you from Pine Haven?"

"No, I'm from Ohio," said Hailee.

"I see. And what do your parents think of your living in Pine Haven?"

"My parents passed away some years ago."

"I'm sorry to hear that." Peyton paused for a moment, then looked at her son. "Nate, do you remember Felicity Wynton?"

Nate gave her a smile that Hailee knew was artificial. "Yes, of course."

Peyton sighed wistfully. "It was always assumed that Nate and Felicity would marry someday," she told Hailee. "The Wyntons are one of Boston's finest families, and Felicity is as lovely as they come." Peyton paused and looked back at Nate. "I ran into Felicity shortly before we left for Montana, and she asked about you. It seems she hasn't forgotten you, either."

Nate closed his eyes, and Hailee thought he might be praying. How would he respond to his mother's less-than-subtle prodding?

"I'm not sure if Nate told you, Hailee," Peyton went on, "but we have high hopes for our son. He's our only child, as you probably know. His father is a partner in my father's prestigious law firm, and it has been long understood that Nate would someday follow in his father's footsteps and become a lawyer, too."

"But God had other plans for me," Nate said, firmly yet gently.

Peyton scoffed. "Fine. As soon as you're finished with this reverend business, you can come back to Boston and attend law school. I'm sure Felicity will wait."

"Mother, I'm not returning to Boston to become a lawyer, nor do I plan to marry Felicity." Hailee admired his calm reaction to his mother's outrageous suggestions.

"Well! That is a disappointment."

"Mother, I am happy here in Pine Haven," Nate replied, his voice ever steady and gentle. "This is my home. Hailee is the woman I love, and I will not return to Boston, except for the occasional visit. Please know that I do this not in deliberate defiance of your wishes but out of obedience to God."

Peyton smiled dismissively. "Well, let's talk about something more pleasant, shall we?"

Hailee couldn't believe her ears, but not because of anything Peyton had said. Had Nate really just declared that he loved her?

"We should probably head back to town," Maxwell said, glancing at his pocket watch.

"Surely, you can stay a bit longer," Nate said. "I thought you might like to take a stroll along the river."

"Oh, I fear your father is right," Peyton insisted. "We're still rather weary from traveling, and it would be prudent for us to rest before tonight's dinner at McKenzie's ranch."

"You are welcome to take the buggy back to my house, then. Hailee and I can walk back later."

"That sounds fine, if you're sure," Maxwell said.

"Of course." Nate turned to Hailee. "Is that all right with you?"

Did he really have to ask? "Yes, of course." Hailee wasn't ready for their afternoon together to end.

"We'll see you a little later, then," Peyton said. "Thank you for lunch."

"You're welcome. See you soon."

As Nate's parents climbed into the buggy, he shook his head. "I'm sorry, Hailee. Sometimes, my mother speaks without really thinking about how her words will affect others."

"It's all right, Nate. I understand that she had plans for you."

Nate sighed. "I keep praying she will understand that it's more important for me to follow God's plans for my life than to uphold the family name by pursuing wealth and prestige above all else."

"She'll understand in time, I'm sure of it."

"I hope so. I keep praying, too, that she and Father will come to faith in Christ, no matter what it takes."

Hailee nodded. She knew what it was like to pray for something continually. Recently, the Lord had answered one of her longstanding prayers—her brother Philip had found her and written to her. Yet she kept praying for the same thing to happen with Reuben.

"Hailee?"

"Yes?"

"I meant what I said when I told my parents I love you."

Hailee swallowed hard. "Nate...."

He silenced her by touching an index finger gently to her lips. "I do love you, Hailee. I know it seems early, but it's true. I thank the Lord every hour that He brought us both to Pine Haven so that our paths would cross."

"Nate?"

"Yes?"

She smiled. "I love you, too."

Nate lifted Hailee's chin and leaned in close, kissing her with unprecedented passion. And she kissed him back with all of the love that was brimming in her heart.

"Wasn't that an odd way to start off the visit?" Peyton asked her husband as they traveled toward town in Nate's buggy.

"I think our son has made his decision clear."

"Are you taking his side, Maxwell?"

"No, Peyton, of course not. You know full well that you and I are on the same page when it comes to the desired future for Nathaniel Junior."

"I only want what's best for him."

"As do I," said Maxwell. He squinted at the road ahead. "How odd. There are two men standing in the middle of the street." He slowed the horses as they approached.

"In this uncivilized area, nothing surprises me anymore," Peyton muttered.

"We'll simply go around them," Maxwell said, steering the buggy toward the middle of the road.

Yet the men moved, too, so that they still blocked their path.

Peyton groaned. "What do they want with us?"

"May I help you?" Maxwell asked as he slowed the horses to a complete stop.

"We need you both to get out," the taller man snarled.

"I'm not sure I understand," said Maxwell.

Peyton gasped as the other man reached up and yanked her husband out of the buggy, throwing him onto the road. "Maxwell!" she screamed.

"When we say we want you to get out, we mean it," the man sneered at Maxwell.

"That goes for you, too, fancy lady," the other man barked at Peyton.

She scrambled down as quickly as she could and rushed to Maxwell, who had managed to get back on his feet.

Clinging to him, Peyton looked back at the buggy and saw the shorter man unhitching the horses. "A buggy will slow us down," he muttered to the taller man. "We just need the horses."

Peyton trembled.

"What is it you want?" Maxwell demanded, holding her close.

"I'll tell you what we want," the taller man said. He swaggered over to them and leaned forward. Peyton held her breath when the stench of his breath hit her nostrils. His teeth were rotten yellow, and his flaxen hair clung to his head in greasy clumps. "Give me your wallet."

"My wallet?" asked Maxwell. "In all my years, I've never had anyone make such a request of me. It must be true, what people say about the West—it is untamed, and thievery is rife, with outlaws committing crimes without a second thought."

"Blah, blah, blah. Save your words." The taller man scowled. "Give me your wallet, old man! Or would you rather have a taste of some lead?" He pulled a gun from his holster and waved it in Maxwell's face.

Peyton burst into tears and watched as her husband, with trembling fingers, reached under his jacket and unstrapped the belt from around his waist. Then, slowly, he removed his brown leather wallet and handed it over.

The man handed the wallet to his partner, who opened it and pulled out a number of bills.

"W-why are you doing this?" Peyton sobbed.

"Shut up," ordered the man with the gun. He turned to Maxwell. "Now, give me your watch."

"My watch?"

"Do you have a hearing problem?" the man asked. He leaned even closer to Maxwell and shouted, "Give me your watch!"

Peyton winced again at the stench of his breath and the sight of spittle spewing from his mouth.

Maxwell looked at Peyton, then handed the man his pocket watch. "It...belonged to my father," he murmured.

"I don't care if it belonged to your second cousin's uncle's brother," the man sneered. He fingered the timepiece with his dirty, calloused fingers. "This oughta bring a good price."

Peyton cleared her throat. "Who are you, and why are you doing this?" she demanded with as much indignation as she could muster. Never in her life had she encountered such ruthlessness. She regretted coming to Pine Haven in the first place. The sooner they removed Nate from this lawless environment, the better.

"You don't get it, do you, fancy lady?" the short-er man said. "You're being robbed. And if you really knew that, you wouldn't keep talking." He leaned closer and brushed her cheek with his finger. "Unless, of course, you're thinking of leaving this wimp of a husband behind and coming with me."

Peyton felt a wave of nausea rise within her. "Please, just don't hurt us. Just let us go."

The man threw back his balding head with a hideous laugh. "Please, just let us go," he said, rais-ing his pitch to mimic Peyton's voice. Then, he leaned in so close that Peyton could see his every pore. "Do you honestly think we are going to just let you go? I've heard too much whining from you, and I've been in your presence for less than ten minutes." Scowling, he raised his arm and gave her a hard, backhand slap on the cheek. "Maybe that'll shut you up!"

Peyton cried out and clutched the left side of her face as she collapsed on the ground.

"How dare you assault my wife!" Maxwell shout-ed. Within seconds, he was at her side. "Peyton, are you all right?"

She looked up at him through teary eyes. He studied her with a look of concern, then gulped and reached out to wrap her in his arms.

The two robbers began to laugh. "Aw, did we hurt the missus?" the shorter one asked.

Maxwell swallowed hard and stood to his feet.

"Whatcha gonna do, old man?"

"He thinks he's pretty tough," said the taller one.

"You will never touch my wife again!" Maxwell shouted.

"Never?" The shorter man scoffed. "Or what?"

Visibly trembling, her husband raised a fist.

"Maxwell, please," Peyton said. "Don't make things worse. I don't want you to get hurt—"

A shot rang out. Peyton gasped as Maxwell toppled to the ground, holding his left arm. She looked frantically from him to the two men and saw the shorter one holding a gun from which smoke was still curling. "No!" she shouted, scrambling to her feet. She ran to Maxwell's side. "Maxwell? Maxwell, can you hear me? Maxwell!"

"Come on, let's get out of here!" she heard one of the men shout. Then, she heard the rumble of horses' hooves as they rode off. But she didn't let her gaze leave her husband.

"Maxwell," Peyton sobbed. His body felt limp in her arms.

"Peyton," he wheezed.

"Maxwell? Keep breathing. It will be all right, darling." Blood covered her hands and dress, but she found that she didn't care about her appearance. All that mattered was comforting the man she loved, who had risked his life to protect her honor.

CHAPTER SEVENTEEN

At the sound of a gunshot, a sick feeling had come over Nate. He'd taken one look at Hailee, whose face had been awash with fear, and then, without a word, the two had turned and started running toward town.

He suspected that whatever had happened had to do with the two murderers at large. Yet nothing could have prepared him for the scene they came upon minutes later. In the road sat his mother, rocking back and forth, with his father in her arms. Her sobs were devoid of hope, which made the situation seem all the more devastating.

"Mother!" he shouted as he ran toward her. When he reached her side, he knelt down. "What happened?"

She gasped for breath and tried to respond, but a panicked moan was all she could manage.

Nate turned to Hailee, who stood behind him. "We've got to get him to Doc Orville! But we can't take the buggy; the horses are gone."

Hailee nodded quickly. "Surely, there is someone nearby who would allow us to borrow a horse and wagon. I'll try the surrounding homes until I find one."

"Thank you."

With that, she took off down the road. As Nate waited for her return, he tried to pray but felt numb. "Help him, Father," was all he could muster, so he repeated it over and over.

About ten minutes later, Nate heard the rumble of wagon wheels down the road. Hailee approached, looking determined, and he thanked the Lord for her courage.

When she stopped the wagon, Nate pried his mother's hands off of his father and, with Hailee's help, lifted him carefully into the wagon. "You're going to be all right, Father," he said, mostly to reassure himself. "Doc Orville will have you better in no time."

Meanwhile, Hailee coaxed his mother to get up. "Come on, Mrs. Adams," she said, her tone urgent yet gentle. "We need to get your husband to the doctor."

Nate turned around and looked at his mother. Her eyes had glazed over, and she looked stunned, unable to register anything that was said.

"I don't think she can hear you," Nate said, ashamed at the panic he heard in his voice. "Mother? Mother, wake up! We need to get Father to the doctor!"

"Nate." Hailee gripped his shoulders firmly. "Take your father into town. He is losing a lot of blood and won't make it if you don't get him to the doctor as soon as possible. I'll stay with your mother and help her; we'll be there shortly."

Nate shook his head. "I can't leave her. Please, let's take her with us now."

"Nate, listen to me." Her eyes penetrated his. "Your mother is in no condition to go anywhere just yet. I can comfort her, and the walk will take her mind off of what she's been through. You need to take your father now, Nate. Now."

She had a good point, yet Nate still worried for her safety. The men who had done this could be anywhere. "Hailee, the men responsible for this might still be out here. I came close to losing my father. I can't afford to run the same risk with you and my mother, too."

"Those men are not going to linger after what they did. They're long gone by now. Please, take your father now. We'll be there soon." Hailee embraced him, then gently pushed him in the direction of the wagon. "Go," she said.

Realizing the wisdom in her words, Nate turned around and scrambled into the wagon. He urged the horse forward and drove as quickly—and as smoothly—as possible. His father's life depended on it.

Hailee watched the wagon travel down the road and disappear around a bend, leaving a trail of dust in its wake. She prayed Nate would make it to town safely and speedily. Then, she turned her attention back to Mrs. Adams, who still sat beside the buggy.

Lord, please give me wisdom and strength to help Mrs. Adams. I don't know what to say or what to do. Please, Lord, guide me now, as You always have, Hailee prayed.

Then, she knelt down beside Nate's mother. "Mrs. Adams?"

She stared vacantly ahead.

"Mrs. Adams? How are you feeling?"

Mrs. Adams blinked and looked at Hailee, and then the words started rushing out in a nearly indistinguishable jumble: "Maxwell? Where is my husband? Is he still alive? Is he all right? It was all my fault! I was so foolish to question those evil brutes. What if he dies? What if...what if...oh, Maxwell!" she exclaimed, then burst into tears again.

Hailee reached out and took the sobbing woman in her arms. Soon, tears trickled from her eyes, as well, and she wiped her eyes on the sleeve of her dress. Her heart broke for this woman, who had watched as her husband was shot and now feared for his life. Her heart broke for Nate, as well, who feared losing his father. Hailee knew the pain of that loss. She'd stood by helplessly as her own parents had died.

The woman's crying slowed, and she leaned back to look at Hailee. "Where is Maxwell?" Her composure was an answer to prayer.

"Nate took him to the doctor."

"Is he...is he going to be all right?"

Hailee took a deep breath. "I don't know," she said. "But we can trust that he is in God's hands."

"What if...what if he doesn't make it?" Peyton gasped. "What, then? I—I don't think he knows that I love him."

"Mrs. Adams, may I pray with you?" Hailee asked.

"Pray?"

"Yes. I would like to lift your husband in prayer to God and ask for his healing. I'd also like to pray for your comfort."

"I—I guess so," she said. "I—I've never had someone pray specifically for me or my husband, or for our needs. Is that really possible?"

Hailee smiled warmly. "Yes, Mrs. Adams." She took the older woman's clammy hands in her own, closed her eyes, and bowed her head. "Dear heavenly Father, we pray that You would put Your healing hands on Mr. Adams and heal his wound. Please guide Doc Orville's hands and give him wisdom and skill to treat Mr. Adams. And, Lord, we also ask You to envelop Mrs. Adams and Nate with Your love and peace. In Jesus' name, amen."

When Hailee opened her eyes, she saw Mrs. Adams blinking at her with an expression of shock. "You...you spoke as if God were sitting right here with us."

"That's because He is, in a sense," Hailee replied, squeezing her hands. "God loves you, Mrs. Adams, and He promises never to leave or forsake you."

Nate's mother nodded, though a hint of confusion remained on her face. After a few moments, she frowned. "It's my fault, you know."

Hailee looked at Peyton. For the first time, she noticed the swelling bruise beneath her left eye. "I beg your pardon?"

"It's my fault that Maxwell was shot." Mrs. Adams looked down at her hands, which were dotted with dried blood, and wrung them together.

"That isn't true, Mrs. Adams."

"But it is," she insisted.

Hailee thought for a moment, searching for words to comfort her. She hadn't seen the incident, so she wasn't sure about the grounds on which Mrs. Adams based her sense of culpability. Still, she was sure that her feelings of guilt were unfounded. "Bad things happen sometimes," she said quietly. "You are not to blame."

"I should have kept my mouth shut!" Mrs. Adams wailed. "And I have many regrets...more than

I can count. How can a life change so completely in such a short period of time?"

Hailee wrapped her arms around Nate's mother and again held her while she cried, her choked sobs shattering the peaceful quiet that surrounded them.

"I...I often speak when I shouldn't," Mrs. Adams went on. "The one man, he hit me, and...and Maxwell tried to protect me. If I had kept quiet, this never would have happened."

Hailee closed her eyes. She felt sure that, even if Nate's mother hadn't said a word, his father would still have been shot. The victims could have been anyone, even Nate and she. "Please don't blame yourself, Mrs. Adams." Hailee rocked her gently, hoping the motion would help calm her down.

Moments later, Nate's mother pulled away and looked at her. "I...I'm sorry I was unkind to you earlier. I shouldn't have spoken about the young lady I'd hoped Nathaniel Junior would marry."

Hailee smiled. "I forgive you."

Her jaw dropped. "Just like that?"

"I couldn't fully understand forgiveness until I needed to be forgiven," Hailee explained. She thought of everything she had learned from Ella, as well as everything she had been learning recently as she'd studied the Bible. "God has forgiven me for my past mistakes, for all of the times I've sinned against Him. If I want to be more like Christ, I have to forgive others when they sin against me, as well."

Mrs. Adams closed her eyes and shook her head, as if she were trying to fathom something beyond comprehension. Several moments later, she blinked and cleared her throat. "I can see from the way my son looks at you how much he must care for you," she said quietly.

Hailee's cheeks warmed with a blush. "I care about him, too."

"I...I'm glad you two are courting." Her voice was barely above a whisper, and Hailee imagined it must have been hard for her to say that when, just over an hour ago, she had been obviously displeased with Nate's choice. "You are pretty, after all," she added, "and you show great mercy. It's no wonder Nathaniel is drawn to you."

"Would you like to try walking a little, Mrs. Adams?" Hailee asked her. "Nate will come back to get us, I'm sure, but we could start out, anyway. It might help to take our minds off of all that has happened."

She nodded and prepared to stand up. "I will agree to walk into town if you'll agree to call me Peyton. 'Mrs. Adams' sounds so formal." She smiled weakly.

Hailee grinned. "I think I can manage that." She reached out a hand to help Peyton to her feet. Then, arm in arm, they started the trek toward Pine Haven.

Nate could feel the adrenaline pumping through his body as he pushed the horses to run faster. He'd been torn between taking it slow to avoid most of the bumps and speeding up to get his father to Doc Orville's office sooner. In the end, he'd chosen the latter. Every so often, he would glance down and see his father's face, solemn and lacking color. *Lord, please, keep my father alive and minimize his pain....*

As the buggy rounded the next corner, downtown Pine Haven came into view. He urged the horses ever faster as they neared Doc Orville's office. "Help!" he shouted as the buggy slowed. "Help! My father's been shot!" Saying those words made him realize for the hundredth time the seriousness of the situation. Yes, his father was breathing, but barely. Nate had never been particularly good at remaining calm during emergencies, and this was no exception.

"What's going on?" Wayne Waterston, the blacksmith, came running out of his shop.

"We need Doc Orville!" Nate shouted. *Lord, please, please let my father be all right.*

Wayne knocked on the office door. Within seconds, Doc Orville emerged from the building. "What is it, Reverend?"

"Doc, it's my father. He's been shot!" Nate jumped down from the buggy.

"Let's get him into the office," said Doc, motioning for help from Wayne and Sheriff Clyde, who had rushed over from across the street.

Nate helped the three men carry his father into the examination room, where they laid him on the table.

Doc Orville gritted his teeth and looked less than optimistic as he surveyed the wound.

"Is he going to be all right?" Nate asked frantically.

"It's too soon to tell, I'm afraid. But I will ask that you go next door and summon Diane. I'll need her help." Doc Orville washed his hands and assembled several tools. "In the meantime, I'm going to try to extract the bullet."

Nate nodded. The wound must be serious if Doc Orville needed his wife's assistance.

After he had gone next door for Diane, Nate climbed back into the buggy, hoping Hailee had been able to help his mother. He still felt guilty for leaving them behind. He also felt guilty for a host of other things, especially for letting his parents wander off on their own without warning them about the outlaws at large. If only he could have convinced them to take a walk with Hailee and himself, they wouldn't have encountered whoever had attempted to take his father's life.

Just then, he saw Sheriff Clyde step up to the boardwalk in front of Granger Mercantile for the second time in two days and address the small crowd that had gathered. "As many of you know, Reverend Adams' father, Maxwell Adams, has been shot, and we believe that his assailants were the two men who recently escaped from the Wilmerville jail. Mr. Victor has sent notice to the authorities in Wilmerville, and we expect Sheriff Harmon and two of his deputies to come as soon as they can." The sheriff paused and looked down at his notebook. "It's rumored that Eustace Hays has a brother in Canfield Falls whom they're counting on to help them get to Oregon. Therefore, we have reason to believe that Eustace Hayes and Rolf Northrop are heading toward Canfield Falls. We are forming a posse to apprehend the two men and bring them here for holding until Sheriff Harmon arrives. Anyone who is able and willing to join us should meet here in fifteen minutes."

CHAPTER EIGHTEEN

*R*euben Annigan tethered his horse to a pine tree by the creek and approached the water. The sun was beginning to set, and the cool breeze was welcome after an uncharacteristically hot and humid day. Reuben squatted down, removed his hat, and splashed water on his face. What he wouldn't give for a hot meal—maybe some steak and potatoes and fresh corn on the cob.

He sat down and pulled the worn map from his pocket and unfolded it. From his estimations, his arrival in Pine Haven, Montana, was still several days, perhaps even a week, away. He traced the line of the journey ahead with his finger. If only it was as short as it appeared on paper. Next, he stood up and went back to his horse, reaching inside his saddlebag to pull out his mother's Bible. *Oh, Ma, how I miss you and Pa*, he thought as he fingered the front cover of the worn tome. *And I don't know if I'm doing the right thing by coming to Montana to find Hailee. But I have to know why she left us.* Reuben placed the Bible back inside his saddlebag for safekeeping. While he had kept it in his possession for all of these years, he rarely took the time to read from it.

The trip from Ohio hadn't been easy, yet Reuben was determined and had learned to get out of any scrape life sent his way. He thought of the note he'd found tacked to a board outside a dry goods store in Cincinnati:

Looking for Philip and Reuben Annigan.
If you have any information, kindly respond to:
Hailee Annigan
c/o Pine Haven School
Pine Haven, Montana

So, his sister had moved to Montana. He wondered what her life was like now. Was she married? Did she have any children? He could still feel the sting he'd felt the day Hailee had left in search of food but never returned....

"Where's Hailee?" Philip asked. "I'm hungry."

"I don't know." Reuben didn't even try to keep the irritation out of his voice. It was dark outside, and Hailee had been gone for several hours. He was concerned for her, of course, but he knew that she could take care of herself, better than anyone else he'd met. Yet worries swirled through his mind. Had something happened to her? Had she gotten lost? Or, had she deliberately deserted them? Life would certainly be easier for her without the burden of caring for two brothers. Still, he couldn't imagine her leaving them behind—especially Philip, whom she loved so dearly.

"I want Hailee," Philip whined. He rubbed his eyes with his little fists.

"She'll be back soon." Reuben reached out and put his arm around his younger brother. If nothing else, she would be back for him.

Without a morsel of food in their bellies, the two boys fell asleep an hour later. When they awoke to sunshine streaming in through the dirty windows, Reuben looked around and saw that Hailee still hadn't returned. Philip began to sob.

"Don't cry, Philip," Reuben urged him. "She'll be back." But, as the minutes turned to hours, with no sign of Hailee, he knew the chances of her returning were growing slimmer and slimmer.

"I'm so hungry," Philip moaned that afternoon, rubbing his stomach. Reuben could see his ribs through his shirt.

"I'll go out and find something for us to eat," he told him. "And, while I'm out, I'll look for Hailee."

"Can I come?"

"No, Philip. You have to stay here, in case—I mean, for when Hailee comes back."

"All by myself?"

"You'll be fine. Just promise me you'll stay inside."

"I promise."

"Good." Reuben thought for a moment. "Pretend it's a contest, and whoever comes back first wins. Stand guard at the window, kind of like you're an army soldier, and watch to see who makes it back first—Hailee or me."

Philip grinned. "All right."

"I'll be back soon," Reuben assured him.

About an hour later, Reuben returned with some bread, only to find that Philip was gone. So, he went out *again and spent the next two hours looking for his little brother. The thought of Philip wandering the streets of Cincinnati with his bad foot upset him. "Where are you, Hailee?" he yelled into each vacant alleyway. Angrily, he kicked at a pebble. "Where are you, Philip?"*

After a while, frustration turned to fear, and Reuben reached up to wipe away the tears that had begun to trickle down his cheeks. He'd never felt so afraid and so alone in his life. If Hailee had come back, Philip wouldn't have left and gotten lost. Now, both of them were gone. Reuben never should have counted on Hailee.

"Young man, are you all right?"

Startled by the voice, Reuben looked up into the face of an elderly gentleman. "Yes," he muttered, continuing on his way.

But he was far from all right. Panic filled every fiber of his being, and he was at a loss for what to do next....

When Reuben had seen the sign outside the dry goods store, he hadn't believed his luck. Yet mixed feelings had warred within his heart. He did love his sister, though they hadn't always gotten along. However, because she'd abandoned her brothers, they'd had to separate, and he hadn't seen Philip since. Moreover, because of Hailee's desertion, Reuben's life had taken a turn for the worse....

"You don't understand!" Reuben shouted at the police officer who stood on the other side of Reuben's cell in the county jail. He'd been there for three days,

ever since the officer had picked him up miles from Gardner Street, where he'd been searching for Philip. "I already have a family! Now, leave me be!"

"Son, I'm sorry, but when we find children wandering the streets, we have to do something to help them," the man said. "Besides, you look as though you haven't had much to eat lately."

"But I don't want to go with that family!" Reuben scowled.

"You should feel fortunate that we were able to find a family to take you in at such short notice," the officer told him. "Not every orphan gets a second chance like that."

"I don't need a second chance!" Reuben insisted. "All I need is to find my brother and sister."

The police officer shook his head. "Cincinnati is a big city. They could be anywhere."

"You're a police officer. You could find them," Reuben replied.

"Believe me, I've tried," said the officer. "But in a city of several hundred thousand, it's like looking for a needle in a haystack. Your best bet right now is to live with a family, who will keep you clothed and fed."

"I told you, I'm not going with them," Reuben insisted.

"Well then, I guess you'll just have to stay here," the officer said with a shrug.

Reuben looked around at his dismal surroundings, and a thought occurred to him. It would be a lot easier to escape from a house than from jail. "All right," he conceded.

The police officer smiled and unlocked his cell. "The family is here now, waiting for you," he said as Reuben followed him down a corridor. "They're friends of one of the officers in this precinct."

Reuben didn't care who their friends were. All he cared about was getting out of this jail and then finding Philip and Hailee. And, when he found Hailee, he'd be sure to tell her that his entire predicament was her fault....

The couple who had taken him in, Wilbur and Minnie Pritchard, had made his life miserable. Wilbur had seen him as a source of cheap labor, while Minnie had viewed him as a nuisance, just another mouth to feed.

"Care for some company?" A male voice interrupted Reuben's reminiscing. He glanced up to see a short, husky man with curly black hair standing before him.

"Uh, sure." Reuben got to his feet. While he was suspicious by nature, he'd met enough decent travelers on his journey to recognize that the man wasn't a threat.

"The name's Hosea Guthrie," the man said as he extended his hand to Reuben.

Reuben shook his hand. "Reuben Annigan."

"Pleased to make your acquaintance. Where are you headed?"

"Pine Haven, Montana. It's a small town west of Wilmerville."

"Can't say as I've heard of it. You have some family there?"

Reuben nodded. "My sister lives there."

"I'm headed north," Hosea told him.

"Family?"

"No, I'm a traveling preacher of sorts—a missionary, I guess you could say. I'm fixing to start a church in a small town called Milner's Ranch in northern Montana. I usually help a church get started, and then, when they find a permanent preacher, I head to the next town and do it all over again."

"Isn't that kind of lonely?" Reuben asked. "Traveling all the time with no place to call home, I mean."

Hosea shrugged. "I meet plenty of interesting people. Besides, there's a lot of folks looking for hope on the frontier. I believe God has called me to help share the source of true hope with them—His Son Jesus Christ."

Reuben remembered Pa reading to them the Bible accounts of Jesus' birth, death, and resurrection. He'd learned about Jesus in Sunday school, too, but he'd long forgotten any specific stories from those lessons. "My pa used to read to me from the Bible when I was young," he told Hosea.

"Every time I open that Book, I learn something new, even though I've read it through nearly twenty times in my forty-seven years." Hosea chuckled. "So, tell me, Reuben, has it been a long time since you last saw your sister?"

"It has." Reuben paused and assessed the man more closely. There was something about him that made him seem completely trustworthy, and Reuben was relieved to find someone he could unburden his heart to. "She and my brother and I were orphans, living in an abandoned hotel in Cincinnati. Our ma had made my sister promise to stay with my brother and me, and she did, for a while. She'd go looking for food—she had to steal, since we didn't have any money—and, in the afternoons, she'd teach us lessons in writing and arithmetic from what she remembered of her schooling. And then, one day, she went out to find food and never came back."

"I'd say that's quite a sister you have."

"That's true, but I still can't get over the fact that she left us. One minute, she was there and we were a family, staying together, just as Ma wanted. The next minute, she was gone. Even worse, I lost Philip, too. He ran away while I was out looking for Hailee. Later, when I was searching for both of them, a police officer took me in and made me live with an unkind family in another town. I left there a year ago and have been on my own ever since. Then, last week, I saw a posting on the board outside a dry goods store in Cincinnati. Hailee must have put it there. It said she was looking for us and indicated that she lives in Pine Haven, Montana."

Hosea nodded. "It's good that you're going to see her."

"I don't know, Hosea. I have a lot of unanswered questions. Besides, we never really did get along very well. I can't help but wonder if we'll just start fighting again as soon as we're reunited."

Hosea threw back his head and laughed. "I was smack-dab in the middle of six children, with two brothers and three sisters. Siblings can be a mite irritating—in fact, I think they're supposed to be."

Reuben chuckled. "Maybe you're right." He paused. "Look, Hosea, I don't mean to burden you with this...."

"You're not burdening me," Hosea assured him. "I don't see anyone else around here I'd rather be speaking to."

"It is pretty desolate," Reuben acknowledged.

"Would you like my opinion?"

"Sure."

"All right, then. I think you have a sister who made a lot of sacrifices to ensure that her younger brothers were fed. I think your sister cared deeply about you and did all she could to keep a promise to her ma. And I think your sister was not the type to desert her brothers on purpose."

"I'm just not sure why she left."

"I think the important thing is that she's all right. So much could have happened."

"That's true." Reuben had never really thought of it that way.

"It just so happens that I have some extra food in my saddlebag. What would you say to a little supper?"

"That sounds good. I haven't eaten in a while."

Reuben and Hosea talked all through supper and late into the night. Reuben was surprised to find himself sharing things with Hosea that he'd never shared with anyone. His new friend was a good listener and offered his opinion when requested.

And so, it was on this warm summer night just outside the Montana border that Reuben gave his life to Jesus.

In the morning, there was no sign of Hosea. Had Reuben not discovered a note in his saddlebag, he might have dismissed his meeting with Hosea Guthrie as an imaginary event. He unfolded the paper and saw a handwritten Scripture, the only trace of the man he'd met the night before.

> *"The LORD bless thee, and keep thee: the LORD make his face shine upon thee, and be gracious unto thee: the LORD lift up his countenance upon thee, and give thee peace."*
> —Numbers 6:24–26

CHAPTER NINETEEN

$\mathscr{N}$ate entered the church and sat down in the front pew. It had been a long day, and the stress from his father's injury had taken a toll on him, emotionally and physically. He leaned forward and buried his head in his hands. Tears filled his eyes. "Thank You, Lord, that my father is going to be all right," he whispered. "I am grateful beyond words for what You have done. And yet, I still feel weighted down. I don't understand it, Father. You performed a miracle through Doc Orville, but I feel as if a heavy burden rests on my shoulders."

"Nate?"

He recognized Uncle Zach's voice and turned around, squinting through the darkened sanctuary. "Yes, Uncle Zach?"

A shaft of moonlight slanting through a window illuminated his uncle, walking up the aisle toward him. "I thought I'd find you here." Uncle Zach sat down beside him.

"Did you catch those two outlaws?" Nate asked him.

"We did. We found them before they reached Canfield Falls. Seems they'd gotten a little greedy and decided to rob a few ranches on their way. Their greed actually helped us, as it gave us a chance to catch up with them, even though they'd had a considerable head start."

"Praise God they've been captured."

"We had a good number of men," Uncle Zach added. "Davey, Jonah, Asa, Billy Lee, Wayne, Sheriff Clyde...the list goes on. Northrop and Hayes are being heavily guarded in the jail until Sheriff Harmon gets here. I think we'll all rest a lot easier when those men are out of our town for good."

Nate nodded. "Thank you for helping to apprehend them."

"Of course."

"Father is going to be all right. He hasn't awakened yet, but his prognosis is good."

Uncle Zach nodded. "Just about everybody in town was gathered outside Doc's office for a prayer vigil. Seems the Lord saw fit to answer those prayers with a miracle."

"I'm so thankful," Nate said, unable to say more due to the tears welling up in is eyes. He willed them to stop, for no grown man cried, especially not in front of a fellow grown man.

"Nate, is something else troubling you?"

"It's my fault my father was shot," said Nate.

Uncle Zach grunted. "How so?"

"It wouldn't have happened if I had been able to convince my parents to stay with Hailee and me a little longer instead of heading back into town."

"Nate, Nate, Nate." Zach put a supportive hand on his shoulder. "You had no control over what your parents did or when."

"That's not the only reason it's my fault." Nate looked down at his boots. "I have been praying for years that my parents would come to the Lord. And every time I prayed that prayer, I would add, 'no matter what it takes.' It's my fault."

They sat in silence for a moment before Zach spoke. "That must be a big burden you are carrying."

Nate looked at his uncle. "What do you mean?"

"It must be difficult being God's right-hand man."

"His right-hand man?"

"Yes—you know, God's assistant. It must be difficult having the weight of someone else's salvation on your shoulders." Uncle Zach paused. "Nate, I know you're a reverend, but it isn't your job to save people. That's God's job. Your job is to do what you are so effective at doing—telling people what Jesus did for them on the cross. You can't save your parents any more than I can. That's up to the Holy Spirit, so don't put the responsibility on yourself."

"I just want so badly for them to know the Lord."

"I know, Nate. We all want that for the people we love."

"My father could have died without knowing Jesus."

"But he didn't. God heard each and every one of the prayers that were lifted up to Him by the people of this town—people who care about you and your family."

"It's wonderful news, I know, yet I still feel burdened," Nate confessed.

"I suppose a wagonload of guilt is responsible."

"It is."

"What about Matthew eleven, verses twenty-nine and thirty?"

Nate bit his lip. He knew those verses well and had even preached on them his second Sunday in Pine Haven.

"Insert your own name into the Scripture," his uncle suggested, "as if Jesus were speaking directly to you."

Nate considered the idea for a moment. It would probably feel a little awkward, but he did as his uncle had suggested and spoke aloud, "Take My yoke upon you, Nate, and learn of Me; for I am meek and lowly in heart: and ye, Nate, shall find rest unto your soul. For My yoke is easy, and My burden is light."

"It's not your fault that your father was shot, and especially not because you prayed for your parents' salvation," Uncle Zach assured him. "God wants us to pray that others will come to know Him. Remember Second Peter three, verse nine, which assures us that the Lord is *'not willing that any should perish, but that all should come to repentance.'* It's not your fault that your parents headed back to town without you. They made that choice themselves and had no idea they were about to stumble upon dangerous men. Let go of the burden of guilt you're carrying and give it to Jesus."

Nate nodded and swallowed hard. "Thanks, Uncle Zach."

"You're welcome, Nate. I'm always here for you."

Peyton sat in a chair inside the front area of Doc Orville's clinic and watched out the window as those who had gathered for the prayer vigil left, in ones and twos, for home. Maxwell had survived the gunshot wound, and Doc Orville had reassured her that

her husband was going to be all right. She had chas-
tised herself repeatedly for believing that competent
doctors could be found only in the city. Doc Orville
had saved her husband's life, and Pine Haven was
the furthest thing from a big city she'd ever seen.

Peyton dabbed at her eyes with her handkerchief. So much had happened today that she wasn't
certain it hadn't been a nightmare instead of reality.

"Peyton?"

She turned to see her sisters, Kaydie and
McKenzie, followed by Hailee.

"We brought you some soup," Kaydie said, extending a small, steaming bowl and a spoon.

"Thank you," said Peyton. "The soup smells delicious, although I'm not sure I could eat even one
bite."

"It's here for you if you need it," said McKenzie,
sitting down beside her. "Just as we are."

Peyton began to sob. "I...I don't deserve your
kindness...any of you."

McKenzie put her arms around her. "Peyton,
we're so glad you came to Pine Haven, and we can't
begin to tell you how sorry we are about what happened to Maxwell."

"It was all my fault!" she wailed.

"How was it your fault?" Kaydie asked as she
lowered herself into the chair on Peyton's other side.

"Because, I...I shouldn't have spoken to those
evil men."

"That's exactly what they were—evil men,"
Kaydie said. "And you are not to blame. They would
have shot Maxwell, even if you hadn't spoken. There's
no reasoning with people like that. Believe me; I know
from experience."

"I know you do, Kaydie, and I'm sorry I wasn't there for you during that horrible time you were married to Darius. I...I wanted to pretend that you hadn't made the choice to marry so far beneath our social stature. I wanted to live the lie that Mother and Father had concocted about your having married a kind doctor who had died of an intestinal illness. I didn't want anything to tarnish our family's reputation. How selfish I was!"

"Now, now," said Kaydie, patting her arm. "It's in the past, Peyton, and I've forgiven you."

"It's in the past," McKenzie echoed.

Peyton looked through teary eyes at her sisters, and remorse filled her tired soul. "I never treated either of you kindly when we were growing up. I am so very sorry."

"Peyton, none of that matters now," Kaydie said.

"It does matter—to me. You see, I was just so... so jealous of the two of you. You always had such fun together, and you were so close. I usually felt left out, but I only made it worse by treating you with such disdain."

"We forgive you," McKenzie said.

"How can you do that so effortlessly?" Peyton asked, bewildered by her sisters' ability to forgive. She thought of that afternoon, when Hailee had shown the same eagerness to forgive. This type of grace was beyond comprehension.

"We can forgive you because we've been forgiven for so much," McKenzie explained. "You should have seen the way I treated Zach and Rosemary when I first arrived in Pine Haven." She shook her head.

"I haven't always made the right choices," Kaydie admitted. "In fact, I still don't! I was so unfair to

Jonah for the longest time, comparing him to Darius, when he couldn't be more different from him."

"And I know you remember how unkindly Kaydie and I often treated you in our youth, Peyton," McKenzie put in. "One particular incident comes to mind, something about a skunk in your bed...."

Peyton felt the corners of her mouth lift slightly in a smile. "Oh, yes. I don't believe I will ever forget the time when you put a skunk in my bedroom. That was none too becoming of a Worthington."

"Can you forgive us?" McKenzie asked. "For that, and for all the times when we weren't kind to you, even as adults?"

Peyton swallowed hard as a strange sensation stirred in her heart. "I...I do forgive you," she said.

Then, she felt McKenzie place her hand on hers. "We love you, Peyton," she said.

"But, what about all of those fights we had as children, the moments we wasted bickering...?"

Kaydie smiled and shook her head. "No one thinks about that now."

"But I do," Peyton persisted.

"All is forgiven, and we want to do whatever it takes to help you through this difficult time," McKenzie told her.

Peyton's choked sobs filled the room, and she was grateful that her sisters and Hailee alone heard them.

Hailee patted her on the shoulder. "It's all right, Peyton," she said gently. "We're here for you."

Peyton allowed the tears to fall as waves of remorse, sadness, guilt, relief, and gratitude hit her all at once. Her legs felt weak, and she was glad she was sitting.

"We love you, Peyton," McKenzie said.

"We certainly do," Kaydie affirmed.

"And we Worthington girls must stick together," McKenzie added.

Peyton nodded. How good it felt to know she had friends in her sisters! She knew what she needed to do next. "If you don't mind, I'd like to go over to the church and see how Nate is doing."

"Of course," McKenzie said. "Would you like us to come with you?"

"Thank you for offering," Peyton said as she stood up, "but I think I should speak to him alone."

She bid her sisters and Hailee good-bye for the time being, then made her way out of the office and started up the street. When she reached the church, she pulled open the heavy door and stepped inside. In the dim light of a lantern at the front of the sanctuary, she could see Nate and McKenzie's husband, Zach, sitting side by side in the front pew.

The door closed behind her, and the two of them turned around.

"Oh! Excuse me, I...I didn't mean to interrupt," she said.

Zach stood up. "I was just getting ready to leave," he said.

"Thank you for all you've done for us, Zach," said Peyton. She realized he was yet another person whom she'd failed to treat with the respect he deserved.

"You're welcome, Peyton. Please let us know if you need anything—anything at all. Rosemary is out at the ranch, keeping an eye on the children, so McKenzie and I will be here most of the night."

"Thank you." Peyton sat down next to Nate as Zach left the church. "How are you doing?" she asked her son.

"Better now, after talking with Uncle Zach."

"He does seem like a kind man. I'm beginning to understand what McKenzie must have seen in him when she agreed to marry him."

"He is someone I really look up to," said Nate.

Peyton nodded. "It isn't easy for me to say this, but I...I want to apologize for trying to control your life."

Nate held up his hand. "Mother, there's no need for that now."

"Nate, please. After what happened to your father, I have come to realize how many people I have wronged...including you, my only son." Fresh tears welled in Peyton's eyes. Never had she cried so much in one day. "I'm sorry, too, for being unkind to Hailee and for insinuating that I disapproved of your courting anyone but Felicity Wynton."

"Mother, I forgive you. Please, don't worry about any of that. What's important is that Father is going to be all right."

Peyton turned and glanced out the window at the dark night. "All of this forgiveness...all of this mercy toward me...I don't deserve it." She turned back to her son. "Do you think God will forgive me, too?"

"Of course, He will!" he said, taking her hands in his. "None of us deserves to be forgiven for the sinful things we do. But Jesus died on the cross so that we would be forgiven and made righteous. When we trust Him as Lord and Savior, we accept the sacrifice He made, and the sins we've committed against Him and others are washed away."

"So, if I ask Him to, He will forgive me?"

"Yes, He will."

"I must admit, I've been ignoring God lately... more like all of my life, I suppose."

"All of us have been guilty of ignoring God and neglecting to make Him the highest priority in our lives," Nate assured her. "Even those of us whose vocations center on Him."

"Your father has been equally negligent, I'm afraid, and yet God allowed him to survive. Isn't that amazing?"

"He is a God of mercy."

Peyton dabbed at her eyes with her handkerchief and then studied her son. Nate, precious Nate. Even as a child, he'd looked for the good in others and possessed an unusual commitment to change the world. She'd always applauded him for seeing the good in others, but only insofar as it would help him defend his clients in a court of law. And she'd always wanted him to change the world. Since before he was born, she'd mapped out a plan for him, presuming to know what would be best for him—for his family's reputation, rather. How wrong she'd been! Only now did she realize how his ability to see good in others helped him to forgive. Only now did she realize that he was changing the world, and in a greater way that she ever could have imagined. He was changing the world for Christ, a mission that had never seemed important to her until today.

Despite her misguided manipulations, the Lord had drawn her son to Himself. Such grace overwhelmed her, and the weight of guilt and conviction soon gave way to a rush of peace in her heart. Today, the Lord was giving her another chance, by way of her own child.

Squeezing Nate's hands in anticipation, Peyton met his eyes. "Will you please tell me what to do so that Jesus can be my Lord and Savior, too?"

CHAPTER TWENTY

Nate couldn't help but feel overwhelmed at the Lord's faithfulness. Not only had He softened his mother's heart toward the things of God, but now, she was asking him to tell her more about Jesus! And it was all on account of his father's life-threatening injury—evidence that *"all things work together for good to them that love God, to them who are the called according to his purpose,"* as Paul wrote in Romans 8:28.

After he and his mother had spoken at length about the Lord, he prayed with her. "Shall we check on Father?" he asked as they embraced.

"Yes," his mother agreed.

Nate stood up and helped his mother to her feet. Then, arm in arm, they exited the chapel and headed down the street toward Doc Orville's office. *Thank You, Lord, for softening my mother's heart and bringing her to salvation*, Nate prayed in the silence. *I humbly ask that You would walk beside her and help her to grow in her faith.*

When they entered the clinic, Doc Orville greeted them. "Mrs. Adams," he said with a nod. "Reverend Nate. Could I have a moment to speak with you both in private?" He gestured to his office door.

"Is—is Maxwell all right?" his mother asked.

"That's what I need to speak to you about."

Nate couldn't find his voice. Mutely, he and his mother followed Doc Orville into his office, where they sat down in the two chairs facing his desk.

"What is it, Doc?" Nate finally asked.

"Your father was shot at close range, and the damage to his arm was...significant. Shattered bone, severed nerves.... We treated the wound as best we could, so I don't anticipate infection, but the truth is...well...."

Nate's mother tightened her grip on his hand. "The truth is...?" she nearly whispered.

Doc Orville smiled uncomfortably. "One of the things I like least about being a doctor is having to be the bearer of unwelcome news." He sighed. "The truth is, ma'am, that your husband will never be able to use his arm again."

Mother gasped.

Nate had the opposite reaction; he could neither inhale nor exhale.

"Now, in a situation such as this, I have a recommendation," Doc went on, his voice gentle, "and that is to amputate."

"Amputate?" Mother screeched.

A wave of panic washed over Nate. Had he heard the doctor correctly?

"Yes," Doc affirmed. "The limb will be a great burden to him. Having it amputated, while inconvenient in many ways, will actually make things easier, not to mention prevent infection and further complications."

"Are you sure this is the right thing to do?" Mother asked. "Surely, there must be another option."

"Believe me, Mrs. Adams, I never make a recommendation lightly. I have thought this through, and amputation is the best course, in my opinion."

"Have you performed an amp—this type of surgery before?" Mother asked.

"I have, and with excellent results. However, as a man of faith, I don't trust in my own abilities but rather rely on the Lord to guide my hands and give me the skill to perform the operation."

"What are the risks?" Mother asked.

Doc stroked his graying beard. "As with any surgery, there is the risk of infection...which can prove fatal."

"No." Nate finally found his voice. "We can't allow you to operate on my father."

"Nate." His mother looked him in the eyes. "Did you hear the doctor? This would be far better than living with a dead arm for the rest of his life."

"I'm sorry, Mother, but I don't think Father would agree. Think of his life after the surgery—the recovery, the humiliation."

His mother turned to Doc Orville. "What can you tell us about the recovery process from such an extreme procedure?"

"It will take time for him to heal, and even longer to adjust to the loss of his arm," Doc acknowledged. "But I will be here to assist him—and both of you—in any way I can."

"When would you perform the surgery?" Mother asked.

"As soon as possible."

"Doc, would you mind giving us a moment?" Nate asked.

"Certainly." Doc Orville stood to his feet and moved toward the door, patting Nate's shoulder as he passed. "It'll be all right, Reverend."

When the doctor had gone, he turned to his mother. He regretted his words even before he spoke them, because he hadn't taken the matter to the Lord in prayer, but he couldn't stop himself. "I don't want Doc to perform the surgery."

"You would prefer another doctor?"

"What I mean to say is, I don't want Father to have the surgery."

"I know, Nate, but I think we should listen to the doctor. He seems to think that your father's life would be a lot easier without a...a dead limb...just dangling there."

"But, what if...." Nate took a deep breath. "What if he doesn't make it? Doc said there is a chance—"

"I know, Nate. I'm not sure what to do, other than heed the doctor's advice." She gripped his hand again. "Before receiving the Lord as my Savior, I might have agreed with you. I'll admit, the old me would have been embarrassed to have a husband with only one arm. But I feel as if my love for your father finally transcends appearances. I simply want him to be comfortable."

Nate couldn't believe his ears. He looked at his mother and saw that her eyes were full of tears. Did she really mean what she'd said? She wasn't worried how an amputation might affect how others viewed her and her husband? Nate felt his own eyes fill with tears as emotions overwhelmed him—gratefulness that his mother had accepted Christ as her Lord and Savior; relief that his father had survived a gunshot wound; fear that he might die of complications from the surgery; and shame for allowing that fear to master him. Even so, he repeated, "What if he doesn't make it, Mother? What then?"

"I don't know."

"I won't—I can't—let Doc operate," Nate said quietly. "I'm too scared." There, he'd said it. Nate Adams, a man of the cloth who had preached many a time on 2 Timothy 1:7—*"For God hath not given us the spirit of fear"*—was afraid. And he'd admitted as much to his mother, to whom he was supposed to be an example of faith.

"Oh, Nate. Come here." His mother took him in her arms. "I'm scared, too."

He felt strangely reassured by his mother's embrace. When was the last time she'd comforted him like this? He couldn't remember.

"You always were such a sweet, sensitive boy," his mother said as she leaned back and studied him. "When you were about five, you received a stuffed bear from your father's father, Grandfather Adams, just before he died. You named the bear Biscuit, remember?"

"Yes, I remember."

"One day, you lost Biscuit." His mother paused for a moment and dabbed her teary eyes with a handkerchief. "You were so upset." She looked down. "Nanny had the day off, and I...I didn't know how to console you."

"Mother...."

"Please, Nate, let me finish. I remember I offered to buy you another bear. After all, they were common and could be found at any one of a dozen stores near our home. But you wouldn't hear of it." She searched his face. "Do you remember why you didn't want me to purchase another bear for you?"

"No," Nate admitted. "All I remember is losing Biscuit."

His mother sniffled. "You told me that Biscuit was different from all of the other bears in the store, that he was special, because he was the only bear that held the memory of Grandfather Adams in his heart. You were only five, and already you had such a tender spirit."

"I loved Grandfather Adams."

"I know you did, Nate. He was very fond of you, as well. And you were such a sensitive child, always feeling things deeper than most children would. I knew that, someday, that quality would make you passionate about your career—and make you an excellent husband, as well. I...I love that about you, Nate—that you care so deeply." She paused. "I'm not sure what made me recall that story, but I think that we ought to let the doctor operate on your father."

"I'm just afraid Father won't make it. And, assuming he does, I don't know if he'll be able to face life with a stump for an arm."

"I know, Nate, but, believe me, he will get past it. We need to put our trust in God, right? You told me earlier that He watches over His children, that they need not be afraid. That applies now, too, I should think."

The irony hit Nate head-on. After all, he was a pastor, considered mature in his faith. His mother had just come to salvation, and, already, she was the one full of wisdom for the situation. Nate sighed.

"You're right, Mother. I guess the gravity of Father's condition has caused my faith to falter a bit. I've just never been so afraid before."

"Nate, God will see us through this, no matter the outcome. I know He will." She paused. "Isn't there a story in the Bible about having faith in difficult times?"

"Yes, many of them. There's the woman with the issue of blood who touched the hem of Jesus' garment."

"And He healed her?"

"He did."

"Really? I'd like to read that story sometime."

Nate smiled. "Should we pray together?"

"Yes. Could I try praying? I've never prayed aloud, and I've prayed only a handful of times in private...."

"I would like that, Mother." Nate reached for his mother's hands and bowed his head. What a blessing it would be to hear his mother pray aloud for the first time.

"Dear Lord, I...um, I pray that You would bring Maxwell through the surgery and heal him completely. Please help Nate to...um...not to worry but to be like the woman who touched Jesus' garment in faith. Help me to exercise that same faith, as well. And thank You, Lord, for...for...." Her voice caught. "For everything. Amen."

"Maxwell?" Peyton tiptoed into the room where her husband had been sleeping since his surgery three days ago. She had so much to tell him. But, for now, she would rest in the fact that he was alive and had lost only his nondominant arm.

He blinked several times and looked at her before reaching for his thick glasses on the table beside him and putting them on. "Hello, Peyton," he said weakly.

"Oh, Maxwell!" Peyton rushed to his bedside and put her arms around him. "I've been waiting for this moment." She buried her face in the blanket covering his chest as the tears fell down her cheeks. "I was afraid I'd lose you," she murmured.

"Peyton?"

"Yes?" She didn't want to move; she wanted to stay here and hold him in her arms forever. They had allowed so many precious years to pass them by without showing each other any love or affection to speak of.

"Did you...did you see what they did to my arm?"

Peyton unclasped her arms and leaned back to look at her husband. Beneath his glasses, his blue eyes revealed intense pain and hurt. "Yes," she answered softly. "The doctor did what he had to, Maxwell. Your arm...well, there was so much damage that the doctor said you would never be able to use it again. The bone was essentially shattered, and there was a high risk of infection setting in if they didn't...."

Maxwell turned his head away, but not before Peyton spied the lone tear sliding down his cheek. "The doctors in Boston would have known what to do, and they wouldn't have needed to amputate it," he said firmly.

"Maxwell, look at me."

He shook his head and kept his gaze fixed on the wall.

"Maxwell, please. I know this is hard, but—"

"You don't know a thing about it, Peyton." He looked at her. "It wasn't your arm."

"Now, you listen here, Maxwell Nathaniel Adams." As Peyton spoke, tears began streaming down her face. "I almost lost the man I love. I was there with you, if you remember. I watched that man shoot you." She paused, fighting for composure. "Now, I know it will be difficult to adjust to having only one whole arm, but I'm just thankful you are alive. You lost so much blood, and...."

Maxwell met her eyes. His were filled with regret. "Peyton, I'm sorry we came here."

"I understand, Maxwell, but I don't feel the same way."

"How can you say that? We were robbed and nearly killed. The first thing I aim to do when I'm released from his place is to tell our son to pack his belongings so that he may return with us to Boston. It isn't safe for him here."

"Nate doesn't want to return to Boston. He loves it here."

"I thought you would agree with me. You've always wanted him to come home. What's happened to you, Peyton?"

"A lot of things changed after the robbery, Maxwell. A lot of things changed in those hours when you were...." She paused. "A lot of people were praying for you, Maxwell. I've never seen an entire community come together in the way they did for you, for us," she continued. "Only a handful of people in this town know us, and most of them are our relatives, yet many more offered support. They held a prayer vigil for you, and...and everywhere I turned, someone was offering to pray with me."

Maxwell scoffed. "With all this talk of prayer, you sound just like Nate."

"I realize that I don't sound like myself," Peyton acknowledged. "I never realized the importance of prayer, or that it puts us in touch with God the Father. But I have experienced the power of prayer firsthand; I've felt the peace that comes when you know that God loves and cares for you. I've never felt a peace like that before, Maxwell. Never." She closed her eyes for a moment, then opened them again and continued. "I spent a good deal of time with McKenzie and Kaydie, making amends. We wasted so many years of our lives fighting and envying one another. In fact, I can't recall one time in our childhood when I enjoyed being around either of them. Now, however, I can't imagine life without them. Everything we did to spite one another is in the past, and we've started anew."

Maxwell furrowed his brow. "Do you honestly believe that, after all the times McKenzie went out of her way to cause you grief? And Kaydie was no better. She followed McKenzie and did whatever she said."

"I know, Maxwell. I remember those days. But, with God's help, I've forgiven my sisters, just as they have forgiven me for being vindictive and always trying to get them into trouble. I wasn't the big sister I should have been to them, any more than they were the younger sisters they should have been to me. But they forgave me without hesitation for all of the mean things I did, and their example was all I needed to extend the same forgiveness to them." She dabbed her damp eyes with her handkerchief. "To see how my nieces, Chloe and Bethany Ethel, have grown up together and remained close friends makes me yearn to have a similar relationship with McKenzie and Kaydie."

"You sound nothing like the Peyton I know," he muttered.

Peyton smiled. "I'm a different person now, Maxwell. I know Jesus." She paused. "I finally understand why Nate loves the Lord so much. Jesus died for me! That's something I never fully realized before. Someone died for me, Maxwell!" The thought still overwhelmed her. "We attended church off and on for so many years, but I always daydreamed during the sermon and paid more attention to whether the other women were dressed fashionably." Peyton shook her head in self-disgust. "I know it will take some time for me to become the kind of woman God wants me to be—Nate says it's a gradual process—but I already feel like a different person from the woman who arrived in Pine Haven last week."

"So, after discussing Jesus with Nate for a few minutes, you are now a perfect, pious Christian?"

"Oh, no, Maxwell. I'm far from perfect. I will still make mistakes, probably a lot of them. But Nate showed me the place in the Bible where it says that I am a new creation in Christ. He also told me that, while I'm a new creation, I will never be perfect this side of heaven. He said that I am like a piece of clay, being continually molded in the hands of the Potter." The excitement she felt made her voice rise in pitch. "I'm not perfect, but I am forgiven. I have been given a chance to start over again, and, this time, I plan to live for Christ."

"I'm not sure what to make of all of this, Peyton."

"I know. I'm not sure, either. All I know is that I look forward to hearing our son preach for the first time. And do you know what else?"

"There's more?" Maxwell raised an eyebrow.

"There is. What would you think about having a second home here in Pine Haven? I have this sneaking suspicion, call it a mother's instinct, that our son will soon ask a certain young woman for her hand in marriage, and it would be nice to have a place in which to stay during the wedding festivities, as well as to watch our future grandchildren grow."

"Two homes?" asked Maxwell. "A wedding? Grandchildren?"

"I know it sounds crazy, but I've seen the way our son has taken to Hailee. At first, I didn't like it one bit, but, now that I've come to know her better, I realize that it would be an honor to have her as a part of our family. Besides, I don't want to waste another second of this life. I've wasted too many years already, and to think that I could have lost you...." Peyton closed her eyes.

"Peyton—"

"I'm serious, Maxwell. There were several times when I wasn't sure you would pull through. I learned how to pray just a few days ago, and I feel like an expert now, because of the countless prayers I've lifted to the Lord on your behalf."

"Really?" Maxwell smiled weakly. "I thought you might not want to stay married to me after you saw my arm."

"Oh, Maxwell. How could you think that?"

"How could I not, Peyton? You're a beautiful woman of great means. There's no need for you to stay with someone like me."

"I know I have been a shallow woman in the past, but I would never leave you on the basis of a handicap. I love you, Maxwell. I'm sorry for taking you for granted and always putting myself first in our marriage." She looked into his eyes. "You mean so much to me, yet I never realized just how much."

"You mean a lot to me, too, Peyton. I couldn't believe my good fortune when you agreed to marry me."

"It was assumed since the time we were three that we would marry someday," Peyton reminded him.

"But you didn't have to say yes. There were plenty of other men vying for your hand. Remember Roderick?"

"Of course, I remember Roderick." Peyton closed her eyes. "I never could have been happy with him."

"Your father liked him."

"My father didn't have to live with him."

Maxwell chuckled, a sound that flooded Peyton with relief. She allowed herself to giggle, which felt good after all that they'd been through.

When their laughter quieted, Maxwell said, "I'm sorry for always putting my work first. I know all those late nights I spent at the office left you lonely. I haven't been the husband you deserve nor the father Nate deserves."

"I've hardly been a model wife or mother," Peyton acknowledged. "Nannies and boarding school are basically responsible for having raised Nate. And now, look at him. He's no longer a boy but a man."

"And a fine man, it seems," Maxwell said. "I suppose he made the right choice in vocation."

"True. As Nate would say, by God's grace alone!"

"You'll have to enlighten me as to what you've learned about God."

"I would love to share what I've learned."

"Peyton?"

"Yes?"

"Do you consider me a coward for failing to ward off the men who robbed us?"

Peyton shook her head. "Maxwell, I think nothing of the sort. On the contrary, I think you were very brave, taking a stand for me." She thought for a moment. "Maxwell?"

"Yes?"

"Do you blame me for getting you shot? After all, it was my words that ultimately prompted that awful man to take his anger out on you."

"I don't blame you at all, Peyton, and I mean that. Those men were of evil intent, and they would have shot anybody; we just happened to be the unlucky ones they encountered." He put his hand gently on the fading bruise under her eye. "I'm just thankful you weren't harmed more than you were."

Peyton smiled. "How is your appetite? Believe it or not, there's a café in town, and I happen to know they make excellent dinners. Shall I place an order for two and bring it back here? I think we have a lot more to talk about."

Maxwell grinned. "I can't think of anything I'd rather do than enjoy a meal with my wife."

Peyton stood up, then leaned down and gave him a kiss on the cheek. "I'll be back soon, then, so don't go anywhere!"

CHAPTER TWENTY-ONE

When he came upon a ranch, Reuben Annigan dismounted, took off his hat, and wiped the sweat from his brow. It had been a long ride today, and he was overcome with exhaustion. Judging from the position of the sun, it was probably around six o'clock. He gazed at the whitewashed two-story home, then out at the vast fields dotted with corrals and outbuildings. *This is probably as good a place as any to stop and ask for directions to Pine Haven,* he thought, shrugging. *Maybe the folks who live here even know where I can find Hailee.*

Reuben's stomach growled. Perhaps the owners of the ranch would hire him for the next day so he could earn food and a place to stay for the night. He had long ago run out of funds, and he hadn't eaten since last night.

Reuben tethered his horse to a fence post out front and climbed the stairs to the porch.

He knocked on the front door, which opened several seconds later, revealing a tall man dressed in fine clothes. "May I help you?"

Reuben cleared his throat. "Yes, sir. My name is Reuben, and I wish to speak with the owner of this ranch."

"You're looking at him," the man said. "Anders Nash is the name."

"Mr. Nash, I've been traveling for days on end, and I was wondering if you might allow me to stay here for the night in exchange for a day of labor tomorrow," Reuben said. "I've worked on farms for much of my life, and I'm a good hand." He hoped that Mr. Nash valued experience over age.

Mr. Nash studied him with a wary expression. "You look awful young. Where're your parents?"

"They died a while back."

"Sorry for your loss, son." He paused. "There's been some criminal activity in these parts, so I don't think my wife would like a stranger staying in our house...tell you what. You can bed down in the barn for the night, but I'll expect some work out of you first thing tomorrow morning. There's a fence in the back pasture that needs mending."

"Thank you, Mr. Nash, sir."

"Have you eaten supper yet?"

"No, sir."

"Well, you're welcome to join us." Mr. Nash gestured for him to come inside. "You don't look like a criminal to me."

"Thank you, sir!" Amazed at his good fortune, Reuben followed Mr. Nash inside. The home was well furnished, and, from what Reuben could see, Anders Nash was a wealthy man.

While a cook and two other hired hands set plates of steaming food around the table, Mr. Nash introduced Reuben to his wife, Rowena, and daughter, Etta Mae, who looked like a sourpuss to him.

"So, Reuben, where are you from?" Mrs. Nash asked as they all sat down around the dining room table.

"Ohio, ma'am." Reuben folded his hands and closed his eyes, expecting them to say grace before the meal. At the sound of clinking utensils, he opened them again and saw that Anders, Rowena, and Etta Mae had started eating. Evidently, this wasn't a praying family.

"What brings you to Pine Haven?" Etta Mae asked him.

Reuben finished chewing and looked across the table at her. "I'm looking for my sister."

"And who might that be?"

"Her name is Hailee Annigan. I've heard she's in these parts. Do you know her?"

Etta Mae arched an eyebrow. "She's the schoolteacher," she said simply.

Reuben took a bite of toast. That would seem logical, considering how Hailee had enjoyed teaching Philip and him when they were younger. "It's been years since I've seen her."

"You must miss her terribly!" Etta Mae gushed.

"I am looking forward to seeing her again," Reuben said.

"I don't mean to pry, Reuben, but why is it that you haven't seen her in such a long time?" Rowena asked, concern in her voice.

Reuben finished chewing and set down his fork. How much should he tell these people he'd only just met? They seemed nice enough. "We were separated some years back, after our ma died."

"I'm terribly sorry," said Rowena. "That must have been so difficult. How is it that you became separated?"

"Rowena, I'm sure the boy would like to eat rather than answer your six million questions," her husband put in.

"Oh, Anders. Etta Mae and I are simply concerned, aren't we, Etta Mae?"

"Terribly concerned," Etta Mae confirmed, nodding.

Reuben looked from Anders to his wife and then to his daughter. Yes, the Nashes seemed like kind-hearted folks and likely were friends of Hailee's. He cleared his throat. "We were so poor after Ma died that we didn't have any food to eat. You see, Pa had died some time before, and Ma worked in a factory to support us. After she died, we had no means of income. Hailee and I did the best we could to care for our little brother, Philip, who had to walk with a crutch because of his bad leg." Reuben thought for a moment about his conversation with Hosea Guthrie, whose words rang through his mind: *"I think you have a sister who made a lot of sacrifices to ensure that her younger brothers were fed. I think your sister cared deeply about you and did all she could to keep a promise to her ma...."*

"That's sounds dreadful. You must have been so hungry!" Etta Mae exclaimed.

"Well, Hailee had to make sure both of us were fed," Reuben said.

"As any good sister would do," Rowena replied.

"Yes. However, since we had no money, Hailee had to steal food for us to eat. Then, one day, Hailee went out to look for food and never came home to the vacant hotel where we lived. I told Philip to stay put and went out looking for her. But I couldn't find Hailee, and then, to make matters worse, when I got home, Philip was gone. I haven't seen either of them since."

"What a shame," Rowena said, glancing at her daughter.

"That is a shame," agreed Etta Mae. "One would never guess from Hailee's upstanding reputation that she once had to steal food."

"It wasn't that she wanted to, ma'am," Reuben explained. "She had no other choice."

"Yes, of course, dear."

Reuben looked down to take another bite. The rest of the meal was eaten in silence, which he didn't mind; he was just glad to have food in his stomach and friends of Hailee's surrounding him.

The next afternoon, after he had mended the fence for Anders Nash, Reuben asked for directions to the center of town, then thanked the Nashes and left. When he arrived in town, he spied the schoolhouse immediately—it was small and white, with a pointed roof and a belfry—and the sight caused his heart to race. A flurry of different emotions swirled in his heart as he faced a long-awaited reunion with his sister.

Reuben tied his horse to the school yard fence and then walked slowly up the stairs of the schoolhouse. He shivered, but whether it was from the cool October air or the anticipation of seeing Hailee again was anyone's guess.

Reuben could hear voices inside the school and wondered whether he ought to wait until the students were dismissed for the day. Surely, that would happen soon, as it was late in the afternoon. So, Reuben turned the doorknob and peeked inside. He saw Hailee right away; she stood near the front of the room, evidently helping a student with an assignment. Since nobody seemed to notice him, he slipped inside and closed the door silently behind him, then studied his sister. She was almost exactly as he remembered her, except that her hair was longer. She was still beautiful—a carbon copy of their mother, with her long, wavy blonde hair, fine features, and slender build.

"Who're you?" a youthful voice chirped.

Hailee looked up and met Reuben's eyes. "May I help you, sir?"

"Hailee."

She narrowed her eyes, a doubtful expression on her face. "Reuben?"

"Yes, Hailee, it's me." He removed his wide-brimmed hat and started toward her. "I'm sorry to interrupt your class, but I couldn't wait—"

"Reuben!" Hailee ran toward him with outstretched arms.

They met in the center of the room and embraced. "I can't believe it's you!" she gasped.

"Miss Annigan, are you all right?" another student asked.

Hailee stepped back and wiped her eyes with her sleeve. "Yes, Bethany Ethel, I'm fine," she said in a quavering voice. "Class, this is my dear brother, Reuben Annigan. Can you all say hello?"

"Hello, Mr. Annigan," the students chorused.

"Hello, class," Reuben answered.

"Bethany Ethel doesn't get that excited when she sees us," said a young boy, "and we're her brothers."

"Yeah," another boy, evidently his twin, agreed. "She always tells us to go away."

"That's because you're both a big nuisance," Bethany Ethel retorted.

"That's the truth," another little girl muttered.

"That's not true," one twin contested.

"She does sometimes cry when she sees us, though, just like you're crying now," the other one said.

"My tears aren't tears of joy," said Bethany Ethel.

"Children, that's enough," Hailee reprimanded them gently. "The reason I am so excited to see Reuben is that I haven't seen him for several years."

"I might feel that way if Tommy and Clint moved to New Orleans for fifty years and then came back to Pine Haven," Bethany Ethel said.

"Reuben and our brother, Philip, and I were orphans, but we became separated, and I wasn't sure if I would ever see them again." She sniffled. "And now, here you are!"

"May we be dismissed?" asked one of the twins, rolling his eyes.

Reuben was actually grateful, since their audience was a bit more attentive than he'd expected them to be.

Hailee glanced behind her at the clock on the wall. "Yes, you may be dismissed. Don't forget to study your words for tomorrow's spelling test!"

Her words gave way to a great commotion as the children jumped up from their seats, pushed in their chairs, grabbed books and slates, and bustled toward the door.

Once the room had emptied, Hailee grinned at him. "Let me get a good look at you. My, you look so much like Pa."

Reuben didn't think he looked too different from the last time she'd seen him, except that he'd cut his curly blond hair and had grown a few inches.

"I can't believe you're here," she whispered. She began to sob with abandon. "Thank You, Lord!" she said, over and over.

Reuben felt a little awkward. "It's good to see you, too, Hailee." He placed a hand on her shoulder, hoping she would calm down before anybody came to see what was going on.

"H-how did you know where to find me? D-did you...did you see one of my posters in Cincinnati?"

Reuben nodded. "I saw one outside a dry goods store."

"I put those posters up all over the city. I prayed and prayed that you and Philip would see them."

"Have you heard from Philip?" Reuben asked.

"Yes, praise God. We've been writing back and forth for the past two months. I'll share his letters with you. It sounds as if he's doing well. He was adopted by a nice family and lives in Cheviot."

Reuben grinned through the tears that had formed, to his chagrin, in his own eyes. "I'm glad for him, but I wish I'd known he was still in Ohio. I could have gone to see him. Cheviot really isn't that far."

"And not only that, Reuben, but his new family paid for a surgical procedure to correct his foot."

"That's great!"

"Oh, how I've missed you, Reuben," Hailee sighed.

"I've missed you, too." Reuben paused and stared at the floor. "There is one thing I need to know. Why did you desert Philip and me?"

"Oh, Reuben, I didn't desert you—at least, not on purpose!" Hailee's heart broke at her brother's insinuation. For all of these years, he'd believed she'd deserted him? She loved him and Philip more than anything.

"I just wasn't sure where you were," Reuben went on. "For the longest time, I thought you'd left us to go your own way. I was angry at you and had it in my mind to tell you so. But, as I was traveling here, I met a man named Hosea Guthrie, who changed my thinking. He told me that you must have had a good reason for leaving."

"I did, Reuben. Please, come, sit down." Hailee gestured to a student desk and then sat down across from him. "The day I last saw you, I went out for some food, as usual. Before I found any, though, I was arrested by the police."

"What?"

"That's right. They finally caught me. Not only that, but they hauled me to jail. A few days later, they took me to The Sanctuary of Promise, where they blocked my every attempt to escape and return to you and Philip. Believe me, I tried to escape, time and again, but they always caught me. Finally, one of the teachers there, Miss Fanshaw, promised to look for you and Philip, but only if I promised not to try to escape."

"So, you decided to remain at The Sanctuary of Promise?"

"Yes. I hated it at first. I kept insisting that I needed to find you and Philip because I'd promised Ma to keep us together. Miss Fanshaw did go looking for you, but she found the hotel abandoned, with no sign of you or Philip." Hailee bit her lip. "I'm so sorry, Reuben. For a while, I hated myself for getting caught. It broke my heart not to be able to go in search of you and Philip, or at least to say good-bye. I never would have deserted you on purpose. I love you," Hailee choked out.

"But why didn't you try to find us after you left The Sanctuary of Promise?"

"I did try. I put up posters all over town. I lived in Cincinnati until just a few months ago, staying at a boardinghouse."

"Why did you leave?" Reuben asked, his voice hushed. He sounded hurt.

"I left because I had the opportunity to live out my dream of becoming a teacher. But I never gave up hope that I'd find you again. I changed my address on the posters so that you would know I'd moved to Pine Haven. I am so sorry, Reuben, if you thought I deserted you." *Please, Father, soften Reuben's heart and mend any brokenness between us*, she prayed silently.

"I'm sorry, Hailee," Reuben finally said. "I thought for sure you'd left us behind on purpose."

Hailee shook her head and reached for Reuben's hand. "I am so happy you came here, Reuben, in spite of the betrayal you felt."

"I am, too." Reuben reached into his coat and pulled out a book. *Ma's Bible!* Hailee recognized it instantly. "I thought you should be the one to have this," he said, handing it to her.

"Oh, Reuben! Are you sure you don't want to keep it?" she asked.

"I'm sure. It belongs with you."

Hailee held the priceless Book to her chest. She could almost hear Ma's voice as she read from its pages.

At the sound of footsteps on the stairs, Hailee glanced up and saw Nate enter the schoolhouse. "Hello, Hailee," he said, then glanced at Reuben with a curious expression. "Is everything all right?"

"Yes, everything's fine!" Hailee smiled. "Nate, I'd like you to meet my brother Reuben. Reuben, this is Reverend Nate Adams."

"Reuben! It's a pleasure to meet you," Nate said, extending his hand. "I happen to know at least two people who have been praying every day that you and Hailee would someday find each other again."

"Make that three," Reuben said as he shook Nate's hand.

Nate turned to Hailee. "Would you and Reuben like to join me for dinner at the café this evening? We can celebrate this reunion."

Hailee smiled and looked at Reuben. "What do you think? Mrs. Moore makes the best apple pies in town."

"That sounds good," he replied. "My stomach is growling already."

"Do you have someplace to stay?" Nate asked him.

"Last night, I stayed with the Nash family."

Hailee attempted to hide her shock. "The Nash family?"

"Yes. Theirs was the first ranch I came upon, and I offered to do some work if I could spend the night. This morning, Anders had me mend a fence."

"Well, Hailee's boarding with the widow Marlen, so if you need a place to stay for the rest of your visit,

I know that my uncle Zach is looking for another hired hand," Nate said.

"Really?" Reuben looked interested. "Now that I've found Hailee, I might just stay awhile. I am a hard worker."

"It's settled, then. I'll introduce you to Uncle Zach this evening after dinner. So, shall we meet at the café at five o'clock?"

"That sounds wonderful," said Hailee.

"Agreed," said Reuben.

Nate leaned forward and planted a kiss on Hailee's forehead. "Five o'clock it is." With that, Nate headed out of the schoolhouse.

"I take it you and Reverend Adams are more than casual acquaintances," Reuben said in a teasing voice.

Hailee felt her face heat. "We are courting, yes."

"I figured."

"This time, you figured correctly." Hailee smiled. "I don't have any plans for the rest of the afternoon. Would you care to talk awhile?"

"Reckon I would."

"I've told you where I've been these past years. What happened to you after I was taken to The Sanctuary of Promise?"

Reuben took a deep breath and began to tell her how he'd been arrested and sent to live with the Pritchards....

"Now, don't go gettin' no ideas," said Mr. Pritchard. He smacked Reuben hard on the back of the head.

"You have chores to do. And then, when you're done with them, you'll have more chores to do."

Reuben surveyed the overgrown farm. He didn't mind hard work; Pa had always said that hard work was good for a man. Made him strong.

However, Reuben soon realized that this wasn't ordinary hard work—it was unending forced labor with a dash of cruelty and little rest.

After a month of labor, Reuben's workload did not let up. "Did he work hard today?" Mrs. Pritchard asked her husband when Reuben dragged his weary body into the house at 10:30 one night.

"Not to my satisfaction," Mr. Pritchard grumbled.

"Then, there will be no food for him."

Reuben's stomach growled at the mere mention of food. He was famished. He'd been deprived of lunch as punishment for accidentally getting the plow stuck for several hours, so he hadn't eaten since breakfast. Now, he would be forced to go without dinner, as well? It wouldn't be the first time. On several other occasions, his meals had been withheld because of his "lack of hard work," as Mr. Pritchard put it. But that wasn't the truth at all. Reuben was a hard worker, strong and capable. He tried his best to please Mr. Pritchard. In the end, his attempts were always futile.

"Please, Mrs. Pritchard, I'm starving," begged Reuben.

"We didn't bring you to live with us so that you could eat all our food," said Mr. Pritchard. "We expect you to earn your keep. But that ain't at all what you're doin'."

"With all due respect, sir, I've worked hard today," Reuben protested.

"No, you haven't. I ain't seen a lazier boy in all my life. And to think we done rescued you from that jail. Stupidity on our part, I say."

"I'm thankful you rescued me from jail, sir," said Reuben, although he was sure he'd rather be behind bars than with the Pritchards.

"Then act like it, boy!" Mr. Pritchard shouted. "Nobody else wanted no criminal like you. Nobody else wanted to take a vagabond off the streets and give him a home. Me and the missus, we done did that, and look at the thanks we get! Just a beggar asking for what he don't deserve!"

Reuben hung his head. It was a similar scenario every day. He'd thought about running away several times before, but Mr. Pritchard's threat rang through his head: "If you ever try runnin' away, I'll find you and send you to the penitentiary, where they'll hang you the first time you don't do as you're told. I swear I'll do it, so don't you doubt me for a minute."

Reuben had been terrified of the thought of the penitentiary. He couldn't imagine anyone allowing a young boy to go there, but Mr. Pritchard seemed very convincing.

Reuben resented the forced labor, the skipped meals, and the beatings he received if he so much as looked at Mr. Pritchard the wrong way. However, he had no choice. For four years, Reuben stayed at the Pritchard home, until the fateful day when he escaped.

It was nearly dark when Reuben finally finished his chores and headed inside for supper. He hoped he'd earned at least a small meal. As he approached the home, he saw that a light was on in the kitchen, and he heard men's voices, which sounded

increasingly loud and obnoxious the closer he came.
Reuben snuck up to a kitchen window and cautiously
peered inside, taking care not to be seen.

Wilbur Pritchard sat at the kitchen table, a flask
in one hand and some playing cards in the other. He
was joined by two of his friends, Kerwin Compson
and Damon Hogan, who usually came over to play
cards and drink whiskey while Mrs. Pritchard was
away at her monthly quilting bee. Reuben shivered. If
ever there was a man more devious than Mr. Pritchard,
it was Damon Hogan. And Kerwin Compson wasn't
much better.

Reuben stood outside the window and listened
to the conversation going on inside the house. His
stomach growled, reminding him that he hadn't eat-
en since breakfast. Yet, he knew he would rather go
without food than suffer the cruel insults he would
receive if he dared set foot inside the house. So, he
decided to eavesdrop while contemplating what to do
next.

"That boy should be done with his chores by
now," groused Wilbur.

Reuben stood on tiptoe to get another view of the
three men. Wilbur's shirt was spotted with sweat,
and his sparse black hair stuck up at random on his
mostly bald head. Kerwin and Damon sat with their
backs toward Reuben, yet, from the sight of their
movements and the sounds of their voices, Reuben
could tell that not one of the men was sober.

"You should get that lazy, good-for-nothin' boy in
here to get us somethin' to eat!" Damon suggested.

"Speakin' o' that good-for-nothin' boy, I've always
wondered, how do you get 'im to stay here? I mean,

I'd like me some free labor, too," Kerwin snarled. "You can't expect me to believe he stays on his own accord."

Wilbur snickered. "As you know, that boy ain't the brightest," he began, tipping his flask to his lips. "I done told him that if he tried to escape, I'd have him thrown in the penitentiary."

"What? Thrown in the penitentiary?" Kerwin asked. "He believes you?"

Damon laughed. "You can't throw no hired hand in the penitentiary jest fer leavin'," he said. "Believe me, I know all about what's required to git thrown into a prison cell!" He cleared his throat with a loud, raspy cough, then spit a wad of phlegm on the floor.

"'Course, I could go and accuse 'im o' stealin' a horse or somethin'," Wilbur said.

Kerwin snickered. "I'd like to see that!"

"Well, I guess it don't matter how I get 'im to stay here, just so long as I do. He's the cheapest hired hand I've ever had!" Wilbur said with a chuckle.

The rage that raced through Reuben's body caused his heart to pound. He sucked in his breath and clenched his fists. How could he have been such a fool? Wilbur had deceived him for four years, and Reuben had blindly endured his brutality. Gritting his teeth, Reuben rethought his course of action but quickly reminded himself that seeking revenge would get him nowhere—except maybe the penitentiary.

However, if Reuben left now, Wilbur, in his drunken state, wouldn't know for at least an hour. And, if he cut through the fields, he would avoid Mrs. Pritchard on her way back from town.

Reuben raced to the barn. He grabbed the threadbare quilt off of his makeshift bed in the hay and filled it with his other set of clothes and his mother's Bible, *which was his only possession. Then, he folded up the corners of the blanket and tied them together into a sort of satchel. It would have been helpful to take a horse, but he couldn't justify stealing. Plus, horse thieves were sent to the penitentiary...or worse. So, Reuben surveyed the area as best he could in the dusky light, then set out across a field, running with a speed he'd never known he had.*

He'd never looked back. He'd managed to find odd jobs in Cincinnati, which had brought in enough money to buy food and to keep a roof over his head, as well as to save up for a horse and saddle. Then, one day, he saw a poster Hailee had hung. Two days later, he bought a horse and headed west....

"I am so terribly sorry, Reuben," said Hailee. She couldn't imagine what Reuben had gone through.

"All I ever wanted was to be adopted," said Reuben. "If I couldn't have Ma and Pa for parents, I thought surely there was someone out there who would want me."

Hailee leaned forward and hugged her brother. *Lord, please heal Reuben's broken heart,* she prayed silently. *And please know how thankful I am that You led me to The Sanctuary of Promise. I didn't see it as a blessing then, but I most certainly do now.*

CHAPTER TWENTY-TWO

Hailee was seated at a café table with Nate and Reuben, enjoying her meal, when Lucille Granger burst in through the front door. "Mr. Nash is calling an emergency meeting of the school board!" she announced to everyone in the restaurant. "Meet outside the mercantile at seven o'clock sharp." With that, she turned on her heels and rushed out again, presumably to alert other townspeople of the event.

"What could this be about?" Hailee wondered aloud.

"I'm not sure, but I guess I should attend," Nate said. "At least we're nearly finished our meal."

When they had paid their bill, the three of them walked up the street to join the crowd gathered outside Granger Mercantile. Evidently, many more people than just the school board members were in attendance. On the boardwalk stood Mr. Nash, who had started to speak.

"...That's why I felt the need to call this emergency meeting," he was saying. "At first, I thought this issue should be handled by the school board members alone, but then, I got to thinking, it's you, the citizens of this town, whose children are being taught by Hailee Annigan. It's high time you folks knew the background of this so-called teacher. That's right—she's a criminal of the law!"

A wave of gasps and murmurs arose from the crowd. Hailee's pulse quickened immediately, and it only increased when she saw countless pairs of eyes on her. The truth about her past was coming to light. Hailee wanted to run away from Pine Haven and never look back. She wanted to forget that she had ever stepped foot in this tiny town. Her heart ached at the thought of being dismissed from her teaching position and never fulfilling her dream. Even worse was the heartbreak she felt at the prospect of having to leave Nate behind. The voices of the townsfolk became meshed in her mind as she allowed herself to go back to a happier time....

A streak of lightning lit up the sky, followed by a deafening roar of thunder. Frightened by the storm, seven-year-old Hailee climbed into her mother's lap and buried her face in her shoulder, pressing her cheek against her mother's. "Your face is so soft," she whispered.

Ma laughed and pulled her closer. "You have a soft face, too, Hailee."

"When I grow up, I want to be just like you, Ma."

"And I couldn't ask for a better gift from the Lord than that of my children."

Hailee glanced up into her mother's eyes. "I am a blessing, and so is baby Philip, but I don't know about Reuben."

"Reuben is a blessing too," Ma insisted. "You two are young now and don't always get along, but, someday, when you're older, I know you'll be the best of friends."

"What will happen when I'm all growned up and I can't snuggle you when I'm scared of the thunder and lightning?"

Her mother patted her on the head. "You must remember that even if I'm not with you, God will always be with you."

"Always?"

"Always."

"What if He gets really tired and falls asleep up there in heaven?"

"You don't have to worry about that, Hailee. The Lord never rests."

"Never?"

"No. He doesn't need to, because He never gets tired."

"Well, I know I would get tired watching all the people in Cincinnati all the time. I get tired just watching Reuben when you ask me to keep an eye on him."

Ma laughed softly. "Not only does the Lord watch over all the people in Cincinnati, but He also watches over everyone, everywhere, even in other countries. He holds the whole world and everyone in it in His hands."

Hailee chewed on her bottom lip. She had to think about that for a minute. "God sure must be busy."

Ma smiled. "Yes, He is."

"And He must have really big hands, like maybe this big." Hailee held her arms far apart. "Pa's hands aren't even that big." She paused and thought for a moment. "But what if one of those people He's holding in His hands falls out?"

Ma planted a kiss on her cheek. "No one ever falls out of God's hands. He holds us always."

Hailee scratched her head. "Always?"

"Always." Her mother smiled again. "Do you know why your pa and I chose to name you Hailee?"

"No."

"Because it means 'heroine' or 'victorious woman.'"

"What's a heroine?" Hailee asked. She loved that she could ask anything of Ma, who always answered with patience.

"A heroine is a woman who is brave and coura-geous. For instance, do you remember the story about Moses' sister, Miriam?"

"Yes," Hailee replied. "She was the one who watched over baby Moses when he was in the basket in the river."

"That's right. And Miriam was a heroine be-cause God used her to save her brother's life. Maybe someday, God will use you to save someone's life, as well."

Hailee thought for a moment. "Do you think the pharaoh will ever make you put Philip in a basket? Because then I could take care of him and save him."

"I don't think so," Ma answered, chuckling. "But you never know the amazing plans the Lord has for His children...."

Hailee closed her eyes. *If only you were here with me now, Ma,* she thought.

Her attention was jolted back to the heated meeting by the sound of Anders's loud voice. "We can't allow a thief—a—a hardened criminal—to teach our children!"

"Anders, please," Nate spoke up. "You're being unfair."

"Reverend Adams! You're the last person I would have expected to stand up for her," Anders sneered.

"Don't listen to him," Davey urged her quietly from where he stood on the other side of Nate.

"It's taking my every ounce of self-control to resist hitting that man square in the jaw," she heard Nate whisper back to him.

"You know I have your back, if that's what you choose," Davey replied. "Better yet, allow me the privilege!"

"Oh, Davey. You know as well as I do, that's not the solution."

"You're right," Davey conceded. "But, if you change your mind...." Hailee saw him wink. "The Cousin Code remains in effect."

"Thanks, Davey."

Hailee returned her attention to the dreaded conversation when Zach Sawyer spoke up. "I do think you're being rather harsh, Anders," he said. "I, for one, believe Miss Annigan to be a competent teacher and an excellent nurturer. And all of us have things in our pasts that we aren't proud of."

"I'll second that," Jonah Dickenson said. "It was years ago that Miss Annigan made the choices she did, and those out of desperation. She is totally reformed, and her past actions have no bearing on her ability to teach our children. My three children are in her class, and I can vouch for the difference Miss Annigan has made in their education and character development. This is true of my twin sons, in particular."

"That's fine and well, Mr. Dickenson," said Rowena Nash, "but I simply do not understand why Miss Annigan made no mention of her past prior to accepting the position."

"Would the school board have even hired her, then?" Sheriff Clyde asked.

"I think this meeting is ridiculous," McKenzie spoke up. "We all know that Hailee possesses outstanding integrity."

"The premise of your argument is unfair," Kaydie added. "If you're going to hold Hailee's past against her, then all of us should have our pasts held against us."

"Say what you will," Anders replied, "but I never would have voted to hire her if I had known about her past."

"I doubt that you know the whole story."

Heads turned toward the voice. Much to Hailee's surprise, it was Maxwell Adams who had spoken. Now, he made his way to the front of the crowd. He carried himself in a stately way, with no signs of self-pity over the loss of his arm or pain from the healing incision.

"Allow me to introduce myself." Maxwell stood up straight and removed his hat. "My name is Maxwell Nathaniel Adams, Esquire, and I am a partner at the prestigious law office of Worthington and Worthington in Boston, Massachusetts."

"We know who you are, and we're sorry about what happened to you," Anders said evenly. "But we don't need any high and mighty city folk speaking on behalf of some wayward teacher. Besides, this is Montana, not Boston, in case you hadn't noticed."

"It seems to me that everyone who wishes to speak should have a say in this matter, regardless of where they call home," Sheriff Clyde said in a firm voice. "Please proceed, Mr. Adams."

"Thank you, Sheriff. As I was saying, I am a partner at the law offices of—"

"You're repeating yourself," grumbled Jasper Richardson.

Maxwell ignored the interruption and continued. "As an attorney, I feel an obligation to bring to your attention several key details in order to shed light on this discussion." He turned to Hailee. "Miss Annigan, were you ever apprehended for theft, and did you serve a sentence of any kind?"

Hailee cast a glance at Nate, who gave her a reassuring smile. So, she looked back at Maxwell and cleared her throat. "Yes, sir. I was apprehended by a police officer and spent several nights in the local jail before I was sent to The Sanctuary of Promise in Cincinnati, where orphans and young lawbreakers are rehabilitated."

"So, allow me to reiterate: you were sent to The Sanctuary of Promise after the discovery of your crime."

"Yes, sir," Hailee squeaked, suddenly aware of the crowd's scrutiny.

"Very well. And the years you spent at The Sanctuary of Promise were the consequence of your having stolen food; is that correct?"

"Yes."

"Very well." Maxwell turned to Anders and Jasper. "I am confident that, if I were to obtain depositions from the teachers at The Sanctuary of Promise, such depositions would substantiate Miss Annigan's claims." He turned his gaze on Hailee once more. "Now, Miss Annigan, when and for what reason did you leave The Sanctuary of Promise?"

"I…I left two years ago, when I was seventeen and too old to stay there, and I then worked in a factory. I could have left earlier, but I decided to stay on at The Sanctuary for a year and help teach the children there, after I was offered the opportunity to gain teaching experience."

"So, you were granted leave and left on your own accord," Maxwell confirmed, "rather than escaped?"

"Yes, sir. I graduated from The Sanctuary of Promise's school."

"Very well." Maxwell nodded. "Do you suppose we could safely assume that you were granted leave because the staff at The Sanctuary of Promise had deemed you fully rehabilitated?"

"Yes, sir."

"Excellent. Now, if we consider the reputable staff at The Sanctuary of Promise to be tantamount to a judge and jury, we cannot ignore that the fact of Miss Annigan's release proves that she has fulfilled her sentence and is no longer considered a threat to society."

"Except that this isn't a court," Anders objected.

"And this ain't no trial," Jasper added.

"Though one might get that impression from Mr. Adams's charade," said Etta Mae Nash. "You use such big words, Mr. Adams. Who can understand them?"

"Please allow me to finish," Maxwell said, his voice ever steady and calm. "Now, Miss Annigan, are you certified to teach?"

"Yes, of course."

"And where did you obtain your teaching certificate?"

"I earned my certificate at The Sanctuary of Promise, where I was trained by the other teachers."

Maxwell looked out at the crowd. "For those of you who may not have heard Miss Annigan's last statement, she obtained her teaching certificate under the tutelage of the teachers at The Sanctuary of Promise—the very institution where she was rehabilitated." Maxwell paused, then continued. "To those of you who question Miss Annigan's character, I would say to inquire at The Sanctuary of Promise as to her credentials. I am sure that those esteemed individuals would be amused, at best, by your attempts to sully the reputation of this fine young teacher."

Anders looked dumbfounded for a moment. Then, he scowled. "Are you finished?"

"Yes," Maxwell said. "Thank you for allowing me my say." He put his hat back on his head, turned, and made his way toward Nate and Hailee.

"Excuse me, may I speak?"

Once again, all heads turned in the direction of a voice unfamiliar to them. But Hailee recognized it immediately. It was Peyton, and she timidly held a hand in the air.

"Go ahead," Anders said gruffly. "Everyone else is."

"Thank you," Peyton replied. "I am new to Pine Haven—"

"Which is precisely why you should have no say in the matter," Rowena declared. "You don't even live here."

"I beg your pardon!" Peyton exclaimed, sounding stronger now. "My name is Peyton Worthington Adams. Reverend Nathaniel Adams is my son. What I was about to say was that I am new to Pine Haven, but, already, I have come to love this town. So many of you have prayed for Maxwell's healing and have been a great source of encouragement to me." Peyton paused. "When I first arrived, I was set on disliking everything about Pine Haven, including Hailee Annigan, once I found out that my son was courting her. It didn't take long for my mind to change. I grew fond of the town and very fond of Hailee. She was there for me after Maxwell was shot and during his recovery. She even prayed with me, something no one had ever done before."

"If you're done expressing your ridiculous sentiments..." Anders cut in.

"Anders, would you please allow her to finish?" Mr. Victor said. "I've been called the most patient man around, but even my patience is beginning to wear thin because of you."

"Thank you," Peyton said with a nod, then turned to address the crowd once more. "I believe you have found yourselves a rare gem in Hailee Annigan. She is kind, selfless, and courageous. When Maxwell was shot, she stayed with me and comforted me while Nate went to seek help." Peyton dabbed her eyes with a handkerchief. "That was after I had treated her in a most inconsiderate manner. Yet she forgave me without hesitation. Will you not do likewise and forgive her for the questionable choices she made as a young girl? She was a defenseless orphan then, and, clearly, she is a different woman now."

"I agree with Mrs. Adams," Asa said. "We must extend mercy to Hailee, whom Rosemary and I have also come to love."

"You think you need to love everybody," Anders said with a scowl. "You don't even have children, yet you act as though the Sawyer and Dickenson children are your grandchildren. Pathetic, I say."

"I would say it's the farthest thing from pathetic," Rosemary spoke up. "It's called loving your neighbor as yourself, which is what Jesus called us to do. We are very fond of our adopted grandchildren and of Hailee, too."

Anders waved off her comment. "I say we relieve Miss Annigan of her teaching position immediately. As far as I'm concerned, she won't teach anyone's children ever again."

The arguments grew more heated, and Hailee was thankful when Nate put his arm protectively around her. "It's going to be okay," he whispered reassuringly.

But Hailee's tears fell, anyway. It warmed her heart to hear so many people speak in her defense, but the harsh criticism from the five who spoke against her—the Nashes and Jasper and Zaida Richardson—injured her very core.

"I would like to say something on Miss Annigan's behalf," Nate said, giving Hailee an encouraging squeeze.

"That doesn't surprise me," sneered Jasper Richardson. "Of course, no one feels like a sermon, Reverend. After all, it isn't Sunday."

"I wasn't planning on a sermon," Nate said calmly. Hailee was amazed at his composure.

"That's a relief," said Anders, "though I am a bit tired and could use the sleep."

"I could give you many examples in the Bible for this situation," Nate began, disregarding the men's remarks. "After all, the Bible holds the answers to all of the problems in life—"

"Of course, you would defend Miss Annigan. You're courting her!" Jasper scoffed.

"Mr. Richardson, we will ask you to leave if you don't allow others to speak without interruption," said Mr. Victor.

"You're the last person I'm afraid of," Jasper replied.

"Mr. Victor won't be the only one hauling you away," Jonah warned him.

In the silence that followed, Nate cleared his throat. "As I was saying, there are many examples in the Bible. However, that's not what I wish to speak about. As many of you know, I am courting Hailee. I have grown very fond of her and care deeply for her. What I am trying to say is that if you relieve Hailee of her teaching position, you'll have to relieve me of my pastoral position, as well."

Gasps filled the air, but Nate held up a hand, indicating that he had more to say. "The reason I say this is because I have made mistakes in my past, as well, and one of them involved the theft of something that didn't belong to me." Nate paused and looked at his mother before continuing. "I was young and foolish, and I allowed myself to be swayed by the opinions of my peers rather than be guided by my conscience. I knew it was wrong, yet I still did it. I'll spare you the details, but I later sought forgiveness from both the man I had stolen from and the Lord. So, if you're going to dismiss someone from her job on the basis of her past behavior, you'll have to find yourselves a new pastor, as well."

"And a new postmaster," declared Mr. Victor. "When I was just a young'un, I broke a vase at the mercantile. No one was around at the time, so it was easy to lie about it. Nobody ever found out it was me. But I knew, and God knew, and, now, you all know. So, you have a liar for a postmaster."

"And you'll lose a member of the school board," Jonah spoke up. "I have had to seek forgiveness too many times to count."

"We all have," said Zach. "As Nate said, if you're going to dismiss someone on the basis of her past mistakes, you had best tell us all to leave Pine Haven and never return."

Lucille Granger glanced around, looking nervous. "I suppose I should admit to gossiping…once or twice," she said. "And so, you may want to find yourselves a new proprietress for the best mercantile in Pine Haven."

Several others spoke in turn, calling themselves unfit to retain their various positions. "Mind if I say a few words?" Reuben put in.

Jasper Richardson frowned. "Who are you?"

"He's the drifter who stayed at my place last night," Anders said. "He's also Hailee's long-lost brother."

"I feel somewhat responsible for this situation," Reuben began, ignoring Anders's comment. "While I was eating dinner with the Nash family yesterday evening, they asked me some questions about Hailee. Believing them to be friends of Hailee's, and that they meant well, I told them how Hailee had stolen food for us to eat as children."

There were several gasps, but Reuben continued. "What I want you all to know is that Hailee never would have stolen food if our lives hadn't depended on it. After our parents died, she was responsible for me and also our little brother, Philip. Hailee and I both looked for work so that we could earn money to support ourselves, but nobody wanted to hire a couple of kids. Sometimes, we managed to find scraps of food in garbage bags in the alleys behind restaurants and stores, but it wasn't enough. So, when the three of us were practically starving, Hailee started stealing food. But she didn't do it as a criminal; she did it out of love for us."

"Of course, stealing is wrong, but a sister who makes such sacrifices for her brothers is to be commended," McKenzie said, taking Hailee's hand in hers.

"Agreed!" chorused Kaydie and Peyton.

"A sister who does whatever she can to take care of her brothers is truly honorable," Rosemary affirmed as she joined the small crowd of supporters around Hailee.

"It's an honor to have Hailee Annigan as our schoolteacher," said Doc Orville.

"Her life does make for a good true story," Lucille agreed.

"I hope Hailee will stay here and teach for many years to come," said Mr. Victor. "Geraldine and I have grown quite fond of her."

"Hailee lives with me, and she has been a great blessing in my time of sorrow."

Hailee turned and looked through grateful tears at the widow Marlen, who smiled at her.

"Sheriff Clyde, you're a man of the law," Mrs. Richardson screeched. "You should arrest this woman for her crimes!"

"I am a man of the law, and I will do no such thing," the sheriff replied. "She has paid fully for her mistakes as a youth. Furthermore, I can attest to the fact that there's no one Marie and I would rather have teaching our children."

"Now, you folks aren't listening!" Anders insisted.

"No, Anders, you're the one who isn't listening," Nate said. "Let's have a vote. All in favor of keeping Hailee Annigan as the schoolteacher of Pine Haven, say aye."

A throng of voices answered, "Aye!"

"Those opposed, say nay."

Six people shouted their opposition, but they were no match for the majority.

"The people have spoken," Nate said, "and it seems pretty clear to me that the town of Pine Haven wishes to keep Hailee Annigan as the teacher."

Cheers erupted from the crowd, and Nate took Hailee in his arms and planted a kiss firmly on her lips. "Thank you, Nate," she whispered.

"For the kiss, or for setting the townsfolk straight?" Nate teased.

Hailee giggled. "Both."

"Excuse me, Reverend Nate? Halloo!" Lucille bustled her way through the dispersing crowd toward them.

Nate grinned at Hailee. "Yes, Lucille?"

"I just had the most fabulous idea!"

"Do tell!"

Hailee stifled a giggle at his sarcasm.

"I'm sure you recall that, in addition to Granger Mercantile, I am the proprietress of the highly successful operation known as Lucille's Love Connections."

"I do."

"Well, then you must recall our discussion a while back about the prospect of my finding you a bride."

Nate scratched his head. "I guess I recall that, Lucille, albeit vaguely."

"Well, I just had the most wonderful thought. Why don't you allow me to arrange a love connection between you and Miss Annigan?"

Hailee smiled at Nate. "I think we'd like that, Lucille."

"Delightful!" Lucille exclaimed. "Meet me in five minutes at Granger Mercantile, the finest mercantile in town. I have a little tablet there, and I'll need some information from you both...."

Lucille's words were drowned out by Hailee's laughter when Nate scooped her off the ground and swung her around. *"Someday, Hailee, the Lord will bless you with just the man He has chosen for you,"* Ella Fanshaw had once told her. That someday was now.

CHAPTER TWENTY-THREE

Reuben buttoned his new coat against the late November air. It certainly felt as if snow was on its way. He gazed up at the cloudy sky. *My first winter in Montana*, he thought to himself. *Who could have guessed that I'd come to live here? Thank You, Lord, for reuniting me with Hailee. You have answered my prayers beyond my greatest imagination.*

It had been almost two months since Reuben had started working at the Sawyer Ranch. He was amazed at how well he'd fit in and how easily he'd caught on to the day-to-day duties. For the first time in his adult life, Reuben had found a place where he felt he belonged. He grinned and shook his head. Things were really coming together. First, he had found Hailee, and they'd reconciled their differences. Then, he'd received a letter from Philip, saying that he would come to Pine Haven for a visit in the spring. That day couldn't come soon enough, in Reuben's opinion, but at least it was something he looked forward to.

Reuben truly enjoyed working on the ranch with Zach, Asa, and the two other hired hands. It was nothing like working for the ungrateful Pritchards. Here, he was respected, trusted, and treated with loving care. And, while Reuben had grown fond of Zach, he had grown even fonder of Asa and his wife, Rosemary. It was easy to why the couple was beloved of so many. Of course, nearly everyone in Pine Haven had welcomed him there.

"Reuben?"

Reuben turned and saw Asa approaching him. "Hello, Asa."

"It's getting a mite cold, eh?"

"That it is. I was just thinking about how this will be my first winter away from Ohio."

"How do you feel about that?"

"I'm amazed, that's for sure. I never thought I would find myself here. It's so different from Ohio. But I'm thankful the Lord led me to Hailee—and to you and everyone else on the ranch."

Asa chuckled and placed a hand on Reuben's shoulder. "My boy, we're glad you are here. My question is, why did it take you so long to find your way? You're a good hand, and we've needed your help for some time now." Asa's eyes twinkled. "Do you think you might be staying on permanently?"

Reuben nodded. "I would say so."

"That's a good thing. A good thing, for sure."

"Why is that?"

"Let me see...." Asa paused. "I suppose I may as well lay it out straight for you. I have a question that's been on my mind for some time now."

"Go on."

"You see, Rosemary and I were talking the other day over dinner, and, well, the truth is, we've grown very fond of you, Reuben." Asa cleared his throat.

"This may not be the proper time, so, if it's not, please let me know. But, you see, Reuben, Rosemary and I were wondering if we might…uh, if we might…."

"Please, Asa, go on." Reuben's pulse quickened as he anticipated Asa's next words.

"We were wondering if we might adopt you."

Reuben gulped. "Adopt me?"

"Yes. But, again, if this isn't the right time—"

"No, Asa, it's a fine time. You and Rosemary would really want to adopt me?"

"As sure as the sun rises each day."

"But I'm already almost grown."

"Ah, my boy, is it really so hard to believe? You are a smart, hardworking young lad. You are thoughtful and kind. What's there not to like? Besides, that you are nearly grown is a plus. You see, I've never been good at changing diapers."

Reuben laughed but quickly sobered. Had he heard Asa correctly? "So, I would be your son?"

"Yes. And I would be your father—not to take the place of your true father, of course. But I would be your father, and Rosemary would be your mother."

"I would like that. I would like that very much!" Reuben reached out his arms and gave the older man a hug. "Thank you, Asa. You have no idea what this means to me."

"And you have no idea what this means to Rosemary and me."

"What do we have to do to make it official?" Reuben asked, releasing Asa.

"I happen to know a fine lawyer named Maxwell Adams. He has already agreed to draw up the adoption papers."

"I think this might be the best day of my life!" Reuben exclaimed, blinking the tears from his eyes. All he'd wanted ever since Ma and Pa had died was to be adopted, to be wanted, by another family. And now, finally, his wish was coming true.

"I suppose we'd best let Rosemary in on the good news," Asa said.

"Rosemary?" Reuben grinned. "You mean, Ma."

"Ah, that's exactly who I mean." Asa chuckled. "Come on, son. Let's go share the happiest news of our lives."

CHAPTER TWENTY-FOUR

JUNE 1894 • PINE HAVEN, MONTANA

*S*tanding at a front window of the Sawyer home, Hailee unfolded the most recent letter she had received from Philip. Her eyes alternated between scanning the words of her youngest brother and checking the driveway for a sign of his arrival.

Dear Hailee,

How are you? I am fine. I was thrilled to receive your letter and the invitation to your wedding! I am happy for you, even if it is hard to believe that my only sister is getting married.

I have some good news of my own. Since Ma and Pa and I were already planning a visit to Pine Haven, we have decided to delay the trip until June so that we will be able to attend your wedding! I can't wait for you to meet Ma and Pa, who are eager to make your acquaintance, as well.

I recently entered a contest to write a story for the local newspaper. I wrote about the new horse I received for my birthday from Pa. His name is Moses. I thought the name was fitting, since I remember asking you time and again to tell me the story of baby Moses when I was little. I will find out next week whether my story was selected.

Please say hello to Reuben for me and tell him I miss him, too.

I look forward to seeing you in June!

> *Your brother,*
> *Philip*

Hailee refolded the letter and slipped it back inside her pocket. Any minute now, Philip would arrive at the Sawyer Ranch. Any minute now, she would hug her youngest brother for the first time in years. The problem was, that minute couldn't come fast enough.

She stepped out the front door and peeked at the side of the house, where Zach, McKenzie, and a host of others were making preparations for the wedding. Her wedding. She couldn't recall a time when she'd felt more blessed. Today, she would see her beloved brother *and* marry the man she loved.

Finally, Hailee heard the sound of gravel crunching beneath wagon wheels. *Please, Lord, let it be Philip!* She turned and squinted at the end of the drive, where a wagon appeared. Reuben drove, and beside him sat a young man with wavy blond hair, a freckled nose, and a sweet smile. Philip.

As the wagon came closer, Hailee longed to run toward it, but her feet refused to move.

"Hailee!" Philip called as the wagon slowed to a stop.

"Philip!" Hailee managed, though tears clogged her throat. Her feet finally obeyed by moving forward, but not without stumbling.

Meanwhile, Philip hopped out of the wagon and ran toward her, arms outstretched.

When he reached her, Hailee embraced him as tears fell freely down her face. "Philip, sweet Philip!"

After a moment, she took a step back and placed her hands gently on either side of Philip's face. "Let me get a good look at you," she said.

Philip grinned. "I'm a little older than I used to be."

"You have grown so much!" Hailee exclaimed. "It's easy to see that you're turning into a fine young man."

"Uh, Hailee?"

"Yes, Philip?"

"Could you please stop squeezing my face?"

"Oh, pardon me." She dropped her hands to her sides. "I just can't believe you're here!"

"Did you see him run?" Reuben asked, joining the two of them.

"Your foot!" Hailee exclaimed. "I had forgotten all about it!"

"The surgery was a success," Philip said with a smile, "and I've been able to walk fine without a crutch for some time, now."

"That's wonderful."

"You look so much like Ma," said Philip. "Our ma."

Hailee swallowed hard. "What I wouldn't give to have her and Pa here today."

Reuben looked thoughtful. "I agree. But it's interesting to me that after they died, we were separated and went in three different directions: Hailee to The Sanctuary of Promise, me to the Pritchards, and Philip, you were adopted by the Llewellyns. But God brought us all here from all of those different places so we could be together again."

"And the Lord allowed all of us to find second families," said Philip. "I'm happy for you, Reuben, and I can't wait to meet Asa and Rosemary."

"They're great," said Reuben. "Asa, my new pa, is so wise, and Ma makes the best biscuits and gravy." Reuben patted his stomach.

Hailee giggled. "We can all see how being adopted by the O'Connells has greatly benefited Reuben!"

"I'll say!" Philip chuckled. "You know, my second ma never gave up hope that I would find you both someday, and she never allowed me to lose hope, either. We prayed every night, and when I saw the posting at the depot when my aunt and uncle were leaving to return to Minneapolis, I couldn't believe it."

"I do think it's wonderful how God gave us second families," said Hailee. "I have found a second family in Nate's parents. As a matter of fact, they have offered to pay our fare so that Nate and I can come visit you, Philip, and then head to Boston for a few weeks so that I can meet Nate's grandfather."

"I'll be counting down the days." Philip smiled. "And, speaking of parents, Ma and Pa can't wait to meet you. They'll be here later, for the wedding."

"The wedding!" Hailee gasped. "Oh my, I must get ready!" She glanced down at her calico dress. Soon, in its place would be the most exquisite bridal gown she'd ever seen. "I can't wait for you to meet Nate, Philip. He is such an honorable man who loves the Lord, and, well, I can't wait to be his wife."

Reuben groaned. "Oh, no. Here comes the lovey-dovey talk." He rolled his eyes. "All she ever talks about is 'Nate this' and 'Nate that.'"

"That's enough from you," Hailee teased. "Just you wait, Reub. Someday, you'll get married, and it'll be my turn to tease you about lovey-dovey talk." She hugged her brothers. "I need to get ready. I shall see you both again when it's time to walk down the aisle!"

"If only the vases I ordered from the catalogue had arrived on time," Nate's mother muttered as she stood back and admired the bouquet of flowers she had placed on each table for the wedding reception.

Nate put an arm around her shoulder. "Mother, please don't fret. Everything looks beautiful."

"I just want everything to be perfect for you and Hailee."

Nate took a step back. "Mother, I'm about to marry the woman I love, and I have my family here to celebrate with me. I couldn't ask for more."

"I know, and I'm glad. I just want the wedding to be dignified, as befitting the Worthington-Adams name—"

"Mother...."

She smiled. "You're right, Nate. That's not what's important. How quickly I tend to forget. What is important is that God brought you together, and that your father, your grandmother, and I are here with you on this most special day." She sighed. "I only wish that your grandfather Worthington could attend, as well, but you know how greatly his health has deteriorated."

Nate nodded. "It will be good to see him in the fall when Hailee and I visit Boston."

"He is proud of you, Nate. He may never say those exact words, but he is proud of you. Yes, he wanted you to study law, as we all did, and he doesn't yet understand the things of the Lord. But I think he realizes now how passionate you are about your vocation, and he admires you greatly for that."

Just then, Nate's father joined them. He placed his arm around his wife and planted a kiss on her cheek. "You've done it again, my dear. It looks as if everything will go off without a hitch."

Mother grinned. "It's going to be a wonderful wedding."

"That it is," Father agreed. Then, he turned to Nate. "I know that you probably have some more preparations before the ceremony, but may I speak with you a moment?"

"Of course," Nate replied. "Shall we go for a walk?" He led his father toward the far end of the Sawyer Ranch, away from the wedding site, where they would have privacy.

They walked without speaking for several minutes before stopping near one of the corrals. As they stood there in awkward silence, Nate realized that he and his father had never had a serious talk, just the two of them—that he could remember, at least—and he welcomed the occasion. "Nice weather today," he said, hoping to get things started.

"I agree. Perfect day for a wedding."

Nate cleared his throat.

"Nate—"

"Father—"

"You go first, son."

Nate nodded. "I don't think I ever fully expressed to you how sorry I am for what happened that day with those two escaped convicts." He paused. "I wish I could have prevented it."

His father shook his head. "It's in the past now, son, and that's where we'll leave it."

"How are you doing? Without your left arm, I mean." While his father seemed happier and less stressed than he had ever been, he appeared to have aged significantly in the past several months. His thinning blond hair showed signs of graying, and a few more wrinkles lined his thin face.

"I'm doing well, all things considered. I'd never realized how much I used my left arm and hand until I lost them."

"It must be difficult," Nate acknowledged, not knowing what else to say. "So, how is work?"

"When we return to Boston, I have a court date for a large case I've been working on for the past several months. There are some sensitive details, but I feel confident that we will prevail in the end."

"I was always impressed whenever I was permitted to watch you argue a case," Nate said. "You have always been dynamic in the courtroom."

His father smiled. "I never thought I'd say this, but I could make the same comment about you in the pulpit."

Nate chuckled. "A chip off the old block, shall we say?"

"That would be an honor." His father paused. "Nate, I've been giving serious thought to some things, and I...well, I know how close you are to your uncles Zach and Jonah. I must admit, I've been jealous a time or two of the camaraderie you share with them, and with that Asa fellow, too. I wish...I wish that you and I could have something akin to that."

Nate was taken aback. He'd never realized that his father wished for them to be closer. Nate had wished for that all his life. He had always wanted to be able to speak with his father about his concerns and celebrations, the way other sons could speak with their fathers. He'd often yearned for his father to set aside his latest legal brief and give his full attention to him, instead.

Nate gulped as he realized how vulnerable his father suddenly seemed. He was a good two inches shorter than Nate, and his stature was thin and frail. No longer did he seem larger than life. "I wish that, too, Father."

"Someday, Nate, you'll be a father, with children of your own. I hope you'll be a better one than I have been."

"Father—"

"Let me finish, son. I regret all of the times when I wasn't there to support or console. I shifted the responsibility of raising you, first to nannies and then to boarding schools. I never took you fishing or read to you, like other fathers do with their sons. I am truly sorry."

Nate bit his lip. True, he'd never once been on a fishing trip with his father. As a matter of fact, he'd never really spent time alone with his father, receiving his full attention, until today. *Please, Lord, give my father and me a second chance*, he prayed. *Help us to rekindle our relationship.*

"We can still go fishing, Father," he reminded him. "You would be amazed at the abundance of trout in the rivers here."

"Thank you, Nate. I would like that."

Just then, Tommy Dickenson ran up beside Nate. "Have you seen Clint? We was playin' hide-'n'-seek, an' I think I lost him for good."

Nate chuckled and looked around. "Have you searched the barn?"

"No—good idea! You should play hide-'n'-seek with us more often, Nate. You're really good!" With that, Tommy bounded off toward the barn.

"Just think—someday, you could have twin boys just like your cousins," Father said with a wink.

Nate laughed. "Hailee and I will welcome children, Lord willing, but I think we'll plan to have daughters."

His father leaned his head back and laughed with an abandon that Nate had never seen him display. He thought of all the years he'd spent never really knowing his father as the man he truly was, not just the man he'd perceived him to be. Nate had caught mere glimpses into his father's life from a distance.

Then, Nate realized another sobering fact: this was the first time he'd laughed with his father. The two of them chuckled until tears rolled down their cheeks.

"Seriously, Father," Nate said, still laughing, "I love my cousins, and I would be blessed to have sons, daughters, or both. All children are gifts, even the ornery ones." He paused. "And I think you'd make a wonderful grandfather."

His father regained composure. "Thank you, son. That means a lot to me. And I hope you know that I'm proud of your choice of Hailee as a wife.

Your mother and I have come to love her like our own daughter."

"She is a remarkable woman," Nate said. "I must admit, though, that I'm a bit nervous about getting married. I tossed and turned all night last night and didn't catch a bit of sleep."

"I think that's pretty normal for a man about to be married."

"Did you feel that way when you were about to marry Mother?"

"Yes, but for different reasons. You see, a lot was expected of me since I was marrying a Worthington— the eldest Worthington, at that. But never mind that. You'll be a fine husband."

"I hope so."

"You will. But there is some advice I'd like to give you, if I may; you know, father to son?"

"Certainly, Father."

"Right now, your ministry is your church. But, once you're married, it's critical that you make Hailee your number one ministry. Be there for her and love her. Give her as much attention as you're able and let her know she's important to you. I neglected to do that with your mother, and it hurt her in ways I'll likely never know."

Nate nodded. "I have prayed and asked God to help me not to let my work come before her."

"The fact that you're aware of the danger makes all the difference," his father said. "For most of our marriage, I gave my all to my work and left nothing for your mother. You were away at boarding school, and she was often at home alone long into the night, while I was still at the office. I realize now how lonely she must have been. Yes, she had her volunteer work and her social activities to keep her busy, but there was a void in her heart that I needed to fill. And I failed to do so."

"I will try to remember that, Father. If you ever see me heading toward that tendency, will you point it out to me?"

"I will. You ought to invite Hailee to do the same thing. Your mother just recently became comfortable confronting me about focusing too much on my work, and I appreciate her candor."

"Speaking of Mother, it sounds as if she's been busier than ever these days with her volunteer work."

"That she is. I think she told you about the charity she recently founded, the Worthington-Adams Christian Ladies' Guild. She's even appointed your grandmother as the co-chair, although I'm not sure what the woman thinks about that!"

Nate chuckled. "I'm proud of Mother. She has grown in her faith, which is an answer to years of prayer."

"Ah, yes. Her faith. Well, I don't know a lot about that, other than to say she is different from the woman she once was—certainly kinder and more compassionate. It has been a bit strange to see her ask God for forgiveness when she errs. I really don't know what to think about it all."

Someday, Father, the Lord will soften your heart. Wouldn't it be something if He used Mother to pave the way for your salvation? Nate thought.

"But, I didn't come here to talk about religion," his father quickly added. "I came here to spend time with my son on the most important day of his life"— he reached inside his pocket—"and to give you this." He held out a gold pocket watch.

"Thank you, Father." Nate took the timepiece in his hand.

"As you know, the watch that belonged to your grandfather Adams was stolen in the robbery and was never recovered. I purchased this one before we left Boston, and I'd like to start a new tradition. Pass it on to your son, and he can pass it on to his son, and so forth."

Nate fingered the ornate timepiece. "I will cherish it always, Father." *Thank You, Lord, for a fresh start with my father*, he prayed. *May I seek to honor him, as I honor You, in all I do.*

CHAPTER TWENTY-FIVE

*P*sst, Hailee! Over here."

Hailee jumped at the voice and turned around. There was Nate, peeking out from some shrubberies beside the house. "Nate! What are you doing?" she whispered, going to him.

He took her in his arms. "Just think, it won't be long until we're married."

Hailee giggled. "That's precisely why I must go and get ready! Your mother and aunts will be looking for me."

Nate leaned forward and kissed her on the forehead. "All right. I'll let you get ready."

"Nate?"

"Yes?"

"I just had the most horrible thought. What if I trip while walking down the aisle?"

He chuckled. "Perhaps, I should just carry you down the aisle to prevent any embarrassment to the parties involved. After all, as a member of the Worthington-Adams family, I have a reputation to uphold."

"Nate, I'm being serious! Suppose my shoe gets caught on my dress?"

"I wouldn't worry about that, Hailee." His blue eyes twinkled. "However, if it does happen, I wouldn't be too concerned."

"Well, *I* would be."

"Do you see that man over there?"

Hailee followed Nate's gaze to a tall, slender man wearing a black top hat.

"Yes."

"He is one of the most highly-regarded photographers in Boston. Mother hired him to travel all this distance to take photographs of our wedding. If, by chance, you do stumble and fall, I'm sure he would be honored to capture the event for future generations to enjoy. Just think—your legend will live on in printed form for our children, grandchildren, and great grandchildren—"

"Nathaniel Adams!" Hailee scolded him with a playful punch in the shoulder.

Nate chuckled. "Just kidding. If you should trip, it will be my privileged duty to catch you."

"Maybe I should just wear this comfortable calico dress," Hailee said in a serious voice. "That way, I shouldn't have to worry about tripping over the train or hem of my wedding gown."

Nate furrowed his brow. "I don't think that's such a wise idea. Think of the commotion you would cause. Several of our esteemed guests might never forgive you for your error in fashion judgment."

"Well, it is my wedding, and I plan to be married only once. Why shouldn't I be comfortable? I'm sure your mother could return the gown for a refund. She would be wealthier, and I would be happier."

"Now, Hailee, you know she chose that gown especially for you, never mind the expense."

"That's true, but I much prefer something simpler. Besides, since a certain reverend has detained me for so long, I may not have adequate time to make myself presentable. I suppose plain old calico will have to do."

Nate looked genuinely concerned now, as if he feared that her words had not been in jest. "Hailee, please, wear the gown. I know you won't trip over the hem."

Hailee giggled then. "I was only teasing you, Nate, to avenge your quip about the photographer. I have no desire to wear this plain dress for something as important as our wedding."

Nate sighed. "That's a relief! I was dreading having to explain that one to Mother." He paused and glanced left and right before looking into her eyes. "In that case, how about a pre-wedding smooch?" Without waiting for an answer, he put his hands on her shoulders and leaned toward her.

When their lips met, Hailee's stomach did a flip-flop, as always. She thought of the countless kisses she would enjoy in the years to come as Nate's wife.

"Eww! That's disgusting!" chorused two youthful voices.

Hailee jerked her head back and turned. There stood Tommy and Clint, staring in horror at her and Nate. "What are you boys doing here?" she demanded.

"We was invited to the weddin', same as everybody else," said Tommy.

Nate cleared his throat. "I think what Miss Annigan means is, why did you sneak up on us like that?" he said good-naturedly. "It isn't exactly polite."

"Oh, we wasn't sneakin'; we was walkin' as loud as we always do," Clint insisted.

"I think you two should be inside, getting dressed in your new trousers," Nate said, "so that you're ready to do your very important job of holding the rings during the ceremony."

"Oh, all right," Tommy muttered. "Come on, Clint. Let's you and me go put on them uncomfortable clothes Grandmother ordered for us."

Hailee giggled. "Well, I suppose I should go put on my 'uncomfortable dress.' I promise to do my best not to trip."

"You'll do just fine," Nate said, giving her one last kiss on the cheek. "I can't imagine a more beautiful bride."

Nate realized that he needed to get ready, too, so he headed inside through the kitchen door. Davey must have had the same idea, for the two of them met in the sitting room. They started to exchange pleasantries on their way up the stairs when they heard the infamous twins.

"Do you know where we're s'posed to go?" Tommy asked.

"No, I'm just followin' you," Clint replied.

Nate stopped and turned around, prepared to go back downstairs and intervene. But Davey grabbed his arm. "Shh!" he whispered. "Let's just listen a little. This could be amusing."

Nate grinned and stepped back to listen in.

"Hmm. I have an idea," said Tommy. "Let's you and me go into the kitchen and see that weddin' cake."

"All right."

Nate exchanged a glance with Davey, and then the two of them crept down the stairs and into the sitting room, where they'd have a better vantage point. Plus, Nate wanted to be nearby in case he did need to intervene. Nothing could happen to that cake—Aunt Kaydie had spent hours baking and decorating it!

"That's a pretty cake," Tommy declared.

"It sure is," Clint agreed. "Look at all that white icin'."

"I wonder what it tastes like."

"Only one way to find out."

"Taste it, you mean?"

"Sure! Ma's always tellin' us to help others, right?"

"Right...."

"Well, we'd be helpin' others by tastin' it because we would make sure it tasted good. We don't want anybody to eat bad cake. After all, we always get to test Ma's gingerbread cookies when she bakes 'em."

"I wonder if this is gingerbread cake."

"Only one way to find out," said Clint.

"I think I should go first," declared Tommy.

"You always get to go first."

"That's 'cause I'm the oldest."

"That's not fair," Clint grumbled.

Nate moved forward, but Davey stopped him again. "It'll be okay," he whispered. "What harm can they really do?"

Nate shrugged and peeked around the corner. He at least wanted to supervise.

Tommy ran a short, stubby finger along the side of the cake. "Whoa, would you look at all that icin'!"

Then, as though he hadn't eaten in days, Tommy devoured the dollop of frosting.

"Now it's my turn," said Clint. He performed the same test. "I think it'll do," he mused, licking his lips.

"We better make it look like we wasn't sneakin' tastes," said Tommy. With the palm of his hand, he smoothed the side of the cake. "There."

"Ma would be proud of us for makin' sure her icin' tastes good," Clint said. "Right?"

"Right," Tommy said with a nod. "She would be very proud." He paused. "These new trousers ain't too bad."

Clint fingered the collar of his crisp white shirt. "These shirts ain't, either. Hey! Let's us pretend like we're the weddin' preacher."

"All right. I'll go first."

"You always go first."

"That's because I'm the oldest," said Tommy. "Now, I'll be the preacher, and you can be Nate and Hailee." Straightening his shoulders, Tommy bellowed, "Dearly loved, thank you for comin' to this here weddin'. Nate, do you take Hailee to be your awful wedded wife?" He paused. "Do you know what comes next after that?"

"I think it has something to do with shoppin' at the mercantile," Clint whispered.

"All right. Nate, do you take Hailee to be your awful wedded wife and to let her shop from the catalog at Granger Mercantile anytime she sees fit?"

"I do," boomed Clint.

"And do you, Hailee, take Nate to be your awful wedded husband and to let him go fishin' whenever he sees fit?"

"I do," squeaked Clint in a high-pitched voice.

"Very well. You're married!"

Nate and Davey could contain their amusement no longer. They burst out laughing. "Not too bad, boys," Nate said as he stepped into the kitchen.

"Not bad at all," Davey agreed.

"We didn't know you two was watchin' us," said Clint.

"Tommy, you ought to think about becoming a reverend," Nate suggested.

"Aw, no thanks, Nate. I want to be a rancher, like my pa."

"And I want to be a fisherman on one of them large boats on the Atlantic Ocean," Clint put in.

"Both of those are admirable professions," Nate acknowledged.

"But don't you worry none, Nate," Tommy assured him. "We'll still tell folks all about Jesus."

Chuckling, Nate nodded. "That's the important thing."

"Why don't you two find your ma and ask her to comb your hair?" said Davey.

"Do we have to?"

"I think you should."

"Remember, you have an important job to do," Nate reminded them, "and you want to look your best."

"Oh, all right," the twins chorused, then shuffled out of the kitchen and into the yard.

Nate laughed. "I don't know about those two. If this wedding goes off without a hitch, I'll be surprised."

"That's okay, just as long as they're ready for the next wedding," Davey said with a wink.

"Is there something you aren't telling me?" Nate asked. "You do know that it's against the Cousin Code to keep secrets from your best friend."

Davey chuckled. "All right, but I don't think you'll be surprised: I want to ask Cassandra to marry me. I figure we'll have a long engagement, so I will have time to talk Pa into giving us a piece of land where I can build us a house." Davey paused. "I guess I'll also need time to talk to Mr. Waterson, see if he'll give me her hand."

Nate grinned. "Should we start praying now for the Lord to soften the old blacksmith's heart?"

Davey elbowed him. "He'll agree once I profess my undying love for his daughter."

"Undying love?"

"Yep. I've loved Cassandra since the first time I saw her, at school. I sat behind her, and I loved to tug on her long braids and then act innocent whenever she turned around."

"Surely, she caught on."

"Sure did, and she started wearing her hair up in a bun." Davey chuckled. "It was then that I knew Cassandra was not only beautiful but smart, too!"

Nate laughed. "Congratulations, Davey."

"Thank you. But I have to ask you...aren't you a little nervous to get married?"

"I am. But I love Hailee, and I know she's the woman God has chosen for me."

"I feel that way about Cassandra, too. I know I want to spend the rest of my life with her."

"I can't imagine my life without Hailee," Nate confessed.

"Would you listen to us? All mushy-like."

"Good thing no one is eavesdropping on us. We'd never live this down!"

"I agree," said Davey. "And, Nate?"

"Yes?"

"Assuming Cassandra says yes, would you be my best man?"

Nate beamed. "Absolutely. It's part of the Cousin Code, after all."

"You look beautiful, Hailee," Peyton said, stepping back to survey her with a rapt expression on her face.

Hailee smiled at her reflection in the mirror. "Thank you for helping me to find this dress."

"Oh, it was my pleasure. I especially enjoyed seeing the look on Lucille Granger's face as we were thumbing through the catalog at the mercantile." Peyton paused. "I know we could have hired someone to sew a wedding gown for you, Hailee, but I wanted something extra special. An event like this happens once in a lifetime, you know."

Hailee turned around and looked behind her, admiring once again the lace bodice, pearly buttons, and long train of her white gown. Never before had she worn something so fancy. It felt as though she'd stepped right out of the pages of a fairy tale book. For the dozenth time that day, tears threatened to fall.

Peyton stepped forward and took Hailee's hands in hers. "I've always wanted a daughter. Now, I shall have one."

Hailee embraced her future mother-in-law. "And I've wanted a mother for so many years. I can't imagine anyone more loving and kind. Thank you for everything."

Peyton smiled. "I forgot to tell you and Nate that Maxwell and I have decided—if it's all right with the two of you, of course—to purchase a second home here in Pine Haven, where we may stay when we visit. Having come so close to losing Maxwell, I don't want to miss out on the lives of the ones who are dear to me any longer. I promise that we will visit only for short periods of time—"

"Oh, Peyton, we would be delighted for you to visit as often as possible, and to stay as long as you're able."

"It's settled, then." Peyton's smile broadened. "And remember, if ever you need anything—anything at all—I'm only a telegram away." She gave Hailee a squeeze and stepped back. "Now, I must go. As the mother of the groom, I have important duties to tend to! I shall see you soon, my dear."

When Peyton had gone, Hailee gazed out the window. The second story of the Sawyer home offered an excellent vantage point from which to watch the guests arrive. It thrilled her to see many of the people she had grown to love, some of them prior to her arrival in Pine Haven. Her eyes misted again when she spied Ella Fanshaw Ulmer, Officer Ulmer, and Dot Pangbourn. She couldn't imagine getting married in the absence of the special women who had seen her through the trials of her past.

Her wedding lacked the presence of only two beloved people. *I miss you so much, Ma and Pa*, Hailee thought. *I wish more than anything that you were here, but I know I shall see you again, someday.*

A knock sounded on the door. "Hailee?"

Hailee turned around. "Come in."

To her delight, Nate's grandmother, Florence Worthington, entered the room.

"Hello, Grandmother Worthington," she said, remembering how she'd been told to address the older woman when they'd met one week ago.

Grandmother shook her head. "I declare! With each passing day, someone new is calling me 'Grandmother.'"

Hailee giggled. "That's because everyone who meets you can't help but love you."

"I don't know about that."

"I never knew my grandparents, so I consider it a special privilege to be able to call you 'Grandmother.'"

"Yes, well, as I told Nate, I liked you from the moment we met, although I'm not sure why. It's not often that I develop an affinity for someone so quickly. Perhaps, it's because I sense in you a certain feistiness not so unlike mine."

Hailee smiled. Yes, she'd heard a lot about Grandmother and her tendency to be difficult, for lack of a better word. "Thank you for traveling all this way to attend our wedding. It means a lot to Nate—and to me. What a blessing it is to have most of our family members in attendance. The Lord is faithful, indeed!"

"The Lord...yes, well, He's all I've been hearing about for months. First from McKenzie and Kaydie, then from Nate, behind the pulpit, and then, most recently, from Peyton, which I never would have expected. When she and Maxwell came back to Boston in the fall, she was a different person."

"I don't think one can ever hear too much about the Lord this side of heaven," Hailee mused.

"I don't know about that, either." Grandmother rolled her eyes. "I do know that I'll hear an earful from Peyton during our trip back to Boston. She is bound to chatter incessantly about her newfound 'love for the Lord,' just as she has ever since her last trip to Pine Haven."

Hailee smiled. "God has a way of softening our hearts by using the ones closest to us." She patted Grandmother's shoulder. "He does love you, you know."

Grandmother looked away. "What is there not to love?" she quipped.

Hailee smiled. *Dearest Grandmother,* she thought to herself, *you don't know it yet, but the Lord is working on your heart....*

"Now then, I didn't come to speak of religious things," Grandmother said. "I wanted to meet with you in private before the wedding because I have something for you." She opened her expensive-looking beaded handbag and pulled out a string of pearls. "Turn around," she said to Hailee.

Hailee gasped. The pearls were beautiful. Obediently, she turned and waited as Grandmother fastened the piece around her neck.

"There, now. Let me see."

Hailee turned back around, reaching up to finger the strand of pearls. They were exquisite beyond imagining.

"They were my mother's," Grandmother explained. "She passed them to me, and now I pass them on to you. As the saying goes, 'Something old, something new, something borrowed, something blue, and a silver sixpence in her shoe.' This, my dear, is your 'something old.'"

Hailee felt a tear slide down her cheek. "Thank you, Grandmother, but...shouldn't you have given this to one of your daughters?"

"Pish posh! It's mine to do with as I please." Grandmother turned away and walked toward the window. "It's hard to believe how accustomed I've become to traveling to this primitive place. No doubt I will return soon, for the wedding of Davey and Cassandra." She smiled down at the yard. "There are the two of them now. That Davey has always been such a precocious child. He's never left the confines of this unsightly town, yet, thanks to his love of reading, he has traveled to more places than most people see in a lifetime."

"I hear he's very smart," Hailee assured her.

"Like his grandmother."

"Yes, like his grandmother."

"You know, this uncivilized town of the Wild West is beginning to grow on me." Grandmother paused and turned back to face Hailee. "But if you breathe a word of that to anyone, I will vehemently deny it."

Hailee grinned. "Your secret is safe with me."

"Very well, then. I hear your brothers downstairs. It must be nearing the time when they will summon you to walk down the aisle. I'll leave you be."

"Thank you again, Grandmother, for the pearls...for everything. The necklace is lovely, and I will treasure it always." Hailee leaned forward and planted a kiss on her wrinkled cheek. "I love you, Grandmother."

"Yes, well. I suppose I love you, too."

Seconds after Grandmother had left the room, Reuben and Philip burst inside. "Well, aren't you a sight for sore eyes!" Reuben exclaimed.

"Was that meant as a compliment?" Philip asked him.

"Of course! Have you ever seen anyone as beautiful as Hailee?" Reuben studied his sister. "You look just like Ma."

"Really?" Nothing could have made Hailee happier.

"You do," Philip agreed.

Hailee held her arms open wide, inviting her brothers in for a hug. "I am so thankful we found each other."

"Careful—don't get your dress wrinkled!" Philip cautioned her.

Hailee giggled. "Thank you, Philip. It's simply that, now that I've found both of you, I never want to let go!"

"I'm not sure Nate would be too thrilled about that," Reuben mused. "Seems to me he's pretty anxious to get married, and I doubt he wants us as part of the deal."

Hailee laughed. "You're right. I'm just so happy you're here."

"Hailee?" Rosemary called from the hallway. "It's almost time. Are you ready, dear?"

"I'm ready." Hailee linked one arm with Reuben and the other with Philip as Rosemary stepped into the room.

"You look beautiful," she said, her voice hushed. "I'll let them know you're on your way."

Minutes later, the music rang through the open fields of the Sawyer Ranch. Mountains in the distance with the last remains of snow on them glittered under the June sunshine. No cloud could be found in the perfect blue Montana sky. Rows of chairs filled with people awaited the ceremony. But all of this was at the periphery of her consciousness. She saw only the man she loved, standing beside the podium next to Reverend Eugene, who had come back to Pine Haven to officiate at the wedding.

When they reached the podium, Philip and Reuben gently released her and took their seats in the front. She beamed at Nate, eager for the ceremony to conclude, yet wanting to relish each moment as it happened.

"Dearly beloved," Reverend Eugene began, "we are gathered here today to witness the union in holy matrimony of Maxwell Nathaniel Adams Junior and Hailee Sophia Annigan. It was an honor for Myrtle and me to be invited here to be a part of this beautiful union. Over the years, I have married several members of the Worthington clan, as I like to call them, and each of those couples holds a special place in my heart, from Zach and McKenzie Sawyer to Jonah and Kaydie Dickenson, and, today, to Nate and Hailee...."

Following the wedding reception, Nate helped Hailee into the carriage. "It looks as though some of your pupils have been busy," he observed.

"Indeed, they have!" Empty cans dangled by colorful ribbons from the rear of the buggy, streamers had been threaded through the wheel spokes, and a large poster painted with the words "Nate Loves Hailee" and numerous red hearts had been attached to the back.

They rode in silence for several minutes, until Nate stopped the buggy beside the creek that ran past their new home. He climbed down and came around to Hailee's side. "May I help you out, Mrs. Adams?"

Hailee giggled. "That would be fine, Mr. Adams."

When he set her on the ground, she bent down and began untying her shoelaces.

"What are you doing?" Nate asked as she pulled off her stockings.

She grinned up at him. "I'll race you to that large rock over there." She pointed to a boulder in the distance.

"A race? On our wedding day? In your wedding dress?"

"What, are you afraid you'll lose?"

"Not a chance."

"What would you like to wager?"

"As a man of the cloth, I prefer not to gamble."

Hailee laughed and extended her hand. "All right, then, I'll be the one to gamble. I'll bet you a kiss that I can win."

"A kiss?" Nate's eyes twinkled. "If that's the case, sure, you can win. Who wouldn't want a smooch from the most beautiful woman in the world?"

Hailee tried to think of a counter to Nate's comment but couldn't. His words warmed her heart rather than provoked her wit.

"So, is there going to be a race?" Nate asked.

"There is. I think I have a good chance. I didn't trip once during the entire wedding and reception."

"Well, then, I think I'll take my shoes off this time."

When his boots sat beside Hailee's dainty shoes, she cast him a wily glance. "On your mark, get set, go!"

As she sped toward the finish line, she considered allowing Nate to win, just this once, but then thought better of it. Holding up her gown so that it didn't drag along the ground, she leaned forward and pumped her legs as fast as she could. Pa had said that she ran like the wind, and she wanted to prove him right.

She reached the rock first, with Nate not far behind. "You won," he said, in between gasps for breath.

"I did," Hailee managed, her heart hammering in her chest.

When their breathing had steadied, Nate took a step toward her. "I suppose now you'll have to make good on your bet."

"I suppose I will." She wrapped her arms around his neck.

"I'd like to make a suggestion."

"And what might that be?"

"That we come here to race as often as possible."

Hailee giggled. "If I didn't know better, I would think you actually liked to lose."

Grinning, Nate leaned down and drew her close.

When his lips met hers, Hailee's stomach fluttered, and, if her heart could have leaped out of her chest, it would have. Nate's arms were tightly wrapped around her, and his kiss was warm and inviting. She expected to wake up any minute from the dream she was certain this was. A few short hours ago, she had married Nate Adams. And now, their future together was but a breath away.

ABOUT THE AUTHOR

$\mathscr{P}$enny Zeller is the author of several books and numerous magazine articles in national and regional publications. She is also the author of the humor blog "A Day in the Life of a Mom, Wife, and Author" (www.pennyzeller. wordpress.com). She is an active volunteer in her community, serving as a women's Bible study small-group leader and co-organizing a women's prayer group. Her passion is to use the gift of the written word that God has given her to glorify Him and to benefit His kingdom.

When she's not writing, Penny enjoys spending time with her family and camping, hiking, canoeing, and playing volleyball. She and her husband, Lon, reside in Wyoming with their two children. Penny loves to hear from her readers at her Web site, www.pennyzeller.com.